| AUTHOR | CLASS |
|---|---|
| SIMONS, P. | 551.6 |
| **TITLE** Weird weather | |

# WEIRD WEATHER

# WEIRD WEATHER

Paul Simons

LITTLE, BROWN AND COMPANY

A *Little, Brown* Book

First published in Great Britain in 1996
by Little, Brown and Company

Copyright © Paul Simons 1996

The moral right of the author has been asserted.

A CIP catalogue record for this book
is available from the British Library

ISBN 0 316 87703 4

Typeset in Times New Roman by M Rules
Printed and bound in Great Britain by
BPC Consumer Books Ltd
A member of
The British Printing Company Ltd

Little, Brown and Company (UK)
Brettenham House
Lancaster Place
London WC2E 7EN

# Contents

# INTRODUCTION: THE STRANGEST WEATHER IN THE WORLD

SO YOU THOUGHT THE weather was just drizzle, scattered showers and the odd storm? Weather forecasts by and large hold few surprises, and it's easy to kid ourselves we know all about it. But what do you make of balls of glowing light the size of footballs seen floating through buildings and aircraft for no earthly reason? They come in a variety of iridescent colours, make no noise, no smell and generally disappear by hitting television sets or any other electrical fittings with a pop. Yet this isn't some sort of cranky UFO story – there are thousands of reports worldwide of these balls, including eyewitness accounts from professors of electrical engineering. But no one knows for sure what these balls are. All we can be certain of is that they are electrical freaks of weather, and probably some rare form of lightning called ball lightning.

There are many other weird and wonderful phenomena you hardly ever hear about, many of which leave scientists scratching their heads to explain. Showers of frogs, glowing trees, giant lumps of ice that fall from the heavens, cities that appear in the sky, huge spectres that are cast on clouds.

*Weird Weather* is a record of some of the most bizarre weather phenomena from Britain and the rest of the world. Some weird weathers are more familiar but have caused spectacular disasters, such as the largest recorded tornado in history on 18 March 1925 which killed over six hundred people in the USA. The worst storm in British history in 1703 killed approximately 8000 people; the worst flood in recorded history in 1887 in China, when the Yellow River flooded, killed an estimated 6 million people; the most lethal hurricane in history in Galveston, Texas, on 8 September 1900 killed around ten thousand people.

Extreme weather can strike in some surprising places and do some weird things. Hampstead in north-west London is prone to flash floods from freak thunderstorms, west London was ripped apart by a tornado on 8 December 1954, the Föhn wind in Germany sends people mad, the Namib desert in southern Africa is fertilized by fog, and Rickmansworth just outside London is one of the coldest places in Britain.

Wherever possible, explanations are given for all these phenomena, although there is a lot we do not know about them.

Also included are extraordinary eyewitness accounts – what does it feel like to be blasted by a million-volt bolt of lightning and survive, watch a ball of light float through an aircraft, or be sucked up in the middle of a tornado?

Even the everyday weather influences the way the living world behaves, affecting the honey-making of bees and the spinning of webs by spiders. And we too are creatures of the natural world affected by weather. Rheumatism, asthma, headaches and much else are affected by air pressure and temperature. Even our mental state responds to the weather, with statistics showing that murder and suicide rates are influenced by wind or atmospheric pressure changes. And even in these sophisticated technological days, weather still affects what we eat and drink, agriculture, the insurance industry and much else in our economy, and, some even argue, our national politics.

Not that there's anything new to weird weather. Britain has been savaged by dramatic meteorology for thousands of years. During the thirteenth and fourteenth centuries the climate grew so bad that more people died from famine than from the Plague which followed soon afterwards. During that terrible period whole seaports such as Forvie in Scotland, Danwich in East Anglia and the ancient town of Winchelsea in Sussex were wiped off the map by violent storms.

And in the 1700s during the Little Ice Age, the winters turned so cold that the Thames froze over, Eskimos visited Scotland, and polar bears reached Iceland on ice floes.

Bad weather has lost battles, destroyed empires and changed the course of history. The Roman Empire began in a warm epoch when harvests across Europe and North Africa were plenty, and fell in a cold period when famine was widespread. The bitter cold of the Little Ice Age sent the Scottish Presbyterians into colonizing Ireland, and the wet summers of the mid-1800s in Ireland brought on the great Potato Blight which triggered mass emigration to America.

But then good climate led to expanding empires – the Roman, Viking and Norman empires all grew when the climate was even warmer than now. These were times when the Romans grew vines as far north as Northumberland, the Vikings colonized Greenland when it was a truly green land.

And what surprises are in store for us in the future? Weird things are going on in our climate right now and hardly a month goes by without some weather record being broken somewhere. It's already affecting wildlife, plants, farming and forestry. The experts are in knots trying to forecast our future climate and whether the global warming we're experiencing is a natural part of the climate or a terrifying man-made problem running out of control. Already the warmer world is raising sea levels and many cities such as Shanghai are nearing the brink of catastrophic flooding. Altogether some 500 million people worldwide are at risk from flooding. As European summers turn milder we are seeing swarms of foreign pests and diseases invading Britain from as far away as Africa. Projecting that sort of mayhem into the future is a little alarming to say the least.

# FREAK
## PHENOMENA

## Showers of Frogs, Fish, Plants and Other Material

IT SEEMS UTTERLY BIZARRE to think of anything other than the usual rain, hail and snow falling out of the sky, but there are many reports of very strange showers from all over the world. Showers of animals, plants and inanimate objects are so numerous that they are now acknowledged as real phenomena. They seem mostly to consist of local showers of young toads or frogs, usually living, and falling from the sky with heavy rain.

Mab Hollands in Shepton Mallet, Somerset, was about nine years old and was walking along a country road when a storm suddenly broke. 'But it was not rain. It was not hail, 'til I realized that it was soft!' she recalls. 'The cattle went berserk and so was the dog. My own hair was heavy with what I briefly thought must be hailstones. As I shook my hair the little oddities simply fell out to the ground.' The 'oddities' were frogs. Meanwhile the cows were panic-stricken and almost stampeded.

Trowbridge open-air swimming pool had a similar shower, when thousands of frogs fell in 1939. But what made that episode so special was that so many people saw it happen. Even today, eyewitnesses who were children then still recall the shower vividly. The day had been overcast and thundery when suddenly the sky opened. 'It was a job to walk on the path without treading on them,' remembers one woman. Even *The Times* carried an account of it.

Another group of eyewitnesses saw a shower of frogs in June 1954. Sylvia Mowday took her eleven-year-old son Timothy and four-year-old daughter Mary to see a naval exhibition at a local park in Sutton Coldfield. The day was overcast but when the sky suddenly became dark and it started raining heavily the Mowdays ran for shelter. And then they saw something unbelievable. As the rain came down in torrents they also saw thousands of tiny thumbnail-sized frogs showering down all around them. 'I thought it was hail, but my son suddenly said "It isn't hail, mum, they're frogs, baby frogs,"' says Mrs Mowday. 'There were literally thousands of them. When we looked up we could see them. They covered our shoulders and umbrellas. This went on for about five minutes . . . but afterwards we were afraid to move in case we trod on them.'

Strange showers like these are more common than you'd think. Apart from frogs, there have been showers of fresh fish and sea fish, tadpoles, pond snails, and pond weeds, young eels and much more throughout the world. And there's nothing new to all these reports. Throughout history there have been persistent stories of showers of things falling from the sky. Pliny the Elder in AD77 reported frogs falling and Athenaeus in the fourth century AD recorded a continuous shower of fish for three days in Greece, so serious that 'the roads were blocked, people were unable to open their front doors and the town stank for weeks'.

Reports of similar showers have come from all over the world, for example:

toads in Brignoles in France (24 September 1973)

frogs in Greece (1991)
frogs in Arkansas (2 January 1973)
flounder and Dover sole in East London (1984)
minnows and sticklebacks in Mountain Ash,
   Glamorganshire (1859)
hazelnuts in Dublin (1867)
snails in Chester, Pennsylvania (1870)
snails in Algiers (1973)
crayfish across Florida (1954)
maggots in Acapulco (1968)
pond mussels in Paderborn, Germany (1892)
jellyfish in Bath (1894)
coal in Bournemouth (1983)
and many, many others.

Experts have tried to dismiss eyewitness testimonies, such as the fall of fish on Dunmarra, 500 miles south of Darwin in the Australian outback in February 1994. But then the respected journal *Science* reported a fish shower from a biologist, A.D. Bajkov, who worked for the US Department of Wildlife and Fisheries. On the morning of 23 October 1947, he saw fish ranging from two to nine inches long falling on trees in Marksville, Louisiana. 'I was in the restaurant with my wife having breakfast, when the waitress informed us that fish were falling from the sky. We went immediately to collect some of the fish. The people in the town were excited,' he wrote. 'They were freshwater fish native to local waters: large-mouthed black bass, goggle-eye, and hickory shad.'

So how can frogs and fish fall from the sky? Many accounts speak of hundreds of tiny frogs blanketing the ground after a downpour, but many of these sightings are unreliable because the animals could have simply come out from the ground during the rain-shower. As for the authentic accounts of things actually *seen* falling from the sky, it wasn't until 1921 that Dr Eugene Gudger at the American Museum of Natural History was convinced of their authenticity. He collected so many reports of these odd stories he knew they couldn't be ignored. He suggested that the showers were caused by tornadoes or waterspouts, the water equivalent of a tornado. These funnels of spiralling air suck up wildlife from ponds, lakes or seas, and dump them miles away on land. There have been eyewitness accounts of tornadoes passing over ponds and rivers and temporarily draining them, so any living thing would be lifted up into the air maybe thousands of feet above into the cloud base.

We have dozens of waterspouts and tornadoes every year in the UK and some of them can be quite strong. For instance, in Baileyhaulwen, Powys, Wales, on 17 May 1983, one tornado reportedly picked up sheep and flung them several hundred feet. Ned Jones, on whose fields the sheep fell, exclaimed: 'I couldn't believe my eyes. They could not run here because there are stone walls and a river in their path.' So lifting a few hundred sunbathing frogs should present few problems to the average British tornado or waterspout.

But one nagging question remains: why are the showers of animals usually only frogs or fish and not everything else in the ponds and rivers – things like stones, rocks, weeds or other animals? Perhaps the vortex of a tornado or waterspout and the thundercloud above it simply drop materials too small or too large for them to carry. This is only speculation, though. On the other hand, there is one recorded case of a whole pond falling from the sky. Ron Newton was a teenager walking in the countryside in Rayleigh in Essex in the 1930s when out of a clear blue sky a dark cloud came over and an intense downpour of rain came down with a shower of small frogs, tadpoles, sticklebacks and pondweed.

There are many other types of mysterious showers. On 13 March 1977, as Alfred Osborne and his wife returned home from a church service, they heard a clicking noise. Suddenly hundreds of nuts fell down from a practically clear sky, bouncing off cars. What's even more puzzling is where fresh, ripe hazelnuts could have come from in mid-March, as they don't mature in Britain until late summer.

Strangest of all is the story of Jack Moody of Southampton, who was sitting in his conservatory on the morning of 12 February 1979, when he heard a 'swooshing' sound on the glass roof and looked up to see a cascade of seeds hitting the house and garden. The seeds were mustard and cress, and were then followed by a few more showers of seeds. They smothered the garden as well. Then next day followed a shower of haricot bean and broad bean seeds. All of the seeds later germinated into proper plants. The explanation may have lurked close to his home, because seeds being packaged in large containers in the docks a few miles away could have blown away.

## Showers of Straw

Hay is quite commonly seen floating in the air and then falling down in showers. Basildon in Essex is not often noted for supernatural phenomena, but on 28th July

1992 it experienced a most extraordinary incident. Just after lunchtime several eyewitnesses reported seeing large clumps of straw falling from the sky. As one star- tled resident observed, 'There were large handfuls of straw like you would put in a rabbit hutch falling out of the sky.' A local estate agent spoke of hay flying hori- zontally through the air, and a local UFO expert went on full alert (flying saucers apparently being quite active along the Thames estuary).

The same day, a similar outbreak of straw showers struck in South Wonston in Hampshire. Again, eyewit- nesses reported straw floating through the sky and then cascading down over fields and villages to earth.

And these two incidents aren't isolated. Ten years ago, a shower of hay struck Devizes in Wiltshire. It was a beautifully hot and cloudless day, as the *Bath and West Evening Chronicle* reported: 'Late afternoon a great cloud of hay drifted high over town. Then it dropped onto the centre of town . . . It was caught in gutters and against buildings and made a big job for the street cleaners.'

Could all these bizarre outbreaks be signs of invading aliens? Probably not, because there is another explana- tion. In Basildon, Glen and Trevor Hudson saw the straw being sucked up from a field and whirled round in a spiral. In the Hampshire incident a local resident, David Kirkwood, saw a vortex cut a 12-foot (3.7-metre) wide swathe through a field. 'It was the most extraordi- nary thing I have ever seen,' he reported to the *Southern Evening Echo*. 'You could see the vortex because it was sucking up the straw from the field.'

In all these cases whirlwinds were caused by hot air spiralling up from the ground, and they are quite capa- ble of sucking up loose straw in their path.

# Giant Ice Falls

Ice has long been a menace, sometimes in a brutally direct way. In 1776 the son of the parish clerk of Bampton in Devon was killed by an icicle which detached itself from the church tower, plummeted down and speared him. The tragedy was marked by a bizarre memorial in the church:

> *Bless my eyes*
> *Here he lies*
> *In a sad pickle*
> *Kill'd by an icicle.*

Following a freak ice-storm over Chicago in March 1978 huge chunks of ice fell a thousand feet or more into busy streets. Police sealed off roads surrounding the city's tallest buildings as ice blocks weighing up to 20 pounds (9 kilograms) smashed to the ground. Fortunately no one was reported injured, although several parked cars were pulverized.

Not so lucky was a pedestrian in Moscow in January 1978. For some time giant icicles had been hanging at great heights from the city's high-rise buildings. One icicle fell and struck a man causing serious head injuries from which he later died.

Ice can also fall from the sky for no apparent reason. On 2 April 1973, a storm struck Manchester. Several witnesses saw a single flash of blinding lightning, while a few miles away hail fell. A short while later a postgraduate student, Mr R. F. Griffiths, walking along a street in south Manchester saw an enormous chunk of

*Lumps of ice have fallen from aircraft, but other ice falls remain unexplained.* © Harrow Observer

ice crash and shatter onto the road. The largest piece of ice measured over 5 inches (127 millimetres) long and weighed 22 ounces (0.62 kilograms), although because it was melting this was an underestimate. Detailed analysis showed it was highly unlikely to have fallen off an aircraft as an icicle, and was probably a frozen collection of hailstones.

Aircraft have sometimes been blamed for the ice – either the ice falls off their wings or waste water is jettisoned. A huge lump of ice crashed through the roof of a house in Isleworth outside London on 16 August 1970. The family of four who lived there were asleep when the block fell. On 25 March 1974 Mrs Nonion Wildsmith of Pinner in Middlesex was cleaning her car at 5.10p.m. when a mass of ice about 18 inches (46 centimetres) across crashed into and cratered the bonnet of her car.

At the same time, more ice blocks smashed roof tiles nearby. The culprit was a 'plane passing overhead, and she successfully claimed compensation from the airline.

Another peculiar event occurred in Timberville, Virginia, USA on 7 March 1976. Robert Rickard writing in the *Journal of Meteorology*, 1977, records the story from the *Daily News Record* (Harrisonburg, Virginia). The sky was clear and Wilbert Cullers and his family were watching television when at 8.45p.m. there was a loud crash which shook the house. A block of ice about the size of a basketball smashed through the thin metal roofing of the house, through the plasterboard ceiling of the living room and fell onto the floor. Deputies from the Rockingham County Sheriff's Department arrived about an hour later and collected some of the ice samples. A neighbour saw the ice and another ice ball fall about 50 yards (46 metres) away, but when he looked up at the sky for any sign of aircraft he saw nothing unusual. Later chemical and physical analysis of the ice at a local college found it was fairly unremarkable; it appeared to be made of tap water.

But these stories are unlikely to explain other cases. Sometimes the ice falls out of a clear sky, such as at Long Beach, California on 4 June 1953 when about fifty ice lumps fell, some weighing 165 pounds (75 kilograms), and the total weighing about 2200 pounds (1 tonne).

Given these enormous sizes, some of the fantastic historical stories of ice falls look less suspicious. The greatest ever natural ice chunk recorded fell at Ord in Rosshire on the evening of 13 August 1849 on the estate of Mr Moffat of Balvullich. The monstrous block was some 20 feet (6 metres) across, and *The Times* reported that it had a beautiful crystalline, almost transparent appearance, formed of diamond-shaped ice coalesced together. 'Immediately after one of the loudest peals of thunder heard there, a large and irregular-shaped mass of ice, reckoned to be nearly 20 feet in circumference, and of a proportionate thickness, fell near the farmhouse.' And of course no aircraft could have been responsible for it.

There are also a few cases of strange objects encased in ice falling from the sky. The *U.S. Monthly Weather Review* reported in May 1894 of a gopher turtle 6 by 3 inches (15 by 20 centimetres) falling, entirely encased in ice, with hail during a severe hailstorm at Boving, Mississippi. More recently, in December 1973, the *Daily Express* reported that frozen ducks had tumbled out of the sky above Stuttgart, Arkansas. It was thought that they had been caught in a tornado, pitched into the sky and become iced over.

In fact, falls of ice may have much in common with the strange showers of frogs, fish, and other objects described earlier. Violent thunderstorms might toss hailstones inside the cloud so violently that several hailstones clump together and become wrapped in even more ice, forming a 'superhailstone'. But this is only a theory.

## *Showers of 'Blood'*

In the early hours of 1 July 1968 a remarkable shower of red rain fell over southern England and the Midlands. People woke up later that morning to find everything outside covered in a thin layer of red sand. It was Saharan sand, carried up in sandstorms and sent aloft in a low pressure system that swept up over North Africa and Spain, sending temperatures soaring up to 90 degrees Fahrenheit (32 degrees Celsius) in London.

Another large fall of Saharan sand occurred in the first week of November 1984 in southern England, brought on balmy 68 degree-Fahrenheit (20 degree-Celsius) winds. The winds also brought other Saharan guests: masses of Pallid Swift, a North African bird used to flying high and which had been swept along in the southerly airstream.

In fact, dust and sand from the Sahara arrives in Britain about two or three times a year on average, but it's usually washed away in the rain that it falls down in. It normally travels to Britain on a strong southerly wind over about 1600 miles (2600 kilometres) in forty hours.

## Tornadoes

Tornadoes are the most violent winds known on Earth reaching some 300 miles per hour (480 kilometres per hour), but only strike a very narrow area. They are often created inside a thundercloud as warm air is sucked upwards and rubs against cold air passing downwards. The rubbing spins the air in between – in the way that water going down a plughole forms a spinning and sucking funnel, so the tornado's funnel spins and sucks up the ground below.

Tornadoes strike in many areas of the world, but

nowhere are they as frequent or as fierce as in the USA, where each year the country is hit by around a thousand 'twisters', killing eighty-nine people on average. The worst hit area is in 'Tornado Alley', a region of the American MidWest running through Kansas, Oklahoma and Missouri. Several hundred tornadoes a year strike here during spring, summer and early autumn, as hot, humid air from the Gulf of Mexico hits cold, dry, polar air masses from Canada. Where the two air masses clash, giant thunderclouds develop – the greater the difference in temperature between the air masses, the more violent the thunderstorm and the more chance of tornadoes, sometimes dozens of them.

One of the worst outbreaks in the USA occurred in the late afternoon and evening of 11 April 1965. A

*Tornadoes are the fastest winds on Earth, capable of blasting towns to smithereens.* © *NOAA/NSSL*

system of at least 37 twisters spread destruction for 9 hours across 6 mid-western states; 271 people were killed and more than 3000 injured, with property damage estimated at 300 million dollars. But the most fatal series of tornadoes hit southern USA in one day on 19 February 1884, when 800 people were reported killed in Mississippi, Alabama, North and South Carolina, Tennessee, Kentucky and Indiana.

But even this horrendous episode is overshadowed by the most devastating *single* tornado in recorded American history. It started at 1p.m. on 18 March 1925 when a tornado took shape near Ellington in south east Missouri. It began as a funnel at the front of a huge thundercloud, but a quarter of an hour later it had grown into a full scale tornado a quarter of a mile (400 metres) across and ripped through Annapolis, Missouri. Then it headed north east in a straight line travelling at 60 miles per hour (96 kilometres per hour) across into Illinois, swelling into a gargantuan funnel nearly a mile (1.6 kilometres) wide. Eyewitnesses said it looked like a colossal inverted cone truncated at the ground with lightning darting through it, accompanied by a constant thundering roar like a giant freight train. It destroyed the town of Gorham with winds so strong that bodies were thrown over a mile (1.6 kilometres) away into the surrounding countryside.

The tornado then picked up speed and crossed into Indiana, completely destroying the town of Griffin and then ripped up a quarter of Princeton (Indiana) before finally dying out. By the end it had left a trail of devastation along 219 miles (350 kilometres) in its three and a half hours' life, killing 689 people, injuring 1980 others, destroying 4 towns, severely damaging 6 others and leaving 11,000 homeless.

The enormous death toll was partly because the tornado was difficult to see. The sky was so dark, the funnel so wide, there was so much debris flying in the air and the storm cloud was so close to the ground that people in its path didn't realize the tornado was heading towards them until it struck. Apart from being the single most destructive tornado in recorded history, the 1925 tornado also established a number of other records: it had one of the longest continuous tracks of 219 miles (350 kilometres), passed in an almost straight line deviating by no more than a degree off course, lasted the longest time and was one of the fastest tracking tornadoes, advancing at about 50 miles per hour (80 kilometres per hour).

Few people have seen the inside of a tornado's funnel and survived, but one eyewitness was Bill Keller from Wellsford, Kansas. In June 1928 a tornado passed directly over his house: 'A screaming hissing sound came directly from the end of the funnel, and when I looked up, I saw to my astonishment right into the very heart of the tornado . . . it was brilliantly lit with the constant flashes of lightning zig-zagging from side to side . . . Around the rim of the great vortex, small tornadoes were constantly breaking away and writhing their way around the funnel.'

Another eyewitness, Dean Cosgrove, from Fort Morgan, Colorado, was in his car in June 1991 when a thunderstorm started brewing up. He told the *American Weather Observer* magazine of an eerie calm at the beginning of a thunderstorm: 'The calm was followed by what I can best describe as a slam of wind and mostly marble-sized hail at what I estimate to be in excess of seventy miles per hour. The force of this windslam made me cover my head instinctively because I felt

sure my driver's side window was going to be blown in.
The wind-slam ended about as quickly as it began. I
looked out the passenger side window and saw the
funnel.'

Britain also has tornadoes. The worst ones reach
wind speeds of up 212 miles per hour (95 metres per
second) resulting in three devastating tornadoes this
century, including one that hit Birmingham in 1931 and
another that hit west London during the afternoon rush
hour on 8 December 1954. The London tornado ripped
a 100–400 yard (90–360 metre) wide track for 9 miles
(15 kilometres) through Chiswick, Gunnersbury, Acton,
Golders Green and Southgate, injuring six people at
Gunnersbury railway station where the roof was
destroyed. A factory at Acton was destroyed and twelve

*One of Britain's worst tornadoes struck west London in
1954, demolishing buildings like this factory.* © Ealing
and Acton Gazette

people injured. As an eyewitness in Acton reported, 'I saw a car flying by my shop fifteen feet in the air. It landed upright without bursting a tyre.'

Prehistoric monuments may also be linked with tornadoes. Dr Terence Meaden of the Tornado Research Organisation in Britain has discovered that prehistoric strips of cleared land known as cursuses at stone circles tend to point in the same directions. Tornadoes tend to pass in the same direction and each cursus, such as the 1.7 mile (2.7 kilometre) Stonehenge Cursus which runs past Stonehenge itself, is about the same direction, shape, length and width as the track of a severe tornado. Maybe severe tornadoes with their roaring sound, sweeping damage and sometimes with hail and lightning, might have been seen as religious signs by prehistoric societies and later commemorated in their stone circles.

### WEIRD EFFECTS OF TORNADOES

Tornadoes have some extraordinary powers. During a tornado at El Dorado, Kansas, on 10 June 1958, a woman was reputed to have been plucked through a window in her house, carried 60 feet (18 metres) away and to have landed safely.

The air pressure inside a tornado is so low it drops to as little as 150 millibars – that's the equivalent of suddenly being shot 5000 feet (1500 metres) high into the sky, as if swept in an instant to the top of Ben Nevis. That vacuum creates horrific damage. There are stories of chickens blown up like balloons and plucked clean by the tornado's funnel, as at Scottsbluff on 30 May 1951, and Flint, Michigan on 8 June 1953.

The violent winds are so powerful they can shoot sand, gravel and even straw like bullets. Pieces of straw can puncture the bark of trees. In one well-documented case, a pine plank was shot right through a solid iron girder supporting the Eads Bridge in St Louis, Missouri, on 27 May 1896.

The vacuum inside tornadoes gives them enormous lifting power. A house in Oklahoma was picked up, turned 90 degrees and set neatly back down again sideways to the road. A spire of a church in Kansas complete with weathercock was dropped 15.5 miles (25 kilometres) away from its base. Five coaches of a train travelling through Minnesota in 1931 were lifted off the track and left 27 yards (25 metres) away in a ditch. A tornado on 26 September 1971 in Rotherham, Yorkshire – an area not noted for violent tornadoes – shoved a 90-ton locomotive 150 feet (46 metres) along a railway track.

The amazing vacuum in a tornado produces vast pressure differences. A pilot flying over Waco in Texas during a tornado in 1953 reported seeing a theatre and a six-storey building burst open like bombs and collapse.

Tornadoes can cut a house in half, demolishing one side and leaving the other untouched, as happened during the west London tornado of 1954. A tornado in Sherman, Texas, in 1896 picked up two houses and shattered them, severely injuring everyone inside.

### TORNADO LIGHTS

On 25 May 1955 at Blackwell, Oklahoma, eyewitnesses saw a tornado with a bizarre lightshow shining out of it.

One witness reported looking up: 'As the storm was directly east of me, the fire near the top of the funnel looked like a child's Fourth of July pin wheel [firework like a Catherine wheel].' According to another witness, Lee Hunter, standing 4 miles (6.4 kilometres) away, the funnel looked as though 'it was a steady, deep blue colour – very bright. It had an orange coloured fire in the centre from the cloud to the ground . . . it looked like a giant neon tube in the air. As it swung along the ground, orange fire or electricity would gush out from the bottom of the funnel.'

Eyewitnesses to tornadoes have seen many other strange phenomena: glowing columns inside tornado funnels, blinking luminous patches in tornado clouds, searchlight beams, ground-level flashes of light.

But what are these bizarre lights? Some scientists remain sceptical that tornadoes have lights at all. But several modern reports plus photographs have lent more weight to the phenomenon of tornado lights. Some of these accounts appear to be of plain forked lightning. Others are probably of ball lightning – glowing spheres of coloured light. On 11 April 1965 in Toledo, Ohio, there were reports of a beautiful electric blue light around a tornado: '. . . balls of orange and lightning came from the cone point of the tornado.'

The destruction of a church in the seventeenth century could have been the combined work of a tornado and ball lightning. On Sunday 21 October 1638, the church of Widecombe in the wilds of Dartmoor was packed for the morning service. Outside, a huge thunderstorm broke out, with torrential rain, thunder and lightning raging. And then suddenly lightning blasted right through the church in a blaze of fire and smoke, the spire fell down, the roof collapsed and several people were killed – somewhere between five and fifty depending on which account you read from the time.

Despite the carnage, it seemed like a case of ordinary lightning because the highest point – the steeple – was the most severely damaged part. But a fiery ball was also seen blazing through the church which according to one account: 'so affrighted the whole Congregation that the most part of them fell downe.' Together with engravings of the time, these accounts all fit the description of a violent form of ball lightning – what might be called a 'fireball'. Severe thunderstorms sometimes drop balls of 'fire' which instantly explode into flames and electrical mayhem on buildings. Even today these fireballs are totally unexplained.

But that isn't the end of the story. One eyewitness saw another bizarre sight – a funnel in the sky. From an engraving made shortly afterwards it fits the picture of a tornado, and indeed, powerful thunderstorms can spawn both tornadoes as well as fireballs.

So maybe the wretched parishioners of Widecombe were hit by an utterly bizarre double whammy of fireball and tornado, which probably remains unique anywhere in the world to this day. But whatever the cause, they were convinced it was divine punishment.

Ball lightning and ordinary lightning don't account for all the bizarre tornado light displays. The best we can say is that tornadoes have powerful electrical discharges. The whirling funnel is like a motor generating an intense electrical field around it, strong enough to create glowing lights.

Possibly the earliest reference to a tornado's lights may have been in the Old Testament, when Elijah was snatched up to heaven in a lightning-filled tornado. A description appears in Ezekiel, Chapter 1, verse 4: 'And

I looked, and, behold, a whirlwind came out of the north, a great cloud, a fire infolding itself, and a brightness was about it, and out of the midst thereof was the colour of amber, out of the midst of the fire.'

## Monsters and Waterspouts

There's a bit of confusion about tornadoes and waterspouts. Basically, tornadoes are born from thunderclouds and when they pass across water suck up a funnel of water. Waterspouts are gentler cousins of tornadoes, created from less violent clouds with weaker funnels of spinning water. They often occur in the warm waters off the Florida Keys where up to five hundred a year are spawned.

The water tornadoes can be amazingly powerful. A tornado that formed at Norfolk in Virginia in 1935 started to demolish the town, crossed a creek sucking up water until the bottom was exposed and then gouged a channel in the mud. As a 'waterspout' it lifted small boats on to the shore, ripped off part of a heavy pier and then went back on land again and destroyed several buildings.

On 7 June 1968, at Diner Key near Miami, a tornado passing across water ripped through a marina, smashing dozens of boats including a 5-ton houseboat which was lifted up 6 feet (1.8 metres), and impaled on a wooden pillar on a pier 100 feet (30 metres) away.

But true waterspouts can be quite impressive. The White Star liner *Pittsburgh* was hit by a huge waterspout in mid-Atlantic in 1923. So many tons of water

*The furious vortices of waterspouts or water tornadoes terrified ancient mariners and helped create legends of sea monsters. From* L'Atmosphère *by Camille Flammarion*

were dumped on her so suddenly her bridge was wrecked.

Sailing through a waterspout is sometimes a terrifying experience, as described by John Caldwell in his book *Desperate Voyage* (Gollancz, 1950). He was sailing his boat *Pagan* in mid-Pacific when he saw a waterspout and deliberately aimed for it.

> *Pagan* was swallowed by a cold wet fog and whirring wind. The decks tilted. A volley of spray swept across the decks. The rigging howled. Suddenly it was dark as night. My hair whipped my eyes, I breathed wet air, and the cold wind wet me through. *Pagan's* gunwales were under and she pitched into the choppy seaway.
>
> I had sailed into a high dark column from 75 to 100 feet wide, inside of which was a damp circular wind of 30 knots, if it was that strong.
>
> As suddenly as I had entered the waterspout I rode out into bright free air. The high dark wall of singing wind ran away.

Weaker cousins of waterspouts are water devils – small whirlwinds that whip across the water and swirl up a small spout of water. A party of anglers was fishing in Loch Dionard in Sutherland on 12 February 1978. After half an hour or so, a wind blew up and they decided to head for the shore. That is when they heard a whooshing sound behind them. A spout of water 10 feet (3 metres) high was bearing down on them. Before they could get out of its path, the boat was lifted out of the water and spun round. It crashed back to the surface facing the other way. The anglers were lucky to get off with nothing worse than a soaking. They watched terrified, but fascinated, as the spout of water swirled across the loch before it fizzled out. When a strong wind blows over the loch and hits the cliffs at a certain angle, it creates a sort of whirlwind that sucks up a spout of water. It can prove perilous for the unwary as the party of anglers found out.

The *Surrey Mirror* reported on 20 April 1979 spouts of water seen on Earlswood Lakes near Reigate, Surrey:

> Picnickers watched in awe as a freak whirlwind struck twice at Earlswood Lakes, spinning water into the air and making a loud roaring noise. One eyewitness, Martin Gaule, said: 'There was a splash, and the water was whipped up in the air about ten feet high and five feet across. It moved towards the middle of the lake and died out.' His friend Ian Bristow then saw another one blow up: 'The water went round and round. You could see fish on top of the water. At first we thought it was a UFO.'

Another account was reported in the *Louth Standard*, 11 May 1979:

> A freak waterspout off the coast of Mablethorpe proved to be the main Bank Holiday attraction in the resort. Miss Gaynor Kirkby, the Foreshore Manager, told the *Standard* that the spout appeared after there had been an isolated flash of forked lightning and a peal of thunder. 'Suddenly it just appeared in the sea opposite the Foreshore Office. It was like steam rising off a boiling sea and travelled parallel to the coast before veering out to sea and disappearing,' she said.

Dr Terence Meaden of the Tornado Research Organisation has been studying water devils, and wonders if
these and their bigger waterspout cousins explain that
other phenomenon of Scottish waters, the Loch Ness
Monster. He believes that the long tapering funnel of a
waterspout or water devil could easily be mistaken for a
monster's head and neck.

> Some of these cases could be explained by a whirl-
> wind spinning on water and throwing up spray.
> The waterspouts in particular are very long, reach-
> ing way up to a cloud above, but their trunks can
> be invisible for a great part of their length. So
> down at the water's surface all you would see is a
> great mass of fuming spray and this can be raised a
> few feet suggesting that there is a body in there.

Sometimes the spouts run erratically backwards and
forwards across the water, sometimes they come to a
halt for a minute or two before moving off again. Add
to that a roaring or swishing noise and you have the
ingredients of a classic water monster. Now go back to
olden days when eyesight was generally a lot poorer,
and waterspouts would look even more monsterish.

Take this other account from the Orkneys, from
August 1910. 'I looked up and saw a creature standing
straight up out of the sea – with a snake-like neck and a
head, like a horse or camel. The wind was light . . . I
reckon we sat watching it for about 5 minutes, when it
very slowly began to sink, straight down in the sea, and
the water closed over its head without a splash.' Dr
Meaden thinks this could have been a water-whirlwind
slowly moving over the water. Not that these sorts of
sightings explain all the Loch Ness stories . . . maybe

there is a monster there after all, but not when the wind blows!

The *Sunday Express* reported another interesting case in 1979. The scene outside the car window as passenger Anne Jones gazed out on the lake was one of tranquillity – until the creature appeared. Then suddenly the surface began to foam and bubble and for a few seconds Mrs Jones found herself watching a huge hump-backed form. Then it vanished beneath the deep dark waters of Bala Lake, which nestles in the shadows of the Berwyn mountains. 'I shall never forget it,' commented Mrs Jones. 'All I saw was its huge back, and froth boiling around it.'

The interesting part of this account was the bubbling and foaming, typical of water devils, and the humps may have been the centre of the ring of bubbles.

Such 'monsters' can have profound effects on the people who witness them. In the book *Inland Waters of Africa*, published in 1933, authors S. and E.B. Worthington declared that the great sea-serpent of Lake Victoria Nyanzna in what was then Rhodesia was 'a powerful influence in arranging the lives of the Jalup and other tribes . . . It announces its coming with a terrible roar and emerges from the lake at certain times to swallow up human beings, canoes and everything in its path.' The authors were sure, though, that the monster was a spout of water, which they witnessed on the lake for themselves.

## Corn Circles

Mysterious circles of flattened cereal crops first appeared in southern England in 1980 and caused immense excitement in the media. There were reports of strange noises, weird lights and the odd behaviour of dogs in the areas of the circles. Were these circles the signs of UFOs? The tabloid press certainly jumped on the circles as evidence that extraterrestrials had visited us. The alternative popular explanation was that 'earth energy' channels had appeared which could knock both people and corn over. In fact, many people claimed to have had strange experiences just by standing in the centre of the flattened corn.

Questions were asked in Parliament, crop circle watches were set up with video cameras and radar to find one actually being formed. The circles became an international sensation, with visitors from all over the world coming to see them. And there was money in it: conferences were organized, videos of the circles made and books published. UFO-crop circle proponent Pat Delgado wrote three books which sold nearly five hundred thousand copies worldwide.

And then the shapes of the corn circles started to become more elaborate: circles with smaller circles on their edges, and circles linked to each other with arms. And then in September 1991 two middle-aged men, Doug Bower and Dave Chorley, announced that they were behind the crop circles: with a piece of string, flat boards and invigorated with bottles of beer they could flatten crops quite easily into symmetrical circles. That Doug and Dave were responsible for all the crop circles is highly unlikely, though, since hundreds of them have appeared each summer, up to twenty per night.

The great crop circle hoax finally culminated in a competition organized by the *Guardian* in July 1992, when crop circlers from all over the world came to Wiltshire for the chance of winning £3,000 prize money.

That was probably the apotheosis of crop circles. In July the following year, the *Guardian* announced the sudden decline of the crop circle. Only forty-five crop circles had been found so far in 1993, compared with more than four hundred in each of the previous two years. 'It is a tragedy on the scale of England's cricket demise for the fledgling, bitterly divided cereology industry and a blow to farmers who have earned more from charging people to inspect circles found on their land than from growing crops,' wrote the *Guardian*'s environment editor, John Vidal.

The enthusiasts – particularly those who made a lot of money out of it all – weren't so easily bowed. Author Pat Delgado was still convinced that the circles were supernatural. 'Some of the circles are genuine. I still believe we have a fundamental mystery.'

More mundane explanations were that the circles were made by the downdraught from helicopters. But for meteorologist Dr Terence Meaden of the Tornado Research Organisation, the circles looked to him very much like the work of vortices of wind that stayed spinning on one spot. Such a novel idea didn't really catch on with other meteorologists because whirlwinds, tornadoes and other spinning columns of air never remain in one spot. But Dr Meaden persisted, especially when eyewitnesses came forward who actually saw stationary whirlwinds flatten crops into circles.

Dr Meaden has long abandoned crop circles, which is

a pity, because no one has yet explained those early eye-witness reports of stationary whirlwinds flattening cereals. It could be that hoaxers alone cannot explain all the crop circles, but we'll probably never know now.

There are several naturally-spinning wind systems like the upward-spiralling whirlwind. When a whirlwind becomes unstable and breaks down it is thought to make crop circles. The same applies to the break-down of lee- or eddy-vortices. Typical eddy-vortices have been watched countless times spinning in the lee of hills and scarps. Excellent examples were seen by Roy Lucas in the lee of Windmill Hill, near Avebury on 16 June 1988, and by Gary and Vivienne Tomlinson in Surrey in May 1990. When the vortices become un-stable they break down and carve out circles in the vegetation below.

David and Elaine Haines of Sturminster Newton, Dorset, reported another very peculiar sight. On Sunday 21 July 1990, at 11p.m. they were travelling home from Westbury, Wiltshire, when they saw what looked like the reflection of the moon: '. . . as we trav-elled on it then looked like four beams of a high-powered torch, but as we went still further we could see it was in fact four swirling shapes, shining white. We turned off the car engine and could hear a whooshing noise. These four spinning shapes went round and round in a clockwise direction.' They reported the sighting to the local police and local RAF station who seemed to think they were reporting UFOs, but neither witness felt it was, and was instead more like a whirlwind.

Brian Hayes writing in the *Journal of Meteorology* records an observation by Barrie Brumpton at 10.30p.m. on Colden Common, Winchester, on 29 September

1991. The weather was very wet and stormy, but during a lull in the rain and wind he saw an 'object' filling the road 150 yards (137 metres) ahead of him. It was on the ground and round at the top, looked like a 'mass of mist' and 'very wet'. It seemed to roll towards him at about 30 miles per hour (48 kilometres per hour). It sounded 'like very heavy rain pounding on the road', even though it wasn't raining at the time, and was clearly visible despite the darkness, so was apparently luminous. It later moved off the road and vanished.

Another line of evidence was published in the *Journal of Meteorology* in April 1992. Dr Meaden and colleagues claimed that when a whirlwind fizzles out it causes an intense wind near the ground and makes a whirl pattern on the vegetation. Meanwhile, Japanese researchers discovered a crop circle in a fully fenced off protected area at a radio transmitter near Tokyo. At the time the circle appeared on the night of 31 August 1991, the transmitting system started performing strangely. There was no sign of any intruders and it was thought highly unlikely that hoaxers were responsible.

## Bible Stories

### THE GREAT FLOOD

'In the six hundredth year of the life of Noah, in the second month and on the seventeenth day of the month, all the fountains of the great deep were opened up: and the flood-gates of the heavens overflowed exceedingly and filled all the face of the earth; and the waters prevailed beyond measure.'

Noah wasn't the first to survive cataclysmic floods. Stories of Great Floods are so old and so varied they seem to be part and parcel of human history. And there might be a good reason for them.

Some ten thousand years ago the last ice age drew to a close. Ice had spread down to the Midlands in Britain in the northern hemisphere and close to South America and New Zealand in the southern hemisphere. When the thaw started, change was at first slow but then came a sudden and dramatic warming. Vast quantities of ice melted in catastrophic floods, inundating early human settlements. Violent storms raged across the globe. Sea levels rose so fast that in less than a thousand years the rising waters cut Ireland from Britain, Britain from the rest of Europe, Russia from North America. These floods may have been the root of the stories of a Great Flood.

## MANNA

When the Children of Israel collected manna from heaven during their exodus from Egypt, did they experience a meteorological miracle? There's been a surprising amount of controversy about the subject, given that the accounts of the phenomenon are somewhat old. Some say the manna was sticky sweet sap oozing out of the tamarisk, a desert shrub. On the other hand, there could be a meteorological explanation.

Showers of nutritious lichen are known to fall in the Middle East. *Leconora esculenta* is a rather flaky lichen which easily peels off the rocks it grows on and rolls around in the wind. There are several cases of people being showered with it and then eating it. In one incident the countryside was covered in the lichen, which witnesses claimed 'fell down from heaven'. Seeing their sheep happily eat it, the locals ground the lichen down into flour and made bread from it.

But possibly the most exotic form of manna to fall to earth was a shower of meat over the backyard of a Kentucky house in 1876. As reported in the local press, *Bath County News*: 'Mrs Crouch was out in the yard at the time making soap, when meat which looked like beef began to fall around her. The sky was perfectly clear at the time, and she said it fell like large snow flakes.' The meat was apparently perfectly fresh and tasted of either mutton or venison. One explanation is that birds may have been hit by lightning and then fallen to the ground ready-cooked. This seems a bit of a long shot, but dead burnt birds have been found falling during thunderstorms.


RED SEA

The parting of the Red Sea could have been another weather-related phenomenon. The Israelites miraculously crossed the sea on a dry seabed and left the Egyptians to drown behind them. One idea is that a strong crosswind blowing across the Red Sea for about two days during a freak low tide could actually part the waters and expose the seabed. A sudden change in wind direction would then let the waters return and these could have swamped the Egyptians.

Another weather-related explanation involves an optical trick. If the Israelites had taken a route north of the Red Sea they would have passed through the Nile Delta.

This area is rich in mirages where baking hot air from the ground is trapped by cooler air above. This difference in air temperatures bends light from the horizon upwards, so images of the Delta's lagoons appear to float as a high wall of water all around. Could Moses have led his people through an illusion of water? The 'sea' would have appeared to part in front and close up again behind them. But if so, what happened to the Egyptians?

Another theory is that a gigantic seismic disturbance sucked out the water from the Red Sea before a colossal tsunami (tidal wave) flooded the seabed. The closest event we know of that fits the time was the cataclysmic explosion of the Greek volcanic island of Santorini nearly 3500 years ago. The Bible supports the idea when it describes how the Israelites' exodus from Egypt was guided by a pillar of fire and clouds which could have been the eruption of the Santorini volcano. The eruption was so violent that the core of the volcano collapsed, sucking in sea water in a spectacular explosion and the tsunami it triggered could have drawn out water from marshes on the northern coast of Egypt and let the Israelites escape. Then about an hour later the water flow would have reversed and the main surge of the tsunami would have ripped into the marshes and drowned the Egyptians.

Whatever the explanation, if the parting of the Red Sea was a freak of Nature it's still a miracle that it happened at just the right time.

SEVEN YEARS

The seven years of plenty and seven years of famine first predicted by Joseph in his dreams and told to

Pharaoh are almost echoed in real weather cycles. There is an eleven-year cycle in sunspots which are reputed to affect droughts. The Chinese were the first to notice these dark spots on the surface of the sun when dust storms left the sky so dark that they were able to look directly at the sun during the day and record the larger spots. They've been recording sunspots ever since for over two thousand years and this provides a marvellous historical record.

The complete sunspot cycle of twenty-two years matches cycles in global climate. Scientists grew particularly excited when they found the same sorts of eleven-year cycle in other places. Botanists studying tree rings found an eleven-year cycle in tree rings which show an annual historical record of weather – generally speaking, the larger the ring the milder the weather. They grew even more excited when they found some notable exceptions to this tree-ring cycle during the years 1645 to 1715. This seventy-year period is known as the Little Ice Age because of its severe cold, and it matched the Chinese records, showing sunspots were less common during this time.

Many scientists still remain sceptical that sunspots can affect weather, partly because the evidence is often unreliable. But one important turning point came in the late 1980s when it was discovered that winter storms regularly followed an eleven-year pattern over the North Atlantic, matching the solar cycle. And in 1994 it was revealed that the Earth's troposphere – where our weather generally takes place – around the tropics grows hotter and cooler in tune with the solar cycles. But the changes in solar energy during the cycle are tiny – only about 0.1 per cent – and many meteorologists are still sceptical.

### THE RED TIDE

When the Israelites were trying to persuade Pharaoh to let them out of Egypt, one of Moses' miracles was to turn the Nile to blood: 'Lifting up his rod, he struck the water of the river, and it turned to blood. And the fishes died and the river was corrupted, and the Egyptians could not drink the water of the Nile.' (Exodus 7: 20–21)

The river of blood may well have been a red tide of microscopic algae. Given plenty of light and a big feed of nutrients, these algae can suddenly proliferate into such enormous numbers they bloom into red tides. The problem is that blooms can sometimes be poisonous and kill all other life in rivers. For humans, the water becomes so foul it is impossible to drink, and eating the dead fish can result in poisoning from the toxins accumulated in them.

Exodus 7: 24 goes on 'all the Egyptians dug round about the river for water to drink'. This suggests the river was dried out, for this is how wells are made in the dried-up beds of wadis in the Sudan and other regions which have seasonal monsoons followed by long dry periods. These dire conditions could have led to freak phenomena inflicted as plagues on the Egyptians. Frogs which normally breed when the flood waters receded now multiplied at a greater rate and then died in great stinking heaps (Exodus 8: 14). This was followed by 'lice' which may have been mosquitoes breeding in stagnant pools of water or fleas that carry bubonic plague ('boils and blains', Exodus 9: 8–11). And finally tsetse flies that breed in swampy areas spread 'murrain' on cattle (Exodus 9: 6–7).

This all suggests that there was a severe drought in Egypt of more than usual severity. Egypt at this period, during the reign of the Pharaoh Rameses II, 1290–24BC, was especially vulnerable to variations in the flow of the Nile making it highly susceptible to drought.

## THUNDER AND HAIL

Exodus 9: 25–6 also describes how 'hail smote throughout the land of Egypt all that was in the field and broke every tree of the field', except in Goshen where the Children of Israel were. Ferocious thunderstorms affect the Nile and Cairo even today. In 1907 a storm at Port Said showered hailstones weighing up to 19 ounces (550 grams). And on 2 November 1994, a ferocious thunderstorm swept the country, killing about sixty people in floods and about five hundred people died when lightning set fire to a fuel depot.

## LOCUSTS

Exodus 10: 13–15 describes an east wind which blew for a day and a night and brought locusts, probably shortly after the hail, and that the locusts ate all the plants 'and all the fruit of the trees which the hail had left'.

Some extraordinary change in pressure systems must have carried the locusts north up from their usual breeding grounds in Saudi Arabia, getting caught in the Egyptian cyclonic circulation. When this depression moved northwards it produced a 'mighty strong west wind which took away the locusts and cast them into the Red Sea'. Spectacular plagues of locusts are still a menace in Africa and the Middle East. For successful breeding the female needs to lay her eggs in wet ground for the eggs to develop. Once the locusts have hatched and fed, they swarm on the hot winds between 68 and 104 degrees Fahrenheit (20 and 40 degrees Celsius).

### DARKNESS

Given all these upsets to the normal weather patterns it is not so surprising that a colossal sandstorm should blow up to produce a thick darkness (Exodus 10: 21–22). Alternatively the khamsin, a strong scorching desert wind, can blanket sand and dust for days and block out sunlight.

### JESUS WALKING ON WATER

A mirage might help explain the miracle of Jesus walking on water on the Sea of Galilee. An inferior mirage creates an upside-down image of the sky, making a shimmer which looks like water, and happens in hot deserts. This could have made Jesus appear to float over real water.

## Ball Lightning

Mysterious glowing balls of light hovering or slowly passing through the air have been reported for thousands of years. The balls vary from the size of a golfball to a football, can float through aircraft, houses or vehicles, and usually appear during or just after thunderstorms.

*Ball lightning is a mysterious glowing light, drawn into houses during thunderstorms. From* L'Atmosphère *by Camille Flammarion*

One June evening in Norwich several years ago, Ron Moore had just returned home from a walk with his wife, Stella, and son, Stephen. The sun was shining, and only the distant rumble of thunder broke the air. Stella went into the kitchen, Stephen to his bedroom at the front of the house, and Ron was just walking down the hall from the garden. Then literally out of the blue came a blinding flash, a huge explosion, and Stephen fell out of his room and lay paralysed on the hall floor.

Stella came out, severely shocked, from the kitchen, paralysed in her hands. Luckily, both her and Stephen's paralysis quickly wore off, but it wasn't until much later that evening that they could talk about what had happened. And the story they told sounds too fantastic the first time you hear it.

Stella had been working at the sink when a glowing ball about the size of a tennis ball floated in through the window, across the kitchen and out the door. It then apparently floated down the hall, before Stephen saw it glide into his bedroom and hover before his eyes, and then he remembered nothing after that.

It all sounds like something out of 'Star Trek'. This, and dozens of other accounts of what has become known as ball lightning, have been explained away as hallucinations, or a trick of the eye following a lightning bolt, rather like the flash of a camera going off. But none of these fit the case of the Moore family, simply because their next door neighbour told them later that he too had seen the ball of light float into their kitchen before the explosion.

Gladys Hughes of Colwyn, North Wales was driving home in her white Fiesta at about 8p.m. one June evening in 1981 when she ran into a bank of mist rolling off the river on the road between Glan-Conwy and Llanrwst in North Wales. Then she suddenly saw a glowing ball of translucent greenish light, about the size of a football, spinning forwards like a wheel with four spikes of light radiating out from it, about a foot away from her side window. Wondering if she'd gone mad or if aliens were visiting from outer space, she slowed down the car, and in perfect synchrony so did the ball. She then accelerated and again the ball kept perfect pace. No matter what she did she couldn't shake the thing off, and only when the mist petered out just beyond Dolgarrog Station did the ball suddenly shoot up and away out of sight.

Fearing her sanity was in question, Gladys didn't even mention this back home, but she got an unexpected surprise at the front door. Her husband was waiting there, and told her that he and his golf partner had both seen something fantastic – a glowing green ball shooting up high into the sky, at about 8p.m.

*The Quarterly Journal of the Royal Meteorological Society*, 1887, carried an article about numerous globes of light seen between 4 and 5p.m. on 17 August on the Dorset coast at Ringstead Bay. A thunderstorm was approaching when the eyewitnesses, Mrs and Miss Warry, walked into a quarry and saw globes of light the size of billiard balls surrounding them on all sides, from a few inches off the ground to 3 feet (1 metre) over their heads moving of their own accord up and down. The women walked in and out of the quarry but the light display carried on.

You could fill a book with the dozens of accounts of ball lightning reported from all over the world.

They have even been seen on board aircraft. This report by the Soviet news agency TASS is of a ball of lightning inside an aircraft on a flight across the former Soviet Union. The ball, 4 inches (10 centimetres) across, appeared on the fuselage in front of the cockpit of an Ilyushin-18 aircraft as it flew close to a thunderstorm over the Black Sea on 15 January 1984:

'It disappeared with a deafening noise, but re-emerged several seconds later in the passengers' lounge, after piercing in an uncanny way through the air-tight metal wall,' TASS said. 'The fireball slowly flew above the heads of the stunned passengers. In the tail section of the airliner it divided into two glowing crescents which then joined together again and left the plane almost noiselessly.'

The radar and other instruments aboard the plane were damaged, and two holes were found in the fuselage, but no passengers were hurt during the episode.

Of course the cynics enjoy picking on the credibility of the witnesses, but they got a very rude shock several years ago when no less than a professor of electrical engineering, Roger Jennison of the University of Kent, witnessed a glowing ball aboard a plane. It came floating down the aisle during a Pan Am flight between New York and Washington, gliding down from the cockpit and exiting gracefully through the rear toilets.

Another physicist, Arthur Covington, saw one in his own home and reported it in the science magazine *Nature*, 18 April 1970:

'We saw a ball of light emerge from the fireplace and slowly drift across the room. It appeared to pass through a curtained, closed window without making any noise or causing any damage. A loud detonation was heard a few moments after the ball vanished.'

So what on earth is ball lightning? Physicists, meteorologists and mathematicians have been locked in unseemly warfare on this one for decades. Their explanations range from glowing micro-meteorites to electromagnetic fields of energy that condense into balls of light at their centre.

The phenomenon is clearly electrical. Several electrical workers have witnessed strange glowing balls during their work, often involving high-voltage equipment. For example, there have been reports of overhead pylon cables collapsing in storms, short-circuiting in a blaze of sparks and sometimes spawning giant balls of light rolling along the cables.

One recent theory, from Dr Geoffrey Endean at Durham University, concerns a spinning mass of charges in the air contained in a much larger but invisible electric field. With the charges all lined up somewhat like little bar magnets, and energy flowing backwards and forwards between them, a glowing ball of light is formed. Unfortunately, ball lightning is so rare and so difficult to recreate artificially using high-voltage equipment, that we may never be certain what it is.

Yet the sheer volume of evidence does point to one very neat story, going some way towards an explanation. Mark Stenhoff of the Tornado Research Organisation (TORRO for short) has been compiling detailed reports on ball lightning for years. Nearly all the accounts happen towards the end of a ferocious thunderstorm, or at the very edge of a thunderstorm so far away that the witness is often unaware of it. The balls frequently precede a colossal bolt of lightning, so powerful that the accompanying thunder is deafening. But once this spectacular superbolt has passed, the storm is dead.

Stenhoff's theory goes like this. Thunderclouds are basically a huge fluffy battery, with a top side peppered with positive charges and the bottom steeped in negative charges. Except that, for reasons we don't quite understand, a pocket of positive charges gets stuck amongst the negative charges on the bottom of the cloud. Unable to discharge until the negatives have shot their bolts, the positive bubble has to wait until the very end of the last act of the thunderstorm to make a positive discharge creating a spectacular flash of lightning, hence the violent thunderbolt. But with the wind in the right direction and all other conditions just right, the positive bubble might start 'leaking' its charges before the final death throe of the superbolt. This leakage shows itself as a glowing ball that is attracted to electrical equipment in confined spaces – hence its floating into aircraft and houses.

Whatever the full story, one thing is for sure. The eyewitnesses all agree that ball lightning is like nothing else on earth, and remains the single most spectacular thing they've ever seen in their lives.

## Fireballs

The thunderstorms of 1992 in Britain felt like something almost primeval: dazzling lightning strikes, ear-splitting thunder and torrential rain. But something else, even more violent and mysterious, came with those thunderstorms. Scientists don't seem to know what they are or even have a word for them, but you could call them fireballs.

One case on the night of 20 July 1992, in Dormansland, Surrey, was typical of many. Ellen Winter and her family were sitting in their conservatory watching the storm overhead, when there was a bang and all the lights in the house suddenly went out. Hearing shouting from neighbours outside, they saw there an astonishing sight: a 6-foot (1.8-metre) hole had been blasted through the roof with flames rising up through it. By the time the fire brigade arrived a large part of the loft was alight and one bedroom badly burnt.

It seemed like something out of *Quatermass*. Neighbours spoke of a huge red ball quite literally dropping out of the sky and plunging straight into the roof before bursting into flames. There was no question of a flash of lightning having confused their eyes because their accounts were all the same, and one of the witnesses had been watching from a long way off. This was not a lightning bolt, nor a meteorite or any other solid object. The closest thing seemed to be ball lightning – spheres of glowing light – but these usually float horizontally and harmlessly through the air. It was clearly something electrical, because all the electrical wiring in the house was burnt out, including television, video and anything else that had been plugged in, and a neighbour next door said she'd been flung across her kitchen by a severe shock during the bang. It also seemed to travel through the house as some sort of electrical field, because the eyewitnesses said they felt their hair stand up. A ball of red light also shot across the darkened living room and hit the cat, which although it wasn't singed has behaved very nervously since.

And this was no isolated incident. That same night, a house in Crawley, Sussex, also exploded into flames.

These extremely violent balls of 'fire' sometimes fall out of the sky during severe thunderstorms, setting fire to the first object they hit. Many houses have been severely damaged by fireballs, yet these are not simply balls of fire, because all the electrics in the houses are also blown up. These are probably some of the most terrifying phenomena known in thunderstorms, yet virtually nothing more is known about them. And yet they strike all over the world.

Take this description from 13 November 1902, in New South Wales, Australia, as reported in *Nature*. At Boort great 'fireballs' fell in the street, throwing up sparks as they exploded. At Longdale a house was set on fire. In Sydney a man in Paramatta was paralysed by a fireball bursting over his head.

In 1984 a 'fireball' hit a street lamp in Armley, Leeds. It then passed down into the ground, blowing up a gas main which then burst a water main.

What makes these sightings so perplexing is that they don't fit the classic picture of ball lightning: glowing balls of light that gently float horizontally, usually into houses or aircraft, often attracted to electrical fittings and which cause no more damage than minor singeing or a burnt-out fuse.

Perhaps fireballs are an extreme version of ball lightning. There are cases of violent ball lightning, as happened in Conwy, North Wales in July 1992. Pat Stafford saw a bright ball fly up the small cul-de-sac she lives in and explode on her neighbour's tree, splintering the bark and leaving a 4-foot (1.2 metre) long gash. The ball then disintegrated downwards in a shower of sparks and seemed to disappear. But then it resurrected itself in three neighbouring houses, setting fire to the hallway of one, blowing up electrical fittings in another, and leaving two neighbours – Pam Wignall and Aileen Owen – slightly burnt and very shocked.

Another violent ball of fire dropped onto Pulham Market, Norfolk, on 7 July 1994. A bright ball of light fell during a thunderstorm, burst into a fireworks display of sparks and exploded inside nearby houses, setting them ablaze. George Kennedy witnessed his bungalow going up in flames. 'It was just one massive explosion,' he explained, 'And then I realized my house was on fire.' The entire attic was set ablaze, and his wife Helen was taken to hospital with what appeared to be symptoms of electric shock. Experts are at a loss to explain what happened, but these were certainly electrical phenomena because phones and other electrical fittings also blew up in other houses along the street.

Perhaps the most spectacular fireball incident struck Sidmouth in Devon on 12 August 1970. The *Sidmouth Herald* reported that scores of people in Sidmouth described seeing a red ball of fire over the town during a violent thunderstorm making a crackling noise, when it suddenly exploded with a deafening noise, sending a shower of lightning down to the ground. Three hundred residents were reported burnt by lightning, and television cables were cut off to 2500 television sets.

The experts are baffled by these violent phenomena. Lightning expert Clive Saunders at UMIST (University of Manchester Institute of Science and Technology) confirms that these phenomena are perplexing, and likely to remain so. 'The trouble is we just don't have enough data,' he observes, although he confirms the 'fireball' observations because his mother rang from Pinner in north London to say she had seen a 'great big red ball' during the thunderstorm of 10 July 1992.

Another UMIST expert, Neil Charman, doesn't know if these fireballs are a type of ball lightning or if they are lumped together with a wide range of phenomena. There are, in fact, many other strange electrical phenomena in thunderstorms, for instance flashes of light which look like rings, pears, necklaces and other shapes. 'These are lightning-like events but they don't fit into an easy category,' he comments. They may be different types of the same phenomenon, or there may be different physical mechanisms.' The problem, as always, is their rarity and the inability to recreate them in the laboratory.

If you are concerned about being hit by one of these 'fireballs', there seems to be little you can do about it. Television aerials and lightning conductors make no difference, and closed windows and doors offer no protection. There's something vastly destructive tucked up in those thunderclouds, and we don't know what it is. You have been warned.

## Things That Go Bang in the Night

Bangs, screams and things that go bump in the night are not what you might expect from a book about the weather, but the following stories could turn out to be more meteorological than paranormal.

At 3.30a.m. on 14 June 1903, in the South African Transvaal, Mr H. Bourhill suddenly awoke to a sound like the firing of a cannon followed by a whizzing noise, then by a second bang. He tried to go back to sleep but then a terrific explosion burst over the house. 'It was a sudden, terrifying report followed by a tearing, rending noise, giving the idea that some large wooden structure was being torn asunder,' he reported. But next day he was astonished to find his house was completely undamaged. Neither could he find any evidence of a meteorite fall. It remained a mystery.

That same year William Butlin, second mate aboard a merchant ship, reported a similar account during a heavy thunderstorm off the Dutch coast. Firstly, he heard a whizzing sound as if a rocket had been fired. Then a deep red and bright yellow fireball fell into the sea followed by three explosions.

And these spooky goings-on have also happened more recently. At 3.45a.m. on 23 February 1977 a massive explosion and flash rocked the village of Ford in west Wiltshire and left all thirty inhabitants terrified. One resident, Derek Robinson, said a rushing noise passed from one side of his house to the other, followed by a loud explosion and a blue-green flash. It seemed to come out of nowhere, although it was raining at the time.

All of these accounts could very well have been 'fire-balls' followed by a massive lightning strike and thunder clap. One theory is that glowing balls of lightning looking like fire are created during particularly intense thunderstorms. On falling to earth these fireballs charge a channel through the air through which a massive thunderbolt can then follow.

Consider also the strange case of the Barisal Guns. One night in 1871 a man was on the deck of a steamer in the mouth of the Ganges near the town of Barisal. The weather was clear and calm. Then far out to sea came the boom like distant cannons at irregular intervals, as if a huge naval battle was in progress. The sounds seem to have come from two different points, as if opposing fleets were exchanging fire. But no warships were near.

Similar natural booms have been reported throughout the world. What is the explanation? Pockets of gas escaping from the ocean, the sonic booms of falling meteorites, rocks cracking under pressure? There is no satisfactory explanation.

## Cities in the Sky

There are no mountains or trains in the Orkney Islands. So when the people of Sanday woke up one day to find that snow-capped peaks and a village with a train had appeared at the north end of their tiny island, they were dumbfounded. It hadn't been there the day before. Yet suddenly, there was a large white building with several smaller houses grouped around it. And the phantom village remained on view for several hours before vanishing at sunset. The islanders were convinced that a trick of light had brought them a glimpse of Norway, 500 miles (800 kilometres) away. Experts agreed that it was a mirage.

Another most fantastic sight hung over the sky of Hastings in July 1797. The coast of France suddenly appeared clear as daylight as if it was just across a bay. Local resident William Latham wrote: 'The coast of France was plainly to be seen without a telescope. I could see the cliffs on the opposite coast 50 miles distant.' Sailors and fishermen could pick out places they had visited on the coast of Picardy, and with a telescope they could even see the French fishing boats at anchor.

Since then two recent mirages have been reported from Hastings. At 7a.m. on 5 August 1987 David Southey clearly saw the coast of France. It was an unusually cool day. Mr F.G. Thomas from Dover was also walking out on the hills at 9a.m. on 5 August 1987. He noted in his diary, 'Visibility excellent, France very clear.' That afternoon, he noted, the lay-by on the Deal Road near Dover Castle was full of tourists 'enjoying the splendid panorama of the French coast'. Then on 31 August 1992 during a spell of cold polar air the mirage was seen again.

And there are many other examples. Sailors in Dublin Bay have claimed to see Mount Snowdon 100 miles (160 kilometres) away. A report on 6 March 1890 gives an account of a large unknown city seen over Ahsland, Ohio. Although some eyewitnesses claimed it to be the New Jerusalem, most people thought it was either Mansfield 30 miles (48 kilometres) away or Sandusky 60 miles (97 kilometres) away.

Mirages are caused by the weather. When conditions

are calm and warm air sits on top of cool air it creates what's called a temperature inversion. Where the two air masses meet it behaves like a mirror, bending light and creating amazing images and revealing places hidden under the curve of the earth.

Sometimes the temperature inversions actually invert the images as well. This was remarkably illustrated in 1957 when passengers on the cruiser *Edinburgh Castle*, sailing up the English Channel, suddenly saw a line of ships on the horizon – upside down, some on top of each other, funnel to funnel and weirdly elongated. What they saw were the images of ships projected from below the skyline.

And mirages are particularly common in cold northern latitudes. When the images of cities are seen over the Orkneys local people are said to explain them away as the crystal and pearl city of the mysterious Fin Folk. In fact, mysterious islands and cities are also seen off the west coast of Ireland. In both cases the nearest cities are hundreds of miles away. Maybe this was the inspiration behind the flying city of Laputa in *Gulliver's Travels*.

Mirages like these, sent over hundreds of miles, are very special because the image has to be bounced several times, trapped in a massive temperature inversion.

Perhaps floating images also inspired explorers. Might the Celts have set off to Iceland from the Faroe Islands almost 300 miles (480 kilometres) away because they saw it in the sky? And did the Viking, Erik the Red, sail straight for Greenland from Iceland about 980AD across 200 miles (320 kilometres) of difficult waters and winds because he was chasing a mirage?

A superior mirage certainly fooled many explorers. In 1818, the British explorer John Ross was searching the cold waters north of Canada for a passage between the

*There are two horizons in this picture – the top one is a mirage called a Fata Morgana.* © *Pekka Parvianen*

Atlantic and Pacific oceans – the elusive north-west passage. But suddenly he found his way blocked by mountains looming above the sea ahead. He plotted them on his map and named them – the Croker mountains. Discouraged, he returned to England and reported that no north-west passage existed.

A year later, his second in command, Parry, sailed straight through the Croker Mountains. They were a mirage, and there *was* indeed a north-west passage.

In fact, dozens of islands marked on old maps don't exist – they were just mirages. Only with aircraft were the world's islands finally mapped out with certainty.

Mirages can also appear as great towering spires and towers. These are called Fata Morgana, after the folklore of Morgana, an evil witch-like creature who tried to thwart heroes by building castles in the air. The Fata Morgana is a mirage sometimes seen in southern Europe, particularly over the straits of Messina which separate Sicily from the Italian mainland. It occurs when an unusual thermal cap in the atmosphere causes images of boats and buildings in the far distance to appear in the sky and to be elongated in such a way that they seem like great towers.

Distant objects appear grotesquely magnified and elongated. A layer of cold air sandwiched between layers of hot air causes images to reflect, build upon one another, multiply, tower and grow until an immense, spectacular mirage hangs in the distance. It is a complicated mirage.

Mirages might also explain some sightings of lake monsters. Dr Lehn at the University of Manitoba pointed out in an article in *Science*, 1979, that mirages can suddenly distort quite trivial objects into monster-like figures. He looked at a distance at a stick frozen in ice on Lake Winnipeg during a strong temperature inversion. At first it looked flattened, and then three minutes later the stick was bent into a new shape. It was a mirage. He also pointed out that these sorts of temperature inversions need still weather, and indeed of 249 cases of Loch Ness Monster sightings 84 per cent occurred during calm conditions. Mirages can make objects stretch, suddenly appear and disappear, and bend.

## UFOs

~

In November 1958 Dr and Mrs M. Moore were driving in their car through the deserts of Dakota when suddenly they looked up and noticed in the sky a 'silvery, cigar-shaped object, like a giant windsock', which accelerated out of view leaving behind it a trail of strange purple clouds. Their sighting was reported to the *Flying Saucer Review* and, like so many other similar accounts, marked down as a highly promising incidence of a UFO.

Many similar sightings have even produced dramatic photographs of huge saucer- or lens-shaped objects in the sky. But they tend to look rather ghostly and suggest something less extraterrestrial to their origins. Later analyses showed that many were in fact unusual clouds called rotor clouds or lenticular clouds. These have an astonishing resemblance to a colossal flying saucer, often with circular rings around them and occasionally luminous if the sun is shining from behind.

Lenticular clouds come from mountains but are fairly unusual. Normally winds passing over mountains lose their strength and become weaker on the leeward side. But occasionally the air on the leeward side bounces up and down like a bobbing wave. Every time the air bobs up a lenticular cloud is formed. Sometimes you can see formations of them dancing in the sky.

Mountain tops are often capped with rotor clouds similar to lenticular clouds, which spin around like piles of plates over the summit and give another illusion of a flying saucer. The clouds can also form a long horizontal cylinder. But these cloud formations don't explain all

*Flying saucers? No, these are lenticular clouds created on waves of turbulent air. © Pekka Parvianen*

UFOs, and another weather phenomenon could come into play.

The UFO era started in 1947 when Kenneth Arnold, flying a plane over the Cascade Mountains in Washington State, saw a chain of nine brightly-lit objects flying like saucers would if you skipped them across the water. The press christened the objects flying saucers and the US Air Force made a serious investigation of the case. Their official explanation of mirages caused by a temperature inversion made not the slightest difference to public opinion.

But mirages create some fantastic UFO-like sights. At midday on 30 September 1986, Yvonne Westgarth was gazing out of a window in her house in south Edinburgh when she saw an amazing sight. A large cigar-shaped missile flew over the houses opposite. It was like nothing she had ever seen before: long, white, with a black band in the middle. It made no noise and lasted about a minute before disappearing. But there was no denying what she saw because she called over her husband and together they drew sketches of the mysterious object.

The only known airborne thing at that time was a British Airways' Boeing 757 Shuttle from London, landing at Edinburgh's Logan Airport. And yet the two eyewitnesses were quite clear that they hadn't seen an aircraft.

So they called in Steuart Campbell, a local scientist interested in supernatural phenomena. He had a hunch that the Westgarths might have seen a mirage. The phenomenon could have been an upside-down image of the aircraft alongside a normal image, giving the appearance of a flying cylinder. The dark band in the middle was the double image of the aircraft wings. When Campbell showed the Westgarths a picture of two halves of a Boeing mounted together they agreed it was a good likeness.

The weather that day of the 'UFO' had suddenly turned warm after a cool spell, creating a sharp temperature difference. A shallow dome of cold air may have been trapped under the warm air, behaving like a concave mirror and creating upside-down images.

It's interesting that before UFOs first materialized, flying ships were seen in the sky by mariners. Mirages can make ships appear to float in the sky, and inspired legends like the Flying Dutchman. This spectre was supposed to haunt the waters around the Cape of Good Hope and was taken as a sign of imminent disaster. It also inspired the opera *Der Fliegende Holländer* by Wagner, in which Captain Vanderdecken gambles his salvation on rounding the Cape during a storm and is condemned to round the Cape forever.

*Before anyone had heard of flying saucers, mariners often saw flying ships – but they're mirages. From* L'Atmosphère *by Camille Flammarion*

## The Bermuda Triangle

If you believe all the stories, the area of sea bordered by Bermuda, Florida and Puerto Rico is the most terrifying place on earth. It's called the Bermuda Triangle, and ships and planes passing through it are supposed to disappear. The blame is put on unknown cosmic forces such as UFOs or bizarre gravitational fields.

That, at least, is what the popular books would have you believe. What they usually leave out is that this area of sea is dangerous for a very atmospheric reason – it's one of the world's worst hurricane regions. Of all weather catastrophes, hurricanes are the most massive and powerful forces. Their winds blow over 74 miles per hour (120 kilometres per hour), reaching up to 200 miles per hour (320 kilometres per hour). Their winds and intense low pressure can whip the sea into waves over 100 feet (30 metres) high. Small wonder that shipping caught unawares can suddenly disappear [see Ships and Cyclones].

In the Bermuda Triangle hurricanes can blow up out of nowhere, head off in unpredictable directions, and of course cause immense damage to shipping before they even touch land.

The coastal waters around Florida are also the world's greatest place for waterspouts, long tapering funnels which suck water off the sea. Up to five hundred a year strike in this part of the Bermuda Triangle, and although they're easily avoided, people often like to try their luck at sailing through them, sometimes with disastrous results [see Monsters and Waterspouts].

## Musical Weather

The weather has an enormous repertoire of sounds and, dare we say it, even music. Thunder is probably the most obvious, a colossal percussion sound produced by the explosive heating of air by lightning. But why is thunder often a long, rumbling reverberation instead of a single, sharp clap? Lightning is a long, jagged zig-zag, and each segment heats the air at slightly different times. So each lightning segment nearest to us is heard before the segments furthest away – the closest part of the lightning is heard as a sharp clap, but the furthest ones are more muffled. The sound waves from all parts of the lightning bolt also bump into each other, giving the impression of a long, rumbling roll.

But thunderstorms also have some subtler sounds. Electrical discharges from pointed objects just before a thunderstorm give off a sizzling or crackling sound and warn of an imminent lightning strike. Two men fishing from a boat on Derwent Water Reservoir, Cumbria, in August 1975, found the tip of one of their fishing rods began to buzz 'like a swarm of bees'.

Crackling sounds from rainfall are another unusual thunderstorm phenomenon. In 1892 *Meteorological Magazine* reported an electrical engineer in Cordova, Spain, who witnessed great drops of electrical rain, each one of which, on touching the ground, walls, or trees, gave a faint crack and emitted a spark of light. The electrical show carried on for several seconds.

The wind section is probably the biggest component of the weather's orchestra. The sighing sound of the wind blowing through woodlands is made by the vibration of conifer needles or deciduous tree twigs. Changes in the wind modulate the pitch and volume of the woodlands, and winds gusting strongly though a forest on a mountain slope sometimes produce a roaring sound.

These wind sounds are all made by wind eddies, much like the eerie howling sound you get around chimneys and corners of buildings, most noticeable inside a house on a dark winter's night when you are more aware of spooky goings-on.

Even hills make their own sound. A writer in the *Edinburgh Philosophical Journal* described sounds heard in a range of hills in Cheshire. They made a hollow moaning sound when an easterly wind blew, while it remained calm on the flats. It's what Sir Walter Scott in his glossary to *Guy Mannering* called the 'soughing of the wind'. The hills probably behave like gigantic organ-pipes – a breeze sweeping down from the hilltops blows across hollows and the wind eddies sound like a moan.

A different sort of wind sound is made from a vortex. People often say they can hear a humming like a swarm of bees when the air is calm, but there are no insects to be seen. The meteorological explanation could be whirlwinds of hot air. But possibly the most terrifying vortex sound is a tornado. Witnesses say that they make roaring sounds like the noise of freight trains or jet aircraft.

Sounds can be carried far and wide. A Mr R.A. Tyssen-Gee wrote in 1977 to the *Journal of Meteorology* that he was camping in Swedish Lapland one summer, when he and his friend believed they heard music one night which they thought sounded like an organ but as they were at least 30 miles (50 kilometres) from the nearest church, it was unlikely that they could have been hearing a distant service.

The distances to which sounds sometimes travel are remarkable. A traveller called Dr Clark reported hearing a cannon firing 100 miles (160 kilometres) from the Egyptian coast, the air being very still at the time. A Dr Arnott mentions a case in which bells were heard at a similar distance by a ship off the coast of Brazil. Mysterious booming sounds like the sound of distant cannons have been heard for centuries – mistpoeffers, brontides, Barisal guns, Hanley's guns – they went by all sorts of names in different parts of the world. But the distant rumbles of thunder or artillery don't seem to explain all these freak sounds and we're still left puzzling over them.

*When the forest murmurs and the mountain roars,*
*Then close your windows and shut your doors.*

As rain approaches, the lower levels of air can be much more uniform and still than on a day of broken cloud cover. The lack of convective turbulence in the air allows sound to travel far and wide. As the storm comes much closer, the roar of the wind drowns out all other noise.

'As I lay awake praying in the early morning I thought I heard a sound of distant bells. It was an intense frost,' the Reverend Francis Kilvert recorded in his diary in the 1870s.

The whole of winter has a cacophony of noises, all somewhat on the melancholic side. Frost is a vicious sound. It's the sharp crack of a breaking tree as its microscopic plumbing is blown wide open by the expansion of frozen water inside. There's the groaning of pack ice as it bumps and jostles its way in the freezing waters at the Poles. There's the sighing of ice splitting open on ponds and lakes.

A Mr H.H. Gibson in 1915 even reported musical snowflakes: 'When during a snowstorm, when the air is absolutely calm at large, snowflakes when falling cause a musical sound. I am doubtful if it is imagination or a fact that the dry flakes falling cause this.'

Whether it was their striking the ground or interacting with the air or with each other is unknown. Certainly, snow squeaks and long ago it was noticed that the squeak changes as the temperature drops: at low temperatures the sound becomes sharper and has a higher frequency. The snow squeak comes from mass breakage of the tiny ice crystals. As the temperature drops these crystals become more resilient and the snow cover as a whole becomes more friable, explaining the higher frequencies .

It was the sound of snow that proved fatal in the Second World War. During the German invasion of Russia in the bitterly cold winter of 1941–2, the Germans often lost the element of surprise because the snow was so noisy. The intense cold made the snow heavily crusted, and as the Germans advanced the Russians, helped by the way that sound travels faster in very cold weather, could hear the sound of the snow being crushed.

## *Psychedelia in the Sky*

### RAINBOWS

Rainbows are usually taken as a sign of optimism and good fortune. 'If you dig at the end of the rainbow you'll find a pot of gold.' Maybe it's because they tend to appear towards the end of a rainstorm when the sun reappears.

But rainbows mean different things in different cultures. The Greeks thought that a rainbow in the morning was a good omen but one in the evening was bad. In Norse mythology, the rainbow was the only means of entering heaven, the 'bridge of the gods' connecting heaven to Earth. The rainbow was also the covenant between God and Noah after the Flood.

To see a rainbow you need to stand with your back to the sun, looking at a distant shower of rain. The bow is formed from the sun's rays bending as they enter the raindrops. Red light is bent less than blue, so the colours separate into the colours of the spectrum. Then the spectrum is reflected off the back of the raindrop, always at the same angle, 42 degrees. So wherever you look, the rainbow will appear as a 42-degree arc and you can never reach its end. There's no crock of gold.

Sometimes a pair of rainbows appears, the second fainter than the first. The second bow forms when sunlight reflects twice inside the raindrops instead of just once.

But very rarely some quite bizarre rainbows appear in the sky. Narrow rainbows that are entirely pink or red have been seen, including one reported by Frederic Palmer in the *American Journal of Physics* in 1945: 'As I watched [the rainbow] the blue, green, yellow and orange portions were quickly wiped out,' described Palmer. 'There remained a bow of a single color, red, only slightly less brilliant than before, and in width about a quarter of that of the original bow.'

Red or purple rainbows have also been seen at sunset. Red is not altogether unexpected as it's the colour of the setting sun, but purple is at the opposite end of the spectrum from red, so makes a puzzling phenomenon.

Rainbows don't even have to be bow-shaped! Sometimes they can be hideously distorted into great bulging umbrella-shapes, growing into bows, thin bands on the horizon or even larger blocks in the sky.

These and many other bizarre rainbows are described by William Corliss in his book *Rare Halos, Mirages, Anomalous Rainbows and Related Electromagnetic Phenomena.*

*American Indians believed a halo around the sun forecast rain – and they were often right.* © *Pekka Parvianen*

## HALOES

On fine, bright, spring days when the sky is milky white with high feathery clouds, the sun can appear strange – it seems to shine through ground glass with a bright ring surrounding it. This ring is a halo, and it happens more often than you think. It is created from veils of cloud so high that all the water in them is frozen into ice crystals. And the secret of the halo lies in the shape of those countless numbers of crystals.

The halo is formed when the ice crystals are shaped like a short pencil – a short hexagonal cylinder. Each crystal is less than one-tenth of a millimetre in diameter, and as a ray of light hits one side of the hexagonal prism it bends the light by 22 degrees. So a thin curtain of countless numbers of these tiny ice crystals all lined up in the same direction in front of the sun deflect the light by 22 degrees and the combined effect is a 22-degree circular ring around the sun. The same halo can also surround the moon.

Haloes like these around the sun were seen by the Zuni Indians of New Mexico as a sign that the sun was inside its wigwam. They believed it forecast rain, and there could be something in that: haloes are made by ice crystals in cirrostratus clouds and cirrostratus clouds often precede rain showers.

Haloes are just one type of optical phenomena formed by ice clouds. Depending on the shape of the crystals, different sorts of illusions can be seen: various rings, arcs, spots or patches of colour, all known collectively as halo phenomena. Several partial and complete solar haloes are sometimes visible at the same time, giving the sun a target and bull's eye effect or branching off with symmetrical legs and wings from the central halo.

## SUN DOGS

If the cirrus clouds are intermittent they can create extra images of the sun known as sun dogs or mock suns. They probably got the name sun dogs because they sometimes have a long horizontal ray of white light sticking out at one end like a dog's tail. A halo will often have sun dogs on either side of it, lined up with the sun. They can be hazy white or rainbow-coloured.

*The real sun is flanked by two false suns created by ice crystals in the sky.* © *Dr Alistair Fraser*

These sun dogs, or mock suns, carried great significance in olden days. One of the most dramatic displays happened just before the Battle of Mortimer's Cross in February 1461 in the English civil war, the War of the Roses. The Yorkist Earl of Mortimer, Edward, faced a huge Lancastrian army when his army of two thousand

*The pub sign at Mortimer's Cross in Herefordshire commemorating the 1461 battle.* © *Paul Simons*

men saw see three suns in the sky. 'Three suns in the firmament shining full and clear', was how the chroniclers at the time saw it, a vision which alarmed the army. But Edward took the sight as a portent of victory. 'These three signs betoken the Father, the Son, and the Holy Ghost,' he told his men, 'And therefore let us have a good heart.' And on 2 February 1461 his army utterly routed the Lancastrians, killing a thousand of the enemy.

That victory was crucial. Edward raced on to London before the Lancastrian queen, Margaret of Anjou, arrived. He was proclaimed King Edward IV on 4 March, and then his army went on to crush Margaret's army decisively. Edward remained king for the rest of his life, but he never forgot his three suns and he took the 'Sun in Splendour' for his personal banner. Probably the only time a weather phenomenon has inspired victory on the battlefield.

The sight in the sky is still commemorated today by the Mortimer's Cross pub, which has a sign hanging outside showing the two sun dogs alongside the banner of York.

### MULTIPLE RAINBOWS

Imagine the sky gradually breaking out into rainbows. At 6.30p.m., 14 August 1994, Bernadette Fallon and Mark Johnson stood on a beach near the furthest tip of Cornwall. The sky was almost clear with only high wispy (cirrus) cloud, and then they saw a small rainbow rising up from cliffs, another one symmetrically placed on the other side of the sun, and yet another more brilliant and longer rainbow higher in the sky.

Then gradually a couple of shorter and fainter rainbows appeared. By 7p.m. when the sun was truly setting it was ringed in a halo, but that wasn't the end of the spectacle. Half an hour later a pale disc of mock sun appeared in the sky. 'The whole display was very beautiful and striking,' wrote the two eyewitnesses, who recorded their vision in meticulous sketches.

*Rare Halos, Mirages, Anomalous Rainbows and Related Electromagnetic Phenomena* by William Corliss is a collection of authentic science reports classified into groups of phenomena, and the nearest description that fitted the Cornish sighting was an unusual halo display. Even though there are many reports of haloes of white light appearing offset from the sun or moon, they rarely show any colour. Apart from ice crystals in the atmosphere, another source of light would probably be needed, such as the surface of the sea reflecting like a natural mirror.

## WHYMPER

On 14 July 1865, a group of mountaineers led by Whymper were the first men to reach the top of the Matterhorn, but on their descent tragedy struck when four of the men slipped and fell headlong down a precipice to their deaths. Later that evening Whymper saw an astonishing sight: a circle of light with three crosses in the sky: 'the ghostly apparitions of light hung motionless; it was a strange and awesome sight, unique to me and indescribably imposing at such a moment.'

Some might say the mountaineer had witnessed a religious experience, but the meteorologists see something very different. Microscopic ice crystals in high-altitude clouds had bent sunlight like cut-glass. If the crystals are all a regular shape, not too small and not too large, they bend light creating a rainbow, or reflect light like a mirror, creating a bow of white light. Whymper had seen the sunlight split into a large bow, part of a horizontal circle with vertical pillars of light crossing it. A similar sort of horizontal band can also be seen when you look at a light through a window wiped with grease in one direction or reflected by finely ribbed glass. The band of light is always seen at right angles to the ripples.

### DIAMONDS IN THE SKY

A vertical pillar of light can often be seen above the rising or setting sun, best of all when the sun is hidden behind a house, so that the eye is not dazzled, This pillar of light is uncoloured, but when the sun is low and has become yellow, orange or red, the pillar takes on the same hue. Both this and the horizontal circle are created by ice crystals all perfectly horizontal and falling very slowly, reflecting the light.

If there are enough ice crystals in the right place they can reflect so much sunlight that they create a sun pillar, a beam of sunlight pointing vertically upwards from the rising or setting sun, looking like the beam of a searchlight.

A report in the *Journal of Meteorology*, 1979, records minute ice crystals falling from the sky for over two hours at Houwaart, Belgium on New Year's Day. The sky was clear of clouds but misty and extremely cold (the previous night the temperature had plummeted to –4 degrees Fahrenheit (–20 degrees Celsius). Needles of

*Ice crystals in the sky can bend sunlight into pillars of light.* © *Pekka Parvianen*

glittering ice were seen in the weak sunshine from the open skies.

### FOGBOWS

Bows can also be completely white! They are called fog-bows because they are made by the very small droplets in mist and fog. When seen from the air fogbows can make a complete circle. (In fact rainbows would appear as complete circles if the ground didn't get in the way.)

Colourless rainbows form on the face of dense banks of clouds. There is no colour in a fogbow because the droplets of water in fog are too small, a hundredth of the size of a raindrop. The same internal reflection takes place as in raindrops but the colours of the resulting rainbow merge completely and form white light. The

*Fogbows are white versions of rainbows, created by mist or fog instead of rain.* © *Pekka Parvianen*

result is Ulloa's Ring – a luminous semi-circular fog-bow, bright white without the distinctive colours of the rainbow. The effect is strange, eerie and unforgettable, like seeing the ghost of a rainbow. Ulloa's Ring is named after Antonio de Ulloa, the first Spanish governor of Louisiana in the mid-eighteenth century, who first discovered the ring.

### DARK BANDS

There is a mysterious phenomenon often linked to haloes and bows, but very difficult to explain. One report by R. White, a maths don in London, in the *Journal of Meteorology*, 1976, described 'a series of dark vertical bands' which swept across a halo. His suggestion is that these 'ripples' were made by the ice crystals in the clouds rocking in a shock wave. Another eyewitness account in the journal *Weather* in 1979 saw haloes created by high cirrus clouds and then suddenly 'narrow dark vertical lines passed quickly through the arc'. The pattern of the lines was irregular, lasted a few seconds and then repeated itself half a minute later.

## Heiligenschein ('Holy Light')

If you look at your shadow in wet grass after a heavy night of dew, when the sun is low in the sky, you may be lucky enough to see *Heiligenschein* or 'Holy Light' in English.

With the sun behind you the light is reflected back off the dew drops like cat's eyes, and *Heiligenschein* appears as a bright ring round your head. And this is why the sixteenth-century Italian, Benvenuto Cellini, who first described it, thought he was having a religious experience – he thought it was a halo. 'An aureole of glory has rested on my head,' he wrote, 'This is visible to every sort of men to whom I have chosen to point it out.' But the key to his religious experience was that he only saw his halo around his shadow early in the morning with the rising sun for about two hours, and when the grass was drenched in dew.

## Sylvanshine

A new phenomenon has recently been discovered by Professor Alistair Fraser of Pennsylvania State University. When he took flash photographs of trees covered in dew at night they revealed the trees' leaves covered in bright lights – but only on some trees and not others.

The flashlight is reflected back by dew drops, a bit like the reflection from car licence plates. But it only happens on blue spruce, juniper, arborvitae and a few other species, because the waxy surface of the leaf needles makes the dew roll up into beads. Light hitting the beads is brought into focus and reflected back out in the direction it came. A camera's flash is caught in an instant.

Alistair Fraser calls it sylvanshine, and it can be seen on cold, dewy nights anywhere these trees grow.

*Water droplets on trees reflect a camera's flash like millions of tiny mirrors (called sylvanshine). © Dr Alistair Fraser*

## The Brocken Spectre

Mountaineers have seen some bizarre and frightening sights on mountain slopes. They've looked up and seen colossal ghost-like shadows looking down on them.

The Brocken is the highest peak of the Harz Mountains in Germany and the Brocken spectre was named after a strange shadow seen at the mountain's summit. It is a giant shadowy figure looming from the mist in the very early morning, or sometimes evening

*These monstrous shadows are made by reflections off mist, like a huge cinema screen. From* L'Atmosphère *by Camille Flammarion*

just before the sun sets. These ghostly shadows alarmed early mountaineers who saw their shadows turn into huge monsters, sometimes with haloes around their heads!

The explanation is simple: it is a person's shadow cast by a low sun onto a bank of cloud or mist. The droplets in the cloud behave like tiny lenses, reflecting shadows like a cinema screen. With the perspective of the light and cloud, the shadow looms into a ghoulish giant. Added to that, the droplets can also split the light and produce brilliantly coloured rings or haloes around the shadow.

These shadows and rings are also called glories, and you can often see them when looking down from aircraft onto clouds below, where they look like complete rings with the shadow of the plane inside them.

## Bishop's Ring

On 27 August 1883, Krakatoa, a small island in the Sunda Strait between Java and Sumatra, blew up with the loudest sound ever recorded on Earth. The blast was heard 3000 miles (4800 kilometres) away in Africa and the shockwave travelled several times round the world and lowered barometers in London.

Dust from Krakatoa circled the Earth and stayed afloat for years, creating stupendously vivid sunrises and sunsets. The dust scattered the light, and with the sun low in the sky red light was reflected back. But the volcanic dust also created beautiful rings of colour around the sun and moon: a bluish-white disc encircled by a red-brown ring.

This phenomenon was called Bishop's Ring after its discoverer, Sereno Bishop. He saw a strange disc of luminous light fringed with colour around the sun in a hazy sky over Hawaii on 5 September 1883: 'Permit me to call special attention to the very peculiar corona or halo extending 20° to 30° from the sun, which has been visible every day with us, and all day, of whitish haze with pinkish tint, shading off into lilac or purple against the blue, I have seen no notice of this corona observed elsewhere. It is hardly a conspicuous object.'

Soon afterwards, many other observers around the world confirmed Bishop's sighting but with curious differences. Some saw a whitish silvery patch enveloped by a brown border, others saw blue and brown, the rings being of hugely varying sizes.

## Blue Moon

Once in a blue moon is a rare thing indeed. To turn the moon blue needs particles in the atmosphere which scatter red light leaving mainly blue behind. Such particles are rare, but on 20 September 1950, a blue moon was seen over Britain and much of the rest of Europe. Not only the moon – the sun also turned blue during the day as well. The particles that created it came from smoke from forest fires blazing away in Alberta, Canada, sending up tiny particles of fine, oily droplets probably mixed with soot. The soot reached Europe in four days, carried on air currents some 3–4 miles (5–6 kilometres) high. Probably the best pale blue, deep blue and even green suns and moons were seen during the years following the eruption of Krakatoa in 1883 (as described in Bishop's Ring).

Closer to earth, the leading Belgian weather expert Marcel Minnaert saw something similar when he looked at the steam puffing out of an old steam engine leaving his local station. He noticed that the sun turned light green then pale blue and then disappeared in the smoke. The smoke from the steam engine was made up of very small drops of water, less than a fraction of a millimetre across, just the right size to scatter the light to create a blue moon.

## Green Flash

Have you seen the sun set at the seaside. Yes? . . . did you observe the phenomenon that occurs at the instant of the last ray of light when the sky is perfectly clear? . . . you will see that it is not a red ray, or rather flash, but a green one, a wondrous green that is not found anywhere else in nature. If there is green in Paradise it must be this green: the true green of hope!

So wrote Jules Verne in *The Green Ray*, published in 1882. He was describing a rare phenomenon – a brilliant emerald glint now known as the green flash. Just as the very top of the sun disappears below a clear horizon, it sometimes hurls a shaft of vivid green light across the sky for just a few seconds. But the effect is so electrifying that it's no surprise that many observers have been mesmerized by it.

The clearest explanation for the green flash is the way air can bend and split light like a glass prism. As the sun sinks below the horizon its last rays are teased apart into its component colours like a rainbow. Red is the usual colour followed by the blues and purples which tend to be scattered leaving just green behind.

And yet if it was that simple then the green flash should be fairly common, and it isn't. There's a valuable clue in that description from Jules Verne, because his green flash happened at the seaside. The atmosphere above the sea is sometimes sharply divided into sandwiches of different temperature and humidity. Each sandwich can be so strong that as the top edge of the sun passes through, it momentarily splits and amplifies the sun's light, producing a green flash rather like some colossal prism in the sky.

## Will-o'-the-Wisp

Folklore tells us of bright, tiny fairies dancing over marshes and wetlands, enticing onlookers to a sticky end. When Hiawatha set off across an evil swamp on a dangerous mission he found some strange business going on:

*Lighted by the shimmering moonlight,*
*And by will-o'-the-wisp illuminated*

*Fires by ghosts of dead men kindled,*
*In their weary night encampments.*

The fairies are folklore but the lights are very real and are called will-o'-the-wisps. They are found in bogs, marshes and sometimes on freshly manured ground when someone stamps on the soil. They are small flames a few inches tall occurring during wet, warm autumn nights. Sometimes they flicker on the ground and others float about a foot off the ground in ghost-like fashion. The dancing isn't quite what it seems, because as one flame goes out another takes its place, but will-o'-the-wisps are far from being fully understood. It's long been thought that the flame is made from methane given off by rotting stuff, but that doesn't explain why the gas spontaneously ignites. The answer may be another inflammable gas called phosphane. It too is given off by decaying matter and bursts into flame as soon as it hits the air. So the burning phosphane could set fire to the inflammable methane, but this is still speculation.

## Smell of Rain

There's something very special about a shower of rain, especially after a dry summer spell. It's not just the cool breeze, or parched lawns soaking up the moisture. No, there's a distinct *smell*, a very special, almost spicy fragrance, which is a bit odd because rain itself has no odour.

In ancient times it was believed that rain became sweetly scented from its passage through the heavens and that even rainbows had an odour. Both Aristotle and Pliny thought that the rainbow smelt sweet. And some people claim to smell rain before it actually arrives:

> *When the ditch and pond offend the nose*
> *Then look for rain and stormy blows.*

There is some truth to this. The atmospheric pressure falls when rain approaches, which triggers the release of fungal spores. Their odour is earthy, cinnamony, and people with a good sense of smell may be able to detect them.

But there's more than just fungal spores involved. Only during the 1960s was the mystery tackled scientifically, when Australian chemists traced the smell down to the soil. They discovered that certain sorts of clay gave off a rich 'rain' smell when the humidity rose above 80 per cent.

They discovered that the perfumed oils from trees were trapped in the soil. Only after a bout of drought do the chemicals build up sufficiently for enough smell to be released during the rain.

Wet soil, on the other hand, is altogether different – producing not so much fragrance as a slightly sodden odour. It's made by fungi such as *Streptomyces*, and comes out in a variety of odours released as the humidity increases.

So no matter whether it is wet earth or dry earth, there's a strong possibility that we might predict rain on the way before it actually arrives by catching a whiff of the earth.

# Pwdre Ser

Pwdre Ser is a strange glutinous mucus which falls to the ground, and was thought to be some sort of meteor – its name comes from the Welsh for 'star-rot', or what the French call *crachat de lune*, 'moonspit'. But it's difficult to see how something soft and glutinous could survive the burn if it was shot through the Earth's atmosphere.

Take the case of Mrs Ephgrave of Cambridge who saw a ball of jelly-like matter glide to earth on her lawn during a heavy rainstorm, about 7.30p.m. on 23 June 1978. It was the size of a football, white, and stayed intact even when she prodded it with a key. But the following morning it had completely vanished.

Reports of pwdre ser go back into antiquity, and even the eminent scientist Robert Boyle wrote about it in 1661: 'I have seen a good quantity of that jelly, that is sometimes found on the ground.'

Explanations for the jelly are still sketchy, but some scientists feel it may be some organic substance dropped to the ground by birds. Terence Meaden of the Tornado Research Organisation believes pwdre ser is a gelatinous goo oozing out of frogs or toads which is caught and then dropped by large birds such as crows. The jelly swells up in heavy rain and might disappear in the night because some sort of animal might take it for food.

Some experts say that the jelly might be created by a blue-green alga called *Nostoc*. This organism consists of cells wrapped in a gelatinous ball, but the slime found in pwdre ser is far too large for the alga.

# *Spontaneous Snowballs*

Snow can play an amazing game. When you first hear about it you think this is some sort of joke, but it's true. Snow can spontaneously make snowballs – balls of snow that suddenly, miraculously roll up of their own accord on snow-covered ground.

*Spontaneous snowballs! These so-called snowrollers form under certain weather conditions. © Esko Kuusisto*

If this smacks of something vaguely reminiscent of crop circles then rest assured that scientists are willing to believe in spontaneous snowballs. Esko Kuusisto at the National Hydrological Office in Helsinki and Charles Knight of the National Centre for Atmospheric Research in Boulder, Colorado, have both studied these bizarre balls. They're called snowrollers, and roll up like loft-insulating material, reaching up to a foot in diameter with a hollow centre. There are no pranksters at work because the snowrollers always leave a squiggly path behind them without any sign of hoaxers' footprints. On good days a whole field can be dotted with lots of snowrollers and their wiggly patterns behind them. Unfortunately, they are rarely seen being formed, but the finished balls have been photographed.

Snowrollers only form in particular conditions. They need a smooth crust of old snow with a layer of light new snow on top. This must be followed by rapid warming and strong winds. Then they start rolling, beginning with a small piece of snow which continues to roll, sometimes erratically, and powered by the wind. As the hollow cylinders of snow move they collect more snow on the outside. Much the same sort of principle lies behind building a snowman.

## Giant Snowflakes

On the afternoon of 10 January 1915, Berlin briefly experienced a very strange snow shower. Huge snowflakes fell amongst the usual common-or-garden ones. These beauties were 3 to 4 inches (8 to 10 centimetres) across. 'Gigantic snowflakes,' trumpeted the weather journal *Monthly Weather Review* of February 1915. 'They resembled a round or oval dish with its edges bent upward.' And they were so heavy they sank through the air with only a mere ripple without the usual delicate fluttering of a lightweight flake.

This wasn't the first report of monster-sized snowflakes. According to a report in *Nature*, a Mr E.J. Lowe at Chepstow had quite a surprise at midday on 7 January 1887. He looked up and saw a sight that he could scarcely believe: snowflakes measuring 3.5 inches (9 centimetres) in diameter fluttering down. He got a grip on himself, fetched a cold saucer, and after weighing it collected ten flakes. Weighing the dish again he recorded the weight of the flakes as one twentieth of an ounce (1.4 grams).

But the real granddaddy of them all – indeed, the world record holder for the greatest snowflake ever recorded on Earth – belongs to Fort Keogh, Montana on 28 January 1887. A magnificent snow shower fell near a ranch belonging to Matt Coleman, and snowflakes were described as 'larger than milk pans' in *Monthly Weather Review* that year. They measured a mind-boggling 15 inches (38 centimetres) across by almost 8 inches (20 centimetres) thick. A mail courier caught in the snowstorm witnessed the fall of these tremendous flakes over several square miles. There's no record of how he felt when he was hit by them.

These giants of the snow world were actually created from lots of ice crystals stuck together. And this is what ordinary snowflakes are made up of – clumps of ice crystals a mere millimetre or so across. But for some reason the clumps can occasionally get out of hand and turn into monsters of hundreds and thousands of ice crystals.

# Noctilucent Clouds

There is a certain type of cloud so rare and beautiful it can only be seen as the sun sets below the horizon on summer days, as the last rays of sunlight reflect off them without any other clouds in the sky. These clouds are silvery white with a bluish tinge, and they are formed seven times higher in the sky than any other cloud, higher even than the ozone layer in the mesosphere, on the boundary of the atmosphere and outer space. They are called noctilucent or night-shining clouds, and they are so special they were only discovered in 1885.

Although noctilucent clouds are rarely seen they are in fact quite common. It's just that you need a clear night with excellent visibility to see them. They also only appear in the summer months, and although it's summer on the ground this is the coldest time of year in the mesosphere 50 miles (80 kilometres) above the Earth's surface. The temperature at these altitudes drops to −200 degrees Fahrenheit (−129 degrees Celsius) and any water vapour in the mesosphere forms ice crystals on the tiny smoke particles left by burnt-out meteors.

Since their discovery in 1885 noctilucent clouds have increased every year. As well as meteors, they also need water vapour which comes from the breakdown of methane. Levels of methane have been steadily rising since the industrial age and some scientists believe that the increasing abundance of methane from agriculture and industry may well be the reason why noctilucent clouds appear to be more common now.

Another low light phenomenon is created even higher in the sky, in fact in space. At sunset or dawn, when the sun is below the horizon and the sky is dark, its last rays suddenly seem to light the sky up in a breathtaking cone of soft white light. It's called the Zodiacal Light, and it is created from the scattering of sunlight on interplanetary dust circling the Earth. The sky has to be very dark and clear and well away from city lights which it is often mistaken for. The best times to see it are after sunset in February and March and before sunrise in October and November.

## Moon and Weather

There are many pieces of folklore about the weather and the moon, and one of the most reliable pieces links a halo around the moon or a 'watery' moon shining through haze, with wet weather.

*Ring around the moon,*
*Rain is coming soon.*

Moonlight passing through high, wispy cirrus clouds (mare's tails) gives the effect of a halo around the moon because the tiny ice crystals in the cloud bend the light. When a storm is coming the high ice clouds will thicken with more ice crystals and so the moonlight is bent into a halo. And because the cirrus clouds often precede a rain front, the prediction often comes true. The brighter the halo, the nearer the storm.

Another good piece of lunar folklore is how clear the moon appears:

*Clear moon,*
*Frost soon.*

A clear moon means the sky is fine and cloudless, and a cloudless night allows the earth to cool quickly because there are no clouds to act like a blanket and trap some of the Earth's warmth. So in winter a cloudless night often leads to frost.

But there's one thing the moon can't do – it can't affect our weather. As the saying goes:

*The moon and the weather*
*May change together;*
*But change of the moon*
*Does not change the weather.*

The only things the moon can do on Earth are to shed moonlight and pull the world's ocean tides by its gravity field. But Robert Currie in America thinks that the moon's gravity also pulls the Earth's atmosphere in an invisible tide, and that in turn affects our weather. He discovered from records going back to the beginning of the nineteenth century that rainfall patterns in the US Midwest match an eighteen-and-a-half year rhythm. This is unlike any solar cycle but it almost exactly fits the weaving movement of the moon north and south of the equator that repeats every eighteen-and-a-half years. This changes the way the lunar tides affect the Earth's atmosphere.

Currie thinks that the US Midwest is especially sensitive to these rhythms because the lunar gravity can tug the prevailing winds blowing down from the Rocky Mountains. And depending on which way the winds are pulled, they create drought or abundant rainfall. Lunar rhythms have also been found in rainfall in South Africa, Australia, New Zealand, United States, hurricanes in the North Atlantic and typhoons in the northwest Pacific, and sunshine in the central and northeastern United States.

# EXTREME WEATHER

# Hurricanes

HOW DO OUR HURRICANE-force storms compare with elsewhere in the world?

A cyclone, typhoon or hurricane is a roaring vortex of wind up to 1000 miles (1600 kilometres) wide created from the heat of the oceans. Blasting its way across sea and land with winds gusting over 200 miles per hour (320 kilometres per hour), picking up enormous quantities of water vapour – about 2 billion tons per day from the ocean. It takes 500 trillion horsepower to whirl this great core of winds at such tremendous speeds – that's the equivalent of exploding an atomic bomb every second, or enough power to meet the entire United States' energy needs for a hundred years.

The strongest winds are found immediately outside the eye where they can rage up to 220 miles per hour (350 kilometres per hour). People often make the mistake of assuming the eye is the end of the storm, only to be lashed by ferocious winds coming from the opposite direction once the eye has passed. Spiralling bands of wind and rain can occur up to 250 miles (400 kilometres) away from the eye. Mariners in olden days would try to follow the eye of the storm for shelter until the storm died out. Often their ships would be covered with exhausted sea birds desperate for protection from the storm all around them.

*Cyclones generate some 500 trillion horsepower of energy – equivalent to an atom bomb exploding every second. © NASA*

But even though the winds rip, blast and tear everything in their path, they're not the most destructive element of the cyclone. The intense low pressure surrounding the hurricane sucks up the sea surface into a bulge of water up to 10 feet (3 metres) high. And this pushes the water ahead of the hurricane into even larger waves, up to 25 feet (7.6 metres) high. And if the hurricane hits land, this distended mass of water is pushed up into a spectacular wall. This is the hurricane's deadliest weapon – the storm surge. Monstrous waves that cause devastating damage by smashing and flooding everything in their path. In a truly cataclysmic scenario of ferocious winds, torrential rain and high tide, the storm surge can rise as high as 40 feet (12 metres) – as tall as a small apartment block –and it's this storm surge that's responsible for 90 per cent of hurricane deaths.

Cyclones claim more lives each year than any other storms, and in Asia the price in lives lost from cyclones can reach unbelievable proportions. The world's greatest recorded cyclone surge was a 40-foot (12-metre) wave along the coast of the Bay of Bengal on 7 October 1737, driven by the wind and magnified by the configuration of the Bay. It swept over the islands and lowlands, up the north end of the Bay of Bengal and over the mouth of the Hooghly River and the River Ganges delta, drowning an estimated three hundred thousand people. A similar sort of disaster happened in 1881 when storm waves generated by a typhoon swept around the Haifong area in China. Some three hundred thousand deaths were reported. In 1876 a cyclone-driven storm tide and waves killed an estimated one hundred thousand people in the Bay of Bengal. Disease following the flood killed another hundred thousand people.

The area at the north section of the Bay of Bengal is particularly vulnerable to wind and wave disasters because the sea floor of the bay slopes upwards and so huge masses of water are driven into shallow shores and over the low-lying land. This area is also densely populated. The most fatal cyclone disaster in recorded history happened on 13 November 1970, when 100 miles-per-hour (160 kilometres-per-hour) winds forced waves up to 15 feet (4.5 metres) tall through the islands of the deltas between the mouth of the Haringhata

River and the lower Meghna of Bangladesh. More than 1 million acres of rice paddies were flooded, a million cattle drowned, and human loss may have reached half a million.

In the Caribbean and America, cyclones are called hurricanes. The most deadly natural disaster in American history was the Galveston Hurricane of 8 September 1900. The resort town of Galveston, Texas, was hit by the hurricane with wind speeds estimated at over 110 miles per hour (170 kilometres per hour) sending a 5-foot (1.5-metre) tidal wave through the town. By night-time half the place was underwater with several buildings collapsing. The death toll was estimated at between ten thousand and twelve thousand. The city learnt the hard way, but now Galveston is probably the world's best protected city from hurricanes. Between Galveston and the sea there is a barrier nearly 11 miles (18 kilometres) long, 16 feet (5 metres) wide at the base rising to 20 feet (6 metres) high. All property was rebuilt 7 feet (2.1 metres) above the natural elevation.

The small Central American country of Belize took even more drastic measures against hurricane damage. On 13 October 1961, the capital, Belize City, on the Caribbean coast was almost totally destroyed by a 10-foot (3-metre) tall tidal wave from Hurricane Hattie. Afterwards the capital was moved 50 miles (80 kilometres) inland to a completely new site called Belmopan, where hurricane-force winds can't reach.

But recent hurricanes have been some of the strongest on record. Hurricane Andrew in 1992 was rated five out of five on the international scale of storm intensity with winds of 200 miles per hour (320 kilometres per hour) and caused over $20 billion of damage. Hurricane Hugo in 1989 caused $8 billion of damage when it struck southern Carolina, and was rated four out of five. Hurricane Gilbert in 1988 devastated Jamaica, the Yucatan peninsula in Central America and the Gulf of Mexico with a five out of five rating. It left two hundred dead and eight hundred thousand homeless. What is odd is that force five hurricanes are only expected once every hundred years, yet two in just four years is a recent serious escalation. Insurance companies in America and Britain were badly hit by the damage claims from these hurricanes and people are wondering whether the Earth is now set on a much stormier course.

*Hurricanes are growing stronger and more frequent – in 1992 Hurricane Andrew caused over $20 billion damage.*
© *NASA*

## Ships and Cyclones

### THE GREAT KAMIKAZE

The terrifying Mongol emperor, Ghengis Khan, established a colossal empire from Austria to China using a fast-moving, well-organized and utterly ruthless army. But there was one place where the great Mongol army came to utter grief. It was Japan, and the weapon that devastated them was a weather phenomenon: the Kamikaze, a Japanese word literally meaning the divine or god winds, which is given to violent storms, possibly typhoons.

In 1274, Ghengis Khan's grandson, Kubla Khan, sent a fleet to invade Kyushu, the most southerly of the main Japanese islands. Nine hundred ships sailed into Hakata Bay and the invaders ransacked the land and terrorized the natives; in other words, a fairly typical Mongol invasion. But then suddenly a big November storm blew up, sinking a large part of the Mongol fleet and forcing the rest to retreat .

But Kubla Khan wasn't daunted. Seven years later he sent back an even bigger fleet of four hundred ships carrying one hundred thousand soldiers and invaded Kyushu again. But just as the invasion had landed on the morning of 15 August 1281, a giant typhoon blew up and completely destroyed the fleet. The survivors who made it ashore were slaughtered by the Japanese. After that the Mongols left Japan well alone. This then became the legend of the Divine Wind – the Kamikaze, later symbolized by the suicide bomber planes in the Second World War.

### THE US PACIFIC 3RD FLEET

The catastrophic damage a hurricane or any other cyclone can inflict on modern shipping was dramatically shown during the Second World War. The US Pacific 3rd Fleet under Admiral William Halsey was sailing off the Philippines on 13 December 1944, having just fought a battle with the Japanese fleet. The battle had left the fleet very low on fuel, and they were forced to refuel even though the sea swell was high. To begin with they had no idea that a typhoon was approaching and when the terrible truth dawned on them the waves had grown so powerful that refuelling was abandoned. They then miscalculated the path of the oncoming storm and sailed straight into the heart of the typhoon. With so little fuel to act as ballast, many of the ships were pitched about like toys. Three destroyers capsized and sank, seven more were severely damaged, over a hundred aircraft were lost and over eight hundred men were drowned. It cost more lives than the naval battle for the Philippines afterwards. It was the greatest loss to the Navy from any storm since 1889; in fact, it was one of the worst losses the US Pacific Fleet sustained during the whole Second World War.

The typhoon that decimated the US 3rd Fleet was simply so small and tight it evaded all the fleet's weather monitoring. In fact, some of the ships of the fleet scattered out on the flanks had missed the typhoon altogether.

## Freak Winds

In 1961 a freak wind blew east across the Pennines with such astonishing force that ninety thousand homes were demolished in Sheffield. Terrified residents looked on in horror as roofs were flung off and their possessions sent scattering. One eyewitness, Douglas Wilson, described how his home was ripped apart. 'The wardrobe was going – clothing, mattress – all went straight through the roof.'

Hills and mountains can conjure up spectacular winds. It was unlucky for Sheffield that they caught the full blast of winds compressed into a vicious sandwich over the Pennines. Luckily it's a very rare event, but elsewhere in the world these sorts of winds are much more common. The mistral is a strong, dry, cold north wind funnelled through the valley of the Rhône between the Alps and the Cevennes. The victims of the mistral lie along the French Riviera and the Gulf of Lyon where the howling winds blast down at up to 93 miles per hour (150 kilometres per hour), smashing roofs, chimneys and walls.

The worst gusts of wind surge across the polar ice-caps. Wind speeds regularly reach 120 miles per hour (190 kilometres per hour) in Antarctica. They are called katabatic wind; from the Greek word meaning 'to go down'. The freezing temperature of the ice sheet chills the air above making it denser and it slides down the slope. In a continuous process, like a never-ending avalanche, warm air rushes in at the top to replace the sinking cooled air below.

But the fastest gust of wind ever recorded on Earth

was at Mount Washington in New Hampshire on 12 April 1934. It measured 231 miles per hour (372 kilometres per hour). The wind there is funnelled between the tops of the mountains and the ceiling of the troposphere – the layer of our atmosphere where all the weather takes place. As it's forced through this gap it speeds up, just like water when you put your thumb over the end of a hosepipe.

## Freak Waves

On the night of 6–7 February 1933 the US Navy ship *Ramapo* was steaming across the North Pacific when a typhoon slammed into it at 78 miles per hour (126 kilometres per hour). And then it faced a monster from the sea. An estimated 112-foot (34-metre) tall wave, as tall as a four-storey office block, rose up out of the sea and smashed down onto the ship. By some sort of miracle the *Ramapo* was not sunk.

The biggest ever actually recorded wave was 65 feet 5 inches (20.4 metres)from trough to crest which took fifteen seconds to pass a weather ship lying close to the track of a hurricane in 1961.

But there are also 'rogue waves' – waves that seem to rise out of nowhere for no apparent reason. Rogue waves can crush ships. On 5 February 1987, the *Fish-n-Fool* fishing boat was anchored off the Californian coast at San Diego. Without warning a 20-foot (6-metre) wave rushed out of nowhere and turned the boat over like a toy. Only two out of twelve people aboard survived.

Even large ships are in danger from rogues. The *Queen Mary* was swamped by one in 1942, and in 1974 a monster wave ripped a chunk of bow off the Norwegian supertanker *Wilford*. But small boats, like ocean-racing yachts, are particularly prone to rogues. In 1984 the 117-foot (36-metre) long yacht *Marques* was sailing in a transatlantic race when a rogue sank it in less than a minute, leaving eighteen out of twenty-seven crew dead.

Even bystanders watching the sea from what seems the safety of the shore can be in great danger. In October 1987 two anglers fishing from a rocky perch on the Cornish coast were suddenly plucked up by a monster wave and washed out to sea. Only one survived. Rogue waves along the north California coast are so dangerous that some sixty-nine people were believed drowned by rogues over a twenty-two-year period.

Rogues are created when two or more waves merge together, often driven by the wind. The new hybrid wave doesn't last long – maybe only a minute or so – but it's far larger than the surrounding sea swell. And rogue waves hitting coastlines are often created when waves are amplified by local tides and offshore rocks.

## Jet Stream

Jet streams are fast ribbons of wind about 6–7.5 miles (10–12 kilometres) up in the atmosphere, about 50–400 miles wide (80–640 kilometres), running at about 250 miles per hour (400 kilometres per hour) in the centre, roughly following the front where cold polar air meets warm tropical air, blowing from west to east in the temperate latitudes. Transatlantic flights often get buffeted by the jet stream going to America and try to avoid it, but can get an extra boost and ride on it going to Europe.

## JAPANESE FUGOS

The Japanese already knew about the jet stream from research on balloons before the Second World War, and they planned on using it to attack the North American mainland with balloon bombs to cause mass panic with bombs, and set fire to the forests of the Pacific Northwest with incendiaries. They developed sophisticated high-altitude bomb-carrying balloons called Fugos which were carried in the jet stream. Of nine thousand Fugos launched, around a thousand reached America, from Alaska to Mexico, as far east as Michigan and Texas in the south-west. Although only six people in America were killed, the military authorities and FBI realized the panic they could trigger in the civilian population and censored all media reports of the balloons. Special Fugo squads were set up across the country to clear up any evidence of the bombs and hush up eye-witnesses.

If the forests hadn't been wet from rain and snow the Fugos would have succeeded in setting them alight. And if, as the Americans feared, the Japanese added germ or chemical warfare to the balloons' arsenal the results would have been catastrophic.

Ironically, the most successful Fugo attack brought down a power line to Hanford – the plutonium plant from which the atom bombs were being made.

*The Japanese floated balloon bombs on the jet stream to attack North America in World War II. © National Archives, America*

### AMERICAN BOMBERS

On 1 November 1944, Captain Ralph D. Steakley flew a B29 reconnaissance mission on the first American high-altitude flight over Tokyo when the crew suddenly experienced extremely heavy winds. 'I found myself over Tokyo with a ground speed of about 70 mph. This was quite a shock, particularly since we were under attack from anti-aircraft guns and were a sitting duck for them. Obviously the head wind was about 175 mph.'

When B29 superfortresses later bombed industrial sites near Tokyo on 24 November 1944 they too encountered problems. 'The greatest hindrance to bombing accuracy was the high winds over the target. At 30,000 feet high velocities up to 230 mph were met.' The winds carried most of their bombs way off target and many fell out to sea. The airforce had to alter bombing tactics to compensate for the high winds and eventually sent their planes in at low altitude.

## Violent Storms in Britain

The British Isles have been battered by huge gales over many centuries. Whole towns have been obliterated and sunk into the sea during particularly violent storms, such as the old town of Winchelsea in 1287, Forvie in Scotland in 1413 and Santon Downham in East Anglia in the seventeenth century.

In 1993, the Holbeck Hall hotel in Scarborough slowly collapsed into the sea when the cliff it was standing on crumbled away. The coast of Britain is being pummelled by sea and storms and much of the north-east coast is disappearing, dramatically illustrated by the collapse of Holbeck Hall. But in south-east England the story is very different, although just as cruel.

*Violent storms have obliterated seaports and changed the landscape. © National Archives, America*

Romney Marsh in Kent was a great bay at the time of the Roman invasion, with Winchelsea, Lydd, Romney and Rye important island ports. Old Winchelsea (or what was called Winchelsey in those days) was a Cinque Port with toll-free trade, a rendezvous for the English fleets, with its fair share of smugglers. It housed several hundred families and a few churches. Then on 1 October 1250 a huge and terrifying storm battered the town. Three large ships and many smaller ones sank, and bridges, windmills and three hundred houses were 'drowned'. The wreckage was strewn for miles.

The Kent writer, Holinshed, described the storm: 'The sea appeared in the dark of the night to burne as it had been on fire, and the waves to strive and fight so that the mariners could not devise how to save their ships.'

A new town of Winchelsea was built a few miles away, but many people stayed behind in the remains of the old town. Then a second tempest in 1287 entirely swept away old Winchelsea and the island it stood on, in what is thought to be the spot where Pontins holiday camp at Camber Sands now stands. Gigantic waves threw so much sand and shingle into the bay that the nearby River Rother changed course completely leaving the ports of Romney, Hythe and Tenterden stranded far inland. Elsewhere, the storms of 1287 flooded East Anglia, helping start the formation of the Norfolk Broads, as well as flooding the continental coasts.

Afterwards, the inhabitants of Romney tried to cut a channel to the river, but it rapidly silted up and they soon abandoned the harbour. They were literally left high and dry. But their misfortune was a huge gain for the surviving ports of Rye and New Winchelsea, although eventually even Winchelsea succumbed to silting. That left only Rye in business and in 1572 it was dealt another incredible stroke of luck when a storm actually gouged out and enlarged its harbour!

But then, all told, Kent has done quite well from its tempests. The silt that stranded so many ports inland also added about 100 square miles (259 square kilometres) of rich new agricultural land to the county.

The deteriorating climate of the fourteenth century threw up some spectacular storms and floods. In about 1385 a storm threw a sand dune across the harbour at Harlech and closed it for good. A similar fate befell Santon Downham in East Anglia in the seventeenth century in what is now the heart of the Thetford Forest. Coastal erosion and silting destroyed a few other ports. Around 1316 the medieval port of Kenfig near Port Talbot was closed by sand blocking the port.

The 'Grote Mandrenke' (drowning) of January 1362 was a North Sea flood that wiped out some fifty parishes off Schleswig-Holstein. Chronicles tell of a hundred thousand deaths, but modern estimates put the numbers at between eleven thousand and thirty thousand. This was probably the greatest North Sea flood disaster in recorded history, with more than half the population of the wetlands along the coast of Jutland and Slesvig (modern Schleswig) drowned. It was fifty years before the dykes could be repaired. The storm was felt across southern England, destroying bell towers in London, Bury St Edmunds and Norwich. Chronicles from the time speak of the uprooting of hundreds of trees, collapsing houses, towers, monasteries, belfries, steeples, orchards and woods, and men being choked by the wind. Coming after the second outbreak of Plague, the storm was taken as some sort of apocalypse. Several modern writers regard this as the worst storm in southern England apart from the storm of 1703.

The medieval town of Forvie on the Aberdeenshire coast in north-east Scotland was buried by sand during a storm in 1413. The Forvie sand dune advanced 600 feet (180 metres) during the storm and the town now lies buried under a 90-foot (27-metre) high dune.

In northern Scotland a great storm in the autumn of 1694 obliterated up to 7000 acres (2800 hectares) of the most fertile area of farmland, the so-called 'breadbasket of Moray'. Sixteen farms and a manor house were inundated. Survivors were reported demolishing the backs of their cottages to get out. The loss of the crops was even more serious to the Scottish economy, which was already suffering such a succession of bad harvests that grain was being imported from the Baltic states. The nearby River Findhorn changed course as a result of the storm, and the small town of Findhorn at the mouth of the river was wrecked. Ever since then a great deal of engineering has been invested in protecting the coast in this area of Scotland from further damage.

But there seems little doubt that the worst storm in Britain in recorded history was that of 26–7 November 1703. The wind blew at more than hurricane force (73–81 miles per hour or 117–130 kilometres per hour) (although technically it wasn't an actual hurricane because they can only occur in the tropics). It was meticulously documented by Daniel Defoe, author of *Robinson Crusoe*. At about 4p.m. on 24 November the wind suddenly increased with terrific gusts. At least 123 people were killed on land by the storm but losses at sea were far greater: eight thousand men were estimated drowned when merchant and naval ships capsized. Over four hundred windmills were wrecked, some because the intense friction of the rotating blades set the timbers on fire. Over seventeen thousand trees were blown down in Kent. Churches also suffered particularly badly: at least seven had their steeples blown down and one church spire in Stowmarket, Suffolk was blown clean off and sent 28 feet (9 metres) down the length of the church before crashing through the roof. The lead of many church roofs was rolled up and carried away by the wind.

Compared to the storm of 1703, the storm of 1987 wasn't quite as severe. The winds which struck south-east England and East Anglia in the early hours of 15 October 1987 just about reached hurricane force, i.e. 77 miles per hour (124 kilometres per hour) for at least ten minutes at Gorleston in Norfolk and at Shoreham in Sussex and Dover in Kent (85 miles per hour or 137 kilometres per hour). Nineteen people were killed. Some 3 million households and businesses were left without electricity, 150,000 telephones were cut off, 19 million trees were blown down and many villages and towns were completely cut off by fallen trees, with 90 per cent of Kent's roads blocked. It's estimated that insurance claims for the night's damage amounted to over £1 billion.

Extraordinary human stories of bravery and luck were recorded that night. A vicar whose house collapsed while he was asleep, fell through the top floor, landed by the telephone, called an ambulance, which just managed to get him to hospital before the roads were blocked by fallen trees.

The captain of a Channel ferry whose ship lost all power after leaving Dover during the storm, ran aground on a concrete slab which penetrated the hull below the waterline. The ship was only saved by the low tide which left it beached high and dry.

What made the storm so strong was its deep low

pressure – the intense pressure difference drew in wind extremely fast. The storm's ferocity was driven by a big kick in the jet stream. It had picked up warm and humid air leftover from Hurricane Floyd in Florida. Then around the Azores it got a second kick from the unusually warm waters of the Atlantic and the storm 'exploded'. It sped across the Atlantic so fast it turned into the worst storm to hit England for two hundred and fifty years. Fears that the storm was fuelled by high sea temperatures has highlighted the warnings about the arrival of the greenhouse effect, which will be dealt with in the last section.

## Lightning

The power of a typical storm about 0.6 miles (1 kilometre) across is equivalent in energy to about ten Hiroshima-type bombs. Lightning is a sudden shaft of electrical discharge of a million volts with a massive current, peaking at between 10,000 and 40,000 amps, travelling at 186,000 miles per second (300,000 kilometres per second).

Lightning heats the air it blasts through up to 86,000 degrees Fahrenheit (30,000 degrees Celsius) and when it strikes sandy soil this intense heat can instantly melt it into a natural glass called fulgurite. The shape of each fulgurite is a cast of the lightning channel, measuring up to 15 feet (4.6 metres) long.

Lightning occurs when static electricity builds up inside a cloud, probably created from ice or water

*Thunderstorms are made from just hot air and water but they generate phenomenal power – each lightning bolt carries a million volts, peaking at between 10,000 and 40,000 amps. © Warren Faidley*

droplets violently colliding with each other. The base of the cloud collects negative charges which need to discharge like a spark jumping a gap.

It's interesting that lightning can also be formed around volcanoes. There are dozens of historical accounts, including the monstrous eruption of Krakatoa in 1883. One sea captain described the nighttime display of lightning branching out from the volcanic plume like 'an enormous pine tree with branches of lightning', and watched as another ship lying 45 miles away was struck. More recently, the emergence of the volcanic Icelandic island of Surtsey in 1963 showed that the billowing steam clouds generated lightning with thunder that sounded like a sharp crack from a rifle shot.

## AMAZING LIGHTNING STRIKES

Rockets have often made explosive meetings with lightning. On 26 March 1987 an Atlas-Centaur rocket carrying a Navy communications satellite was launched in Florida but triggered off a lightning bolt by flying straight into a storm cloud. The lightning punched through the nose cone, befuddled the computer and sent the missile, which started to break up, hurtling off in the wrong direction. Mission control had to detonate the $160 million package into oblivion .

Just three months later, the prophetically named Wallops Island launch pad in Virginia suffered a lightning bolt which triggered the launch controls to three rockets in possibly the world's most spectacular fireworks display. Two of the rockets shot 2 miles (3.2 kilometres) before plunging into the sea, whilst a 16-foot (5-metre) Orion roared into life, raced across the ground for 300 feet (91 metres) before it too drowned in the ocean. Ironically the rocket was packed with scientific instruments designed to study lightning. Shocked NASA officials claimed it was the first time that lightning had ever triggered a lift-off. After that, NASA prohibited any rocket launch during electrical storms.

Apart from rockets, aircraft have long been vulnerable to lightning attack. Although aircraft are designed to conduct lightning around their shell and leave the interior insulated it doesn't always work. On 24 March 1979 lightning knocked the nose-cone off an Allegheny Airlines 111, flying from St Louis, Missouri, to Indianapolis with seventy-four passengers on board; the airliner made a safe emergency landing.

But maybe the most terrifying explosions are made by a much more organic reaction. The heat of a direct lightning hit can instantly boil the water inside a tree trunk, the scalding vapour blasting the tree into smithereens with the force of something like 550 pounds (250 kilograms) of TNT.

But there's even worse in the desert. The giant candlestick cacti typical of John Wayne's movies have such a voracious thirst they can absorb up to a ton of water. But all that water can also turn them into bombs. Being the tallest objects in the deserts, they are extremely vulnerable to lightning. With one strike their water can instantly turn to steam, the cactus explodes and the spines coating its stem are sent hurtling out in a shower of vegetable shrapnel. There are no statistics on injuries caused by exploding cacti.

There are also cases of high-altitude flashes. It started with reports in *Nature* science journal in 1977 of a satellite recording random split-second light flashes over the Earth's surface. These superbolts strike during severe thunderstorms and are a thousand times greater than normal lightning. The discovery was made by optical sensors on Vela satellites which were designed to detect intense flashes from nuclear explosions. The flashes didn't seem to fit lightning, but there is a phenomenon known as rocket lightning where bolts of lightning shoot out of the tops of clouds into the sky. High flying pilots have also recently reported sighting lightning bolts shooting upwards from the tops of clouds, some of them arcing round and back into the tops of the clouds. Whether these flashes are linked to mysterious bursts of electromagnetism isn't known. In November 1993 powerful pulses of electromagnetic energy were picked up by the Alexis satellite, also designed to detect nuclear explosions. Most of the radio bursts were found over South Africa and South America.

Another remarkable discovery was made about large-scale thunderstorms by scientists at the University of Alaska flying in high-altitude aircraft. Eugene Westcott and Davis Sentman recorded colossal flashes of red light bursting out from the tops of thunderclouds. 'They look like carrots or tall jellyfish,' Wescott said. 'They appear brightest where they top out, so you have the jellyfish body at the top with tentacles trailing down.' They also recorded jets of blue light puffing out of the cloud tops, but what these and the red 'jellyfish' are is a mystery – all Westcott can suggest is that the electricity from thunderstorms interacts with the upper atmosphere like a sort of giant neon tube.

*Over a hundred people a year are killed in the United States by lightning. © Pekka Parvianen*

But perhaps the weirdest recent discovery about lightning was a research paper on the effect of nuclear power stations. According to a report in *Atmospheric*

*Environment* in 1994, nuclear installations give off Krypton-85, a chemically inert radioactive gas. Krypton-85 also makes the atmosphere conduct electricity more easily and helps create thunderstorms. Whether more thunderstorms strike over nuclear plants hasn't been analysed yet.

It's a myth that lightning never strikes the same place twice. The Empire State Building and the Eiffel Tower are struck on average twenty to thirty times a year because lightning usually seeks out the highest object. Tall or isolated trees, telegraph poles and exposed hill tops are dangerous places to be in a thunderstorm, and churches, castles, houses have all been blown up by lightning, hence the reason church spires carry lightning conductors.

In 1750 the Eddystone lighthouse near Plymouth was destroyed by fire from a severe thunderstorm, and when it was rebuilt in 1761 it was the first building in Britain to be protected with a lightning conductor.

One of the worst recent disasters was the explosion at an oil refinery in Wales early in the morning on 24 July 1994. A severe thunderstorm swept Wales and England, when lightning hit the Elf and Gulf refineries during an intense thunderstorm at Milford Haven in Pembrokeshire in Wales starting fires which raged for hours. Then at 1p.m. another lightning strike ripped into the Texaco oil refinery triggering an explosion which could be heard 10 miles (16 kilometres) away. Flames 100 feet (30 metres) high shot out and left firemen battling for twenty-four hours to control the blaze. Although the refinery was ripped apart, workers on the site suffered only minor injuries.

However, far worse hit Egypt that year. On 2 November, a ferocious thunderstorm swept the country, killing about sixty people in floods. But at Durunka, a small town in southern Egypt, lightning triggered a bizarre and apocalyptic chain of events. A lightning bolt struck a train carrying fuel oil, derailing it near to an army oil depot, setting off a fireball of ignited fuel which surged on the torrential rainwaters of the thunderstorm through the town, ripping through hundreds of homes. It's thought that about five hundred people died in the inferno, many of asphyxiation in the smoke and fumes. The rescue effort was severely hampered by the torrential rains, which turned the roads into rivers of mud.

Perhaps the worst recorded lightning disaster in history happened on 27 October 1697, in Athlone, in the heart of Ireland. A ferocious storm broke out during the small hours, and then, following three terrifying claps of thunder, a searing bolt of lightning hit Athlone's Castle, striking the arsenal and blowing up 260 barrels of gunpowder, 1000 hand grenades, various incendiaries, 220 barrels of musket balls and pistol balls, followed by great stores of pick-axes and assorted ironmongery. This vast bomb blew up in the air with such a huge explosion it demolished the castle and set fire to the surrounding town, completely destroying sixty-four houses and burning almost all the rest, thanks largely to their thatch roofs. The damage to property was so severe that the entire castle and town had to be rebuilt. Yet, surprisingly, only eight people were recorded as killed and about thirty-six injured, of which one sobering account added: 'None Killed of Note'.

But the disaster is still shrouded in some mystery. Apart from the accounts of ordinary lightning, this description from the time includes: 'Just above the Castle, and at the last of three Claps, in the Twinkling of an Eye, fell a Wonderful and Great Body of Fire, in figure Round . . . [which fell] down the Magazine took Fire and blew up the Granadoes.' Exactly what this fire-ball was remains very much a mystery, since even today we don't know whether it is ball lightning or some other phenomenon.

Churches have had a long, but rarely happy, association with lightning. Before lightning conductors were invented, churches with steeples were highly dangerous places to be during a thunderstorm. In fact, you could hardly hope to find a worse building for lightning protection: churches were often built on high spots on the landscape with a steeple rising towards heaven, and this makes them ideal for attracting lightning.

One German book published in 1784 reported that lightning hit 386 churches in Europe during a thirty-three-year period. Casualties were particularly high amongst bell-ringers, because for six hundred years ringing church bells were used to ward off lightning. Unfortunately bell-ringers were often electrocuted and the German survey reported 103 sextons killed during bell-ringing in storms.

And yet even in 1749 when Benjamin Franklin invented the lightning rod to ground lightning strikes harmlessly, the Abbé Nollet, a French churchman and philosopher, declared lightning rods 'dangerous'. He argued, 'Bells, by virtue of their benediction, should scatter the thunderstorms and preserve us from strokes of lightning.'

But bell-ringing during thunderstorms persisted long after the dreadful consequences were scientifically clear. Even in the early twentieth century the countryside still echoed to the hapless bell-ringer warding off the evil powers. Ironically, the last church bell known to have been rung against thunder was in the Austrian Alps in

1914, just before the outbreak of the First World War.

Perhaps the unluckiest church was at Steeple Ashton in Wiltshire. On 25 July 1670 a bolt of lightning from an intense thunderstorm blasted a crack through the church steeple. Repairs were soon started but months later on 15 October when it was almost finished another terrible storm let rip a shaft of lightning which hit the steeple, killing two workmen and totally demolishing the steeple and badly damaging much of the rest of the church. The church was repaired, but the steeple was never rebuilt. And then on 20 June 1772 the vicarage at Steeple Ashton was struck by another violent burst of lightning. Two vicars staying there suddenly saw a ball of fire between them which exploded with a deafening bang with thick smoke. One reverend's shoulder was badly hit and he collapsed with burns to his legs, whilst the other was lucky to escape with slight cuts. Even now Steeple Ashton still attracts fate. In June 1973, 84-year-old Henry Bolt was standing in his kitchen when he was thrown across the room from the blast of a nearby thunderbolt which blew up a barn full of straw next door and set fire to it. But was it divine retribution, or just bad luck for having a village on high ground prone to lightning strikes?

York Minster suffered what some took to be a divine strike in July 1984. A thunderbolt seared down into the roof of the South Transept which later collapsed in flames. More than one churchman claimed the fire could have been retribution just three days after the consecration at the Minster of the Bishop of Durham, the Rt. Rev. David Jenkins, had made controversial remarks about the Christian faith. But police ruled out deliberate intent. The restoration of the Minster took over four years at a cost of over £2 million.

What made the York Minster catastrophe even more bizarre is that the sky directly above was clear; the nearest thunderclouds were some way away. The proverbial bolt from the blue has struck on many other occasions, sometimes coming straight down in a vertical line from the sky. One theory is that a thundercloud is full of negative charges at its base and positive charges at the top. At the end of a thunderstorm the negative charges have discharged as lightning to the ground, but the positive ones are left literally hanging in the air, sometimes long after the thunderstorm has gone. These charges go to earth in one massive ear-splitting thunderbolt. These end-of-storm lightning strikes sometimes come with ball lightning, and one idea is that the path of the ball electrifies a channel in the air which the positive bolt then follows.

*Lightning as a fertiliser – 100 million tons of nitrogen are washed down each year by lightning.* © *NOAA/ NSSL*

### BENJAMIN FRANKLIN

Few weather experiments have ever caught the public's imagination, but the story of a thundery day in June 1752 is a legend that led to thousands of lives being saved. It happened in a field near Philadelphia where editor and publisher Benjamin Franklin flew a kite high up to the thunderclouds. Suddenly the twine holding the kite began to bristle and Franklin saw a small spark jump from the kite. He had discovered electricity in the air; little did he realize that he had also come perilously close to blowing himself to smithereens in the process.

*Benjamin Franklin's famous kite experiment showed that lightning is an electrical phenomenon. From* L'Atmosphère *by Camille Flammarion*

Franklin already had a pretty good hunch that lightning was electrical. As he concluded, 'The electric fluid is attracted by points. We do not know if this property is in lightning. But since they agree in all the particulars wherein we can already compare them, is it not probable that they agree also in this?'

And so from those early experiments lightning rods earthed in the ground became a standard protection from lightning strikes. Franklin was hailed a genius.

But not all Franklin's ideas worked. His invention of a bed suspended by silk ropes to insulate the sleeper from lightning strikes on houses didn't catch on. Fortunately neither did 'Franklin wires' for insulating ladies' hats – trailing metal wires which could have given their wearers a terrific headache during thunderstorms.

But one other Franklin myth still persists today. He was convinced that only pointed metal rods were good lightning conductors. Yet recent work now shows that the sharp tips aren't as good as blunt tops, and so light-ning conductors are now made with mushroom-shaped tops.

### STRANGE EFFECTS OF THUNDERSTORMS

In July 1980, fishermen on a boat off the coast at Whitby, Yorkshire found their hair standing on end for twenty minutes. Lightning then struck only metres away from the boat, at which point their hair fell flat. A sim-ilar incident happened to two men fishing from a boat on Derwent Water Reservoir, Cumbria, in August 1975, when not only their hair stood on end but also their fishing lines and fishing flies rose up in the air too. The tip of one of the fishing rods began to buzz 'like a swarm of bees'.

Animals also seem to get warning of an impending lightning bolt. Mr P. F. Burrows of the National Rivers

Authority wrote to the *Journal of Meteorology* that while he was driving in the Chiltern Hills during a thunderstorm, he noticed two horses quietly grazing on an open hillside when suddenly for no obvious reason they bolted to the far end of the field. About fifteen seconds later a lightning strike hit the place where they had originally been standing.

There are many accounts of phones, faxes, answering machines and television sets blown up by lightning strikes. It's hardly surprising: outdoor telephone cables carry electric current easily, and television aerials on roofs are ideal lightning conductors.

But the static electricity of a thunderstorm has caused some much weirder effects. In 1993 the *Journal of Meteorology* reported that a car stalled at a road junction just before a lightning bolt struck just a few metres away. As soon as the lightning struck, the car started again without any further problems.

Even more worrying, lightning has stalled aircraft. According to a report in *Lightning protection of aircraft* (NASA Ref Publn 1008, October 1977), a plane had taken off from Presque Isle, Maine, and had been in cruise speed for fifty minutes when a large thunderstorm was seen. As the plane approached the storm there was a noticeable drop in power. 'A few seconds before the lightning bolt hit the plane all four engines were silent and the propellers were windmilling,' explained the co-pilot, but then they were saved when the engines surged back to power again as soon as the lightning struck.

Pilots have had even more terrifying experiences. In August 1959 US Marine Lt Col. William Rankin was flying 46,000 feet (14,000 metres) above the Carolina coast in his F-8U Crusader single seater jet fighter when his engine failed and he was forced to bail out.

Unfortunately he jumped into a thunderstorm, and by the time his pre-set parachute opened at 10,000 feet (3000 metres) he was being tossed around in ferocious winds in the thundercloud. 'It hit me like a tidal wave of air, a massive blast, as though forged under tremendous compression, aimed and fired at me with the savagery of a cannon,' Lt Col. Rankin later described. 'I was buffeted in all directions – up, down, sideways, clockwise, counterclockwise, over and over . . . I was rattled violently, as though a monstrous cat had caught me by the neck and was determined to shake me until I had gasped my last breath.'

A mature thundercloud drives winds up inside itself up to 70 miles per hour (113 kilometres per hour), gusting to 150 miles per hour (240 kilometres per hour) with downdrafts rushing out of the cloud up to 30 miles per hour (48 kilometres per hour). The turbulence is so great that aircraft wings have been ripped off, so the chances of a human surviving are fairly remote. Lt Col. Rankin was showered with hail, snow and rain, and was tossed around for forty-five minutes – a descent three times longer than normal. But miraculously his parachute remained intact and he eventually fell safely onto a field, got to a hospital and only suffered shock and frostbite.

Lt Col. Rankin's astonishing escape was in marked contrast to five German glider pilots caught in a thunderstorm over the Rhön mountains in the late 1930s. They were forced to bail out when the gliders were violently tossed around in the thunderstorm. They were caught in winds which threw them up into the top of the cloud where they were coated with ice and froze to death.

FOLKLORE

Lightning is an awesome spectacle, even in this age of scientific enlightenment, so it's small wonder that in olden days it was also a religious experience. According to Greek mythology, thunderbolts had been invented by Athena, goddess of wisdom, forged by the ironsmith Hephaestus, but were actually thrown by Zeus, father of all gods, to punish the arrogant. The sites of lightning strikes were revered by the ancient Greeks and that's why they occasionally built their temples there.

A long-held myth was that there was magic in wood which prevented lightning from striking, and the idea persisted in Europe until the nineteenth century. That's why in England and Germany the traditional Yule log used to be tossed into the fireplace, to ward off lightning. The French and Flemish believed that a chunk from a lightning-struck tree could ward off lightning from under their beds. Innkeepers thought that thunder turned beer sour and laid bars across their barrels as a preventive measure. Holly bushes were supposed to protect houses. People stepping outside in a storm would carry a nettle, an acorn or a sprig of rosemary as a charm.

Even today myths about lightning persist. Some people open doors during a thunderstorm, but this isn't just a myth, it's plain dangerous: there are quite a few accounts of lightning striking the insides of buildings through open doors.

Milk is supposed to go off if left out during a thunderstorm, but like most other myths there isn't a shred of evidence that electricity from the thunderstorm causes it. In fact, the atmospheric electricity might even preserve the milk. The souring of milk is caused by bacteria which are fairly quiet at temperatures below 45 degrees Fahrenheit (7 degrees Celsius), but they become increasingly active with rising temperatures, which probably explains the link with thunderstorms. Warm, humid weather usually precedes a summer thunderstorm, and it is probably this warmth and not the electricity in the air which helps turn milk sour.

### PEOPLE HIT BY LIGHTNING

In the United States, an average of about one hundred and fifty people are killed by lightning each year, a quarter of them while sheltering under trees which present dangerous targets for lightning. Yet thankfully only about five people a year are killed by lightning in Britain, although some of the escapes have been hair-raising.

Take the case in July 1982 of Maureen Wingrove in Maidenhead, Berkshire, who was making tea with her kitchen window slightly ajar. A proverbial bolt from the blue ripped through the open window, striking the metal tea strainer she was holding and hurling her several feet backwards. Fortunately she was only left with minor bruises and shock.

In August 1992, twelve-year-old Brian Linkin from Faversham in Kent was watching a thunderstorm raging outside from his bedroom window – also left slightly ajar – when lightning blasted the metal window frame in a shower of brilliant sparks, jumped onto the radiator, and threw him backwards. He was found by his father lying unconscious on the floor, but was left only with temporary muscle cramps across his stomach where he'd been leaning against the radiator. His GP later claimed that Brian's rubber-soled trainers had probably saved his life.

Lightning can seek out virtually any aperture in a house and penetrate deep inside. A few years ago a cottage in Lincolnshire was hit by a bolt down its chimney. The lightning passed right down the flue, then flashed out of the fireplace, across the kitchen, past the astonished family sitting there and blasted the larder, where it fused cake tins together and roasted an uncooked ham. If you find that difficult to swallow, the cake tins are now in the Lincoln Museum.

Geoffrey Hart from Wherwell near Southampton was in his home in August 1992 during a thunderstorm when suddenly all the lights went out. He went to the utility room to get a torch. 'As I stretched my left arm in to get it from a shelf there was a flash and a tremendous bang. I was thrown against the door and landed on my back on the floor about four feet away.' It's thought that lightning struck the television aerial which came down to earth and hit Mr Hart.

Most indoor lightning casualties occur to people talking on the phone, particularly in rural areas, because outdoor cables can catch a lightning strike and send the electrical current surging down into the phone itself. Television sets can blow up in thunderstorms because outside aerials make perfect lightning conductors, with metal spikes sticking high up from rooftops. They can pass a lightning strike down indoors straight into the television, although no one has been reported as hurt by watching their set explode.

The next most dangerous indoor situation is in a kitchen, because of the metal pipes, taps and sink units which can pass current. One Derbyshire village was hit by a particularly violent lightning bolt in May 1992, blowing one woman across her kitchen as she was making a call. The rest of the village suffered blasted fax and telephone answering machines, leaving British Telecom with a fine mess to repair.

And of course open windows and doors are an open invitation to a direct lightning strike. One man in Somerset was in his bedroom when a thunderbolt ripped a hole more than 4 feet (1.2 metres) square through the main wall of his house just a few feet from where he was standing. 'I just could not believe what was happening,' he reported. 'Everything in the house was thrown into chaos. Electrical appliances exploded, plugs, radiators and pictures were ripped off the walls.'

A Tuscon housewife was standing in the middle of her living room between the front and back door while her friends were sitting on a sofa against a windowless wall. Suddenly a large bolt of lightning flashed through one door and out the other, injuring the woman and knocking her to the floor. The others in the room were not hurt. The lightning had flashed between the open doors.

Umbrellas can be dangerous in a thunderstorm. Mrs Decoster from Everberg near Brussels was walking in a street when she heard a booming noise and her umbrella was torn from her hands. She felt something like a 'burning fire' around her and fell to the ground. The umbrella was completely scorched but Mrs Decoster only suffered minor marks.

Some are just very unlucky cases. One farmer was driving his tractor in New York State when he was hit by lightning. One hour later, the ambulance carrying him to hospital was also hit by lightning, causing the ambulance to crash and killing the farmer.

But the all-time record is a park ranger in Yosemite National Park, California, who has been hit seven times by lightning, apparently without serious repercussions. Roy Sullivan was first struck by lightning in 1969 when his eyebrows were burnt, then in 1970 he was left with burns to his left shoulder, in 1972 his hair was set on fire, in 1973 his hair was set alight again, in the same year he suffered a damaged ankle, and in 1977 he suffered chest and stomach burns. On another occasion he was sheltering in a ranger station from a thunderstorm when lightning struck power cables into the building and hit him. He died in 1983 of natural causes.

Three times as many males as females are killed by lightning because more men do outdoor work or recreation. One surprise is that twice as many anglers are killed as golfers by lightning, although golfers are more likely to suffer non-fatal injuries. Injuries from being hit by lightning usually include burns and electrocution, but there are cases of individuals being cooked from their insides, as was the case of a golfer struck at Baltray near Dublin on 7 April 1984. Tony Cosgrave was struck so severely that his clothes and shoes were completely burnt off and he was rushed to hospital and operated on immediately. But during the operation surgeons discovered that his bowels suffered several perforations – it appeared that the lightning had heated gases in his bowels and they had literally exploded. A brass buckle on the golfer's belt had probably given the lightning a convenient entry into his abdomen. And yet after these horrific injuries the victim recovered and several months later carried on playing golf.

The advice to avoid lightning is clear. Stay away from metal fixtures in the home or outdoors. Avoid exposed shelters, open fields, open boats, lone trees and large trees in woods. Get off golf carts, bikes, horses, and take cover. Do not swim.

Out of all the people prone to lightning disasters, you'd expect golfers, farmers and anyone else in the open countryside to be most vulnerable. But spare a thought for policemen. Their metal spiked helmets make little lightning conductors, and at least two PCs have found themselves engulfed in lightning on top of their heads. Luckily, they've been left unhurt because the rest of the helmet seems to take the blast quite well.

Others have not been so lucky. Entire sports teams have been felled by lightning. On 26 September 1981 at Lydney, Gloucestershire, all twenty-two players on a football pitch were thrown to the ground when lightning struck the pitch. Five casualties were taken to hospital and one later died.

Animals are more prone to being hit by lightning, possibly because they have four legs and so take up a larger area of ground which can be hit. Farm animals also tend to huddle together during a storm, presenting a bigger target for one lightning strike. The worst known case of animals killed this way was on 22 June 1918 when lightning struck a flock of sheep in an open field in the Wasatch National Forest, Utah, and killed 504 of the animals in one fell stroke.

But not all people hit by lightning suffer. *The Daily Telegraph*, June 1980, reported that a sixty-two-year-old man blinded in an accident nine years previously regained his sight after being struck by lightning near his home in Falmouth, Maine, on 4 June. Edwin Robinson, a former truck driver, was sheltering under a tree during a thunderstorm when he was knocked to the ground by the blast. He lay unconscious for twenty minutes but when he awoke his sight had returned. Doctors confirmed that Mr Robinson could see for the first time since he went blind.

Although lightning causes fatalities, injuries and damage, it also replenishes the earth with nitrogen. The heat of the lightning flash produces nitrous oxides which are washed down and fertilize the soil – 100 million tons of nitrogen are returned each year by lightning.

## ST ELMO'S FIRE

People can even glow without being hit by lightning. In 1983, five policemen in Swindon were almost blown to smithereens by a side-flash from a lightning strike. They were wrapped in a blue aura 'like something out of "Star Trek"' and left tingling for hours afterwards, but were otherwise uninjured, according to the local paper. Their thick rubber-soled boots had apparently kept them insulated.

The phenomenon is caused by a build up of electro-static electricity called St Elmo's Fire, named after an early Christian Italian bishop, Saint Erasmus, (abbreviated to Sant' Ermo) and adopted as patron saint of Mediterranean sailors.

At midday on Tuesday 21 December 1976 at Dover a thunderstorm passed by. The prefects of the Dover Boys' Grammar school were playing their annual football match against the masters. There was a flash of lightning instantaneous with a loud clap of thunder. Play stopped because the hair of three of the players – two prefects and a teacher – was glowing and standing up. This electrical discharge was presumably a type of St Elmo's Fire; it surrounded the heads only. They did not feel anything and were unhurt, but they reported hearing a popping sound like the repeated snapping of fingers. No damage was reported in the area.

*The Meteorological Magazine* of 1897 reported a most bizarre case of St Elmo's Fire:

On January 4 during the worst of the great wind and snowstorm at Huon, the air was heavily laden with electricity. The cottonwood trees in front of the Chicago and North-western offices presented a very strange and novel appearance. The trees were buried in snow almost to their tops, but at the end of each twig on every branch in sight was an electrical spark about as large as a common field pea. On taking hold of a twig the spark extinguished, but on withdrawing the hand the spark reappeared. Dispatcher Wilson, who wore a glove with a hole in the thumb, took hold of a twig, and the spark transferred itself to his thumb and back to the twig when he let go. There was no shock experienced, says an American contemporary, in handling the twigs, and the light did not waver or tremble, but was quite steady. The trees looked as if a colony of fireflies had settled upon them.

St Elmo's Fire is defined as an ungrounded luminous corona visible around an object or person in humid, pre-thunderstorm conditions.

St Elmo's Fire may be manifested in quite large areas. It has been blamed for igniting the fire that destroyed the airship *Hindenburg* on 6 May 1937 at Lakehurst, New Jersey, and some experts have speculated it may have been behind the York Minster fire in July 1984.

But one of the strangest reports came from Yellowstone Park, Wyoming, cited by William Corliss (*Lightning, Auroras, Nocturnal Lights and Related Luminous Phenomena*, 1982). William Sanborn was looking on a violent thunderstorm in September 1949: 'I watched the ridge for a moment and was amazed to see what can best be described as a hazy patch of blue light coming over the ridge and moving down the hill slope toward the flats around the lake.' As the patch of light steadily approached and enveloped the amazed spectator he felt a weird sensation like static electricity. 'It kept low to the ground . . . Each twig on the sagebrush was surrounded by a halo of light about two inches in diameter . . . There was a marked tingling sensation in my scalp, and brushing my hair . . . caused a snapping of tiny sparks.'

Even large structures like houses can be enveloped in St Elmo's Fire. A report from Rapura, New Zealand, on 8 November 1930 spoke of an entire house 'wrapped in a blue flickering flame for an appreciable period'. In a field, three horses were also enveloped in blue flames.

Even mountain peaks can glow at night. The Andes mountains are especially good for these glows, but they've also been seen over peaks in the Alps, Lapland Arctic, the Rockies and in Mexico. They aren't caused by lightning because they can happen under cloudless skies and can last for hours, and they usually occur during dry weather. They can be rays, streamers, flashes, or steady glows over the mountain peaks or ridges. They are usually yellowy white and, rarely, green or orange.

The so-called Andes Glow might be a giant form of St Elmo's with the peak of a mountain acting as a point for electrical discharge. Measurements on Mexican volcanoes reported in the journal *Weather* in 1970 revealed large electric fields over the peaks. But St Elmo's should give a thinner glow over the mountain tops, and it's difficult to explain the rays, beams and haloes also seen.

And one report from Chile described intense glows during an earthquake [see Earthquake Lights].

Towards the end of the Second World War pilots from all over the world started reporting cases of fireballs alongside their aircraft. The Americans called them Foo Fighters and these strange balls became absorbed into UFO stories. They looked like balls of fire of various colours, that kept pace with the aircraft no matter what the speed or however hard the pilot tried to outmanoeuvre them. These were either ball lightning or St Elmo's Fire, but it's difficult to explain how the balls could stay ahead of or behind the aircraft.

It's interesting that a physicist, Dr M.W. McDowell, reported to the journal *Weather* something similar when he was driving his car. A storm was approaching when suddenly a bright ball of red, blue and white light the size of a football enveloped the aerial of his car. There was no noise, no damage, and not even any radio interference. He thought it might have been St Elmo's fire, although it also has similarities with the ball lightning experience of Gladys Hughes from Conwy, North Wales [refer back to Ball lightning].

### BEAD LIGHTNING

On rare occasions lightning bolts seem to come down as a necklace of luminous balls. *The Marine Observer*, 1930, reported the following case from 26 July 1929 in Balboa Channel, Panama:

> A flash of lightning on the port hand appeared to enter the sea about 100 yards from the vessel. It appeared as a stream of molten metal being

poured from a height into the sea and of about one or two feet wide. It first made a peculiar shattering noise (as a china plate would make on a stone floor), then, as it broke up the noise was a sizzling sound (as fat being thrown on a fire). On breaking up it appeared as a disjointed spinal column.

One report came from Johannesburg, South Africa, on 5 December 1935:

During the height of the storm, a particularly bright flash struck the ground about a hundred yards away; the flash struck appeared to be approximately a foot wide and to last for at least a second. After the flash had died away, there remained a string of bright luminous beads, of which there were twenty or thirty, which appeared to be about a quarter of the width of the flash, that is, say, three inches in diameter.

*Nature* carried an eyewitness account in 1895 from a William Crawford: 'On September 9, 1895, I was cycling near Pitlochry,' he described.

At ten o'clock there suddenly came on a terrific thunder-storm. Crash succeeded crash, and the lightning, of all colours, blazed almost continuously. But the chief peculiarity was the occurrence of eight strange flashes of a chain formation, with large elliptical links, and of a golden-yellow colour. These flashes were not rapid in their passage, as ordinary lightning is wont to be; but one of them took slightly over a minute to pour from the clouds to the edge of the valley opposite me. Two of these chains of living, burning gold passed between adjacent clouds, while the remaining six came to earth, one in the field just beside me.

There is no ready explanation for this bead lightning phenomenon.


## *Sport and Weather*


During the first Wimbledon tennis championships in 1923 it rained every day. With only the Centre Court protected with covers in those days, the other courts became waterlogged.

Wimbledon 1985 was one of the sporting world's great embarrassments. 'Before play started on the very first day', recalled Chairman of the All England Lawn Tennis and Croquet Club, Buzzer Hadingham, 'suddenly there was an enormous explosion. We were all wondering what the hell it was, it sounded just like a bomb.' A huge lump of masonry had been blown off the main building by lightning and landed only a couple of feet from a girl. Then in the second week of the championship, an inch and a half (3.8 centimetres) of rain fell in just twenty minutes, but luckily Met. Office forecaster Bill Giles came to the rescue. He phoned the tournament referee to warn him of an imminent heavy storm blowing up out of a blue sky, and the groundsmen managed to cover the courts just before a deluge of rain fell. Two feet (0.6 metres) of water flooded the spectators' tunnel leading on to the Centre Court. And the following year Jimmy Connors was actually struck by lightning, but luckily suffered no more than brief shock.

Play stopped rain for the South-east Asian Hockey Championships in Malaysia, January 1974, when witch doctors were called in to keep rain off.

Two German hang-gliders who jumped off a mountainside in southern Germany on 3 August 1979 were blown several thousand feet high by a thunderstorm. Their gliders were badly damaged and they landed by emergency parachutes 25 miles (40 kilometres) from their target.

A Birmingham hang-glider pilot was trapped hanging upside down in a tree for more than an hour after a mini-cyclone smashed him into a tree in a freak hang-gliding drama. Firemen had to chop down an oak tree to rescue forty-six-year-old Ian Hazelhurst.

Dozens of sporting mishaps have been caused by lightning and thunderstorms. One of the worst incidents of metal conducting a lightning bolt was in July 1955 at the Royal Ascot races. Lightning ripped along metal railings in a series of blue sparks, injuring forty-five people and killing two.

'My word . . . a huge flash of lightning and then that enormous clap of thunder which frightened the life out of me. You could actually hear the lightning crack then, really rather nasty.' So said Harry Carpenter just before the start of the 1987 Boat Race, after lightning narrowly missed the Cambridge boat.

In recent years the 1987 World Athletics Championships in Rome, 1989 Barcelona World Cup and 1990 Split European Championships were flooded out by torrential rain.

Cricket gets more than its fair share of thundery

weather, as during the July 1989 Test Match when the field was left flooded and only ducks and streakers dared waddle in it.

On 10 August 1975 a cricket umpire from near Berwick was struck by lightning which welded solid an iron joint in his leg. On 2 June 1975 snow prevented play at Buxton in Derbyshire and interrupted play at Colchester in Essex.

The worst affected sport for lightning, by far, is golf. Players on wide open landscapes, holding metal rods in their hands, make ideal little lightning conductors. The 1991 US Open sadly suffered a fatality when a spectator was struck by a lightning bolt deflected off a tree.

On 24 October 1975 lightning struck two golfers during the Wills Masters tournament in Melbourne, Australia, as they were walking along the fairway under their umbrellas. Jerry Silverstein and John Evans were shaken but unhurt. Then, as Guy Wolstenholme was approaching the spot where his ball was lying the wind struck, blowing the ball past him back up the slight slope. A box from a nearby television tower sailed a foot or two over his head and he was bowled over for 25 yards (23 metres) along the turf. Two scoreboards were also blown down, and a dozen huge gumtrees uprooted from various parts of the course.

Television weather forecaster David Brookes was struck by lightning whilst sheltering during a round of golf at Cambridge in April 1979 when lightning hit his umbrella. 'I had forecast rain but I was not expecting lightning. I was so shaken I had to adjourn to the club house for a brandy.'

The most famous golfing incident hit by lightning was during the Western Open golf championship in Chicago on 27 June 1975. Lee Trevino was sitting on the edge of a green by a lake waiting for a shower to pass over. Suddenly, out of the blue, lightning threw him 18 inches (46 centimetres) into the air and he blacked out. 'There was a loud, steady ringing in my ears like a tuning fork, my hands were flailing and I could not breathe. Then I fell back on the ground and blacked out,' he later recalled in his autobiography *They Call Me Super Mex* (Hutchinson, 1983). Trevino was taken to hospital; four burn marks were left on his shoulder where the lightning had left his body. Evidently the lightning had flashed off the lake, shot through the metal club shafts and passed up his back. Though his back continued to give pain for several years he returned to form eventually. Other golfers on the course didn't suffer nearly as badly as Trevino, but other strange things happened. Lightning knocked a club out of Bobby Nichols' hands and Arnold Palmer's club was sent 40 yards (36 metres) down the fairway.

*Great Britain II*, the leading yacht in the Whitbread Round-the-World Yacht Race was hit by lightning in the closing stages of the third leg from Auckland to Rio de Janeiro in February 1978. The lightning struck during a storm and two crewmen were thrown to the deck, but neither were injured. Just afterwards both men reported seeing the masts glowing brightly. All of the electrical apparatus was burned out except for the radio transmitter. The compasses were sent haywire, so the crew had to navigate by the sun and stars. *Great Britain II* arrived in Rio and won the race just thirty-four minutes ahead of its nearest rival.

Plans by a Newport businessman to spend the summer cruising in his £40,000 yacht went up in smoke on 18 May 1981 when the boat was hit by lightning 20 miles (32 kilometres) off the Devon coast. The lightning struck less than twenty-four hours after Cyril Binning had taken delivery and launched the yacht. The 34-foot (10-metre) yacht was set ablaze from bow to stern, the radio was knocked out and all the emergency inflatables destroyed. Mr Binning and his companion Jim Warrington were rescued by a coaster alerted by the flames. 'We heard an almighty bang,' Mr Binning explained. 'I could see that the aerial had gone from the top of the mast, and then the cabin suddenly filled with an awful toxic smoke. Within seconds the whole yacht was enveloped in flames.' The boat sank.

Storms in July 1992 struck during the British pigeon-racing's 'Grand National', a 500-mile (800-kilometre) race from Nevers in France back home to lofts in Britain. But of a field of 3,400 birds only twenty-nine flapped their way home. The rest were lost. Among the missing pigeons were some of the sport's finest racers, including the previous year's winner owned by Ron Hodson, from Humberside. As he summed it up: 'It's like losing a member of your family.'

A hang-glider pilot, Nigel Sumpter, had a lucky escape at Pendle Hill near Burnley when he was caught in a whirlwind and plunged 40 feet (12 metres) to the ground. The glider was completely wrecked and the pilot suffered back injuries but recovered. He was lucky not to have been killed.

One of the worst ever sporting disasters was the Fastnet Yacht Race of 1979. The race sails every two years in August from the south coast of England to the south-west of Ireland. The weather at that time of year is normally calm, but the race of 1979 was a catastrophe. On the night of 13–14 August, a sudden storm hit the race with 40-foot (12-metre) waves. Of the 307 yachts that started off, 85 finished, 194 retired, 23 were abandoned and 5 sank. Dozens of ships and aircraft searched for survivors and 136 were rescued but 15 crew were drowned.

## Weekend Weather

There's an old Shropshire saying:

*Friday's a day as'll have his trick,*
*The fairest or foulest day of the wik [week].*

So much for folklore. After all, how can the days of the week affect the weather when the week is purely a man-made invention? But there *is* some truth in the saying – different days of the week do indeed behave differently.

It was a weather buff called Dr Ashworth of Rochdale, Lancashire, who found the days of the week exerted some sort of weird force on the weather. He spent years pouring over rainfall figures for Rochdale and found that Sunday had the least rain of the week. His mindboggling journey through the weather archives also revealed that rain tended to fall during working hours on weekdays, and it rained more on Sunday nights than during Sunday days.

The pattern was unmistakable, but why? Dr Ashworth found only one answer – Rochdale's rainfall mirrored its industrial activity. Rain tended to fall during factory hours, when chimney smoke sent up tiny particles of dirt. These helped the water vapour in the atmosphere condense into raindrops – a sort of accidental version of cloud seeding to make rain.

Of course, things have changed since Dr Ashworth's days in the 1920s but in January 1995 in the scientific journal *Nature*, an Australian meteorologist, Dr Adrian Gordon, of the Flinders Institute for Atmospheric and Marine Sciences in Adelaide, discovered that weekends are colder than weekdays. His charts of global satellite readings going back fourteen years showed a steady cooling from Thursday to Sunday, picking up again on Monday. The hottest day of the week is Wednesday and the coldest is Sunday. Again, it was caused by industrial activity. There's more pollution during the week, and it tends to ease off towards the weekends, although in this case it's a long weekend starting on a Thursday.

## Hailstorms

It all starts when heat rising from the ground forms turbulent cumulonimbus clouds with strong updrafts of wind. The tops of these supercell clouds can reach up to 10 miles (16 kilometres) high where the temperature falls to as low as –112 degrees Fahrenheit, (–62 degrees Celsius). At this great height, water vapour sucked up by the strong updraft freezes. As the newly formed ice pellet becomes heavier it begins to fall, collecting more water droplets which freeze onto it. The powerful updraft shoots it up the cloud again and it gets coated in more ice. Eventually the hailstone becomes too heavy for the updraft to support in the air and it plummets to the ground. Because hailstones are made up of coats of ice, they look inside like an onion with layers of ice. If the updraft is weak, only small stones the size of peas will form. But a strong updraft of 100 miles per hour (160 kilometres per hour) or more creates monster hailstones.

The most severe recorded hailstorm in Britain probably struck Hitchin and Offley in Hertfordshire on 15 May 1697. Hailstones were described as big as a man's hand, about 4 inches (60 millimetres) diameter in Hitchin and 4.4 inches (110 millimetres) in Offley, with some reputed to be 5.6 inches (140 millimetres). At least one death was caused, the ground was torn up and great oak trees split.

The largest hailstone ever recorded in the USA fell at Coffeyville, Kansas, on 3 September 1970. It weighed 1.67 pounds (766 grams), had a diameter of 7.5 inches

*Hail damage causes up to $25 million property damage each year in the United States.* © *NOAA/NSSL*

(190 millimetres) and a circumference of 17.5 inches (440 millimetres). It was preserved in a freezer and sent for verification to a government climate research laboratory in Colorado. The storm caused widespread damage to houses and crops.

The largest hailstone ever recorded in the world fell on 14 April 1986 in Bangladesh, weighing 2.25 pounds (1 kilogram). The hailstorm that produced it also killed ninety-two people at Gopalganj.

The worst hailstorm on record struck the Moradabad and Beheri districts of India on 30 April 1888. Hailstones as large as cricket balls were recorded to have killed 246 people. Some of the victims were directly hit and pounded by the hail and others were buried in the large drifts of several feet of hail and died of cold exposure. More than 1600 animals were also killed.

Hail has caused air disasters as well. *The Daily Telegraph* reported that on 4 April 1977, a DC9 crash-landed on a highway near New Hope, Georgia, USA, with the loss of sixty-eight lives. The pilot had reported to Atlanta airport that as the plane was descending for landing it hit a severe hailstorm and an engine failed. Then a few minutes later he radioed that a cockpit window had shattered and his second engine was on fire. He tried to land on a small rural highway but as the plane came down its wings sheared trees and telephone poles, fuel tanks ruptured and the plane veered into a shop and burst into flames.

A hailstorm in Alberta Province, Canada, left a trail of destruction 140 miles (225 kilometres) long and 5 miles (8 kilometres) wide on 14 July 1953. Hailstones as large as golfballs shredded plants, and stripped trees and shrubs of their leaves. One wildlife official, Allen Smith of the US Fish and Wildlife Service, described the scene as 'a picture of unbelievable destruction –grasses and herbs were shredded beyond recognition and beaten into the earth'. Some 36,000 wild birds were killed. But that wasn't the end of the devastation. Four days later another horrific hailstorm in the same area destroyed a further 27,000 wildfowl.

Hail damage causes up to $300 million crop destruction and up to $25 million property damage each year in the United States. In the past decade hailstorms have been responsible for sensational losses in many parts of the world. In 1976 a hailstorm over Sydney caused losses of $40 million, followed three years later by a hailstorm over Adelaide causing $20 million damage.

In January 1980, Johannesburg was hit by an unusually violent hailstorm, particularly heavy over Jan Smuts Airport. Most of the airliners outside on the apron suffered severe damage and the insured loss was around $10 million. Another storm in November 1983 caused $15 million damage, and a series of hailstorms in November 1984 totalled $30 million.

All previous records were broken by two large hailstorms in North America in 1981, one in May over Texas and Oklahoma with an insured loss of nearly $200 million and one over Alberta in Canada with $100 million.

But all these were surpassed in a spectacular manner by a hailstorm in Munich in July 1984. Within minutes and without warning, this hailstorm wreaked massive damage to plants, buildings and vehicles. The ferocity of the hailstorm was beyond anything in recorded history. The insurance losses totalled $500 million, but the final bill with losses to the economy caused by damage to uninsured buildings and public property is reckoned at a staggering $1 billion. This is a figure that ranks alongside earthquakes, storms and floods.

The sky over Munich on the morning of 12 July 1984 was bright blue as in the previous few days, although a little cooler. The afternoon had been very hot, reaching 80 degrees Fahrenheit (30 degrees Celsius), and that helped trigger updrafts in the clouds reaching hurricane force. At 8p.m. hailstones 2–2.4 inches (5–6 centimetres) across started falling. The largest was 3.7 inches (9.5 centimetres), 10.6 ounces (300 grams), and they hurtled down like bullets with a terminal velocity which may well have reached 93 miles per hour (150 kilometres per hour).

The east side of the city fared worst with catastrophic damage made worse by gale-force winds and torrential rain which fired the stones almost horizontally, smashing them into walls and windows. The hailstorm took no more than twenty to thirty minutes to pass, but piles of hailstones up to 8 inches (20 centimetres) high could still be seen the next morning. The storm moved on to outlying farming areas and by 10p.m. had pretty well died out. It had a track of almost 186 miles (300 kilometres) and an area of damage 930 square miles (1500 square kilometres).

Large agricultural areas were flattened. Maize was particularly badly affected and in many fields not a single stalk was left standing. Trees were torn down and stripped of their leaves and bark, branches were broken off, the year's conifer growth lay ankle deep in the forests like a thick green carpet.

The worst-affected part of the city outskirts is also home to greenhouses and garden crops in large numbers which were virtually completely destroyed. The broken glass was so widespread all the plants and soil inside the greenhouses had to be stripped out.

The roofs on about seventy thousand buildings,

*In 1984 hail wreaked $1 billion damage over Munich, including this field of pulverised crops. © Munich Re Insurance*

windows, awnings, façades, advertising signs, aerials and everything else liable to damage was torn off or damaged. The hailstones and rain led to flooding in homes and factories.

Some quarter of a million cars parked outside were badly damaged, ranging from dents to craters, smashed windows and headlights and slashed and soaked upholstery. Twenty-four airliners were damaged at Munich's International airport and over 150 smaller aircraft were smashed at four small private airfields. A new Boeing 757 which had just landed suffered the worst damage – fuselage and wings and especially wing flaps had holes bored right through them, costing $7 million to repair alone.

Some four hundred people were injured. Many people were injured from hits on the head, shoulders and arms and it was a miracle no one was killed. The place was teeming with people in parks and beer gardens on the summery evening. But many small animals were killed, especially birds.

But there is a silver lining to hailstorms. One particularly violent episode of hail on 9 August 1843 in Norfolk smashed thousands of greenhouses and windows, flattened thousands of acres of crops, and wrecked farm buildings. The farming communities were devastated but left without financial compensation. As a result, a local insurance group was established in Norwich to protect farmers from further hailstorms. The company quickly grew and became today's Norwich Union, the third largest insurance group in Britain with capital of £27 billion.

British farmers in the early 1900s thought that shooting debris into the sky with special anti-hail guns would prevent hailstorms. Unfortunately the guns were useless, and onlookers were often injured as the gun pellets returned to the ground! In 1902 eleven people were killed by hail guns in Austria alone, but nonetheless an international conference on hail guns in 1905 in Italy attracted sixty-five delegates from six countries. And even in 1966 the journal *Weather* reported that explosive rockets were still being used to suppress hail in northern Italy, Austria and Kenya.

## Deluges

Deluges are relatively short, sharp falls of rain, often – but not always – leading to local flooding.

Britain's record deluge was at Martinstown, near

Dorchester in Dorset on 18 July 1955, when 11 inches (279 millimetres) of rain fell in a fifteen-hour storm. This is a sizeable downpour, bearing in mind that the average rainfall of London is 24 inches (610 millimetres) a year. Yet the flooding at Martinstown was not severe because the underlying chalk absorbed most of the rainwater. But on 15 August 1952 the worst flash flood in recorded history in Britain hit Lynmouth in north Devon. Nine inches (250 millimetres) fell in twelve hours and triggered floods which ripped down through the town in a torrent of water, causing thirty-four deaths and destroying the town.

Built-up areas are more prone to severe rainstorms because they give off more heat, and Hampstead in north-west London is particularly prone to flooding because it also sits on top of a hill where water vapour can more easily condense into clouds. On 14 August 1975 Hampstead experienced a remarkably intense slow-moving rainstorm when 6.84 inches (171 millimetres) of rain fell in about three hours, drowning one man, flooding a hundred homes and causing damage estimated at over £1 million. To show how localized the storm was, the London Weather Centre just 2 miles (3 kilometres) away had only 0.2 inches (5 millimetres) of rain.

This hardly compares with a flash flood in Willow Creek, Oregon, in 1903, when a cloudburst sent a 20-foot (6-metre) high tide of water through the town of Heppner. In less than an hour more than two hundred people were drowned and almost a third of the town washed away .

More recently another deluge struck Big Thompson Canyon, 50 miles (80 kilometres) north-west of Denver, Colorado. On Saturday 31 July 1976, the State of

Colorado was celebrating its centenary with a long weekend. Thunderstorms had been forecast for late afternoon, but the weather was sunny. By now three thousand people were in the canyon. At 6p.m. a thunderstorm struck and then it behaved very oddly. Usually wind blows a storm away, but in this case there was no wind and the storm stayed in the same place – at the top of the valley leading to Big Thompson Canyon. Over the next four hours, the storm burst with 10 inches (250 millimetres) of rain onto the ground below. The usual *annual* rainfall is 14 inches (356 millimetres).

Within minutes 50 million tons of water were roaring down the canyon. As the surging waters ripped through the canyon they smashed up cars and bulldozed mud, rocks, and other debris into a 20-foot (6-metre) high battering ram. The deluge annihilated everything in its path. The flood killed 139 people and 6 others were never found. Many of those that died were trapped in their cars and search teams found cars buried 6 feet (1.8 metres) beneath the bed of the river. Over 400 homes were destroyed, and a further 138 damaged. In just a few hours the flood caused $35.5 million of damage.

# Floods

Throughout history and to the present day, flood is by far the worst of all natural disasters. In fact, floods account for 40 per cent of all deaths caused by acts of nature worldwide.

The greatest ever flood in human times was probably

the legendary 'Great Flood' of Noah fame – a biblical catastrophe which rocked the world. If the flood did happen, it may have been triggered by the melting icecaps following the last Ice Age [see The Great Flood].

But the worst floods in recorded history have all struck China, and on such a catastrophic scale they are difficult to comprehend. Ancient Chinese literature describes how in about 2297BC massive rains burst the Huang Ho (Yellow River), Wei and Yangtze rivers, flooding almost the entire North China Plain and turning it into a huge inland sea. But a more devastating flood may have struck in 1332 when the Yellow River burst and drowned about 7 million people, with possibly a further 10 million dying of famine resulting from the ruined harvest. It may be no coincidence that the Black Death plague, which eventually swept Europe a decade later, appeared in China at this time.

The floods in China have continued into more recent times. In September to October 1887 the Yellow River flooded 50,000 square miles (129,500 square kilometres) killing an estimated 6 million people. In 1931 heavy rains triggered six devastating flood waves on the Yangtze River, destroying twenty-three dams and dykes, flooding 35,000 square miles (91,000 square kilometres) and leaving 40 million people homeless (casualty figures are unknown).

In the United States, floods cause about $2 billion damage on average *each* year. In May 1993 the Mississippi River burst its banks after three times the normal rainfall fell. It was the worst flood in the United States for sixty-six years, with over 13.9 million acres (5.6 million hectares) of land under water. 35,500 homes were destroyed. The damage was put at $15.6 billion.

Most people were evacuated in time, but over fifty people were killed.

Northern Europe, too, has suffered great numbers of floods. The 'Grote Mandrenke' (drowning), as the English called it, of January 1362 was a North Sea flood that wiped out some fifty parishes off Schleswig-Holstein. Chronicles tell of one hundred thousand deaths, but modern estimates put the numbers at between eleven thousand and thirty thousand. This was probably the greatest North Sea flood disaster in recorded history, with more than half the population of the wetlands along the coast of Jutland and Slesvig (modern Schleswig) drowned. It was fifty years before the dykes could be repaired.

On 31 January 1953 disastrous floods struck eastern England and the Netherlands, with eighteen hundred lives lost on the continent and about three hundred in Britain. They were caused by high tides clashing with a storm surge in the North Sea which drove the water over the top of sea defences along the east coast.

## The Drought Hazard

What makes deserts special places is drought. A desert is officially classed as a region with less than 10 inches (254 millimetres) of rain each year. Drought this bad has made a third of the world intensely hostile for humans to live in.

The Sahara Desert is the hottest and sunniest desert in the world – 3,500,000 square miles (9,100,000 square kilometres) in area, larger than the whole of the United States not including Alaska and Hawaii. The Sahara reached the highest temperature known on Earth – 136.4 degrees Fahrenheit (58 degrees Celsius) recorded in Libya in 1922.

Strange as it may seem, the largest desert in the world is Antarctica. Although it's mostly covered in snow and ice, the interior of the great ice continent only gets about 5 inches (127 millimetres) precipitation a year – just slightly more than the Sahara. It looks as though it gets much more because the snow stays trapped and builds up over millions of years into a gigantic ice sheet up to 2 miles (3.2 kilometres) thick. A few parts of Antarctica, though, are completely dry. Here the bare rock has been left naked by the winds.

Most deserts can become searingly hot, but it's difficult to imagine the intense heat extremes that a place like Death Valley can reach. At the height of the summer just half an hour after sunrise the temperature can reach 126 degrees Fahrenheit (52 degrees Celsius). And it stays that hot throughout the day until sunset brings the relief of night and it drops to only 106 degrees Fahrenheit (41 degrees Celsius). Death Valley is both a gigantic heat-trap and, a basin. In fact, it's the lowest desert in the world, lying 282 feet (86 metres) below sea level, the lowest point in the western hemisphere. In one scorching heatwave Death Valley scored the world record for the longest and highest temperature – 134 degrees Fahrenheit (57 degrees Celsius) over several hours in 1913.

Deserts and droughts are never permanent, and even the history of the Sahara holds surprises. Radar images from the Space Shuttle reveal bedrock 15 feet (4.6 metres) under the Sahara showing evidence of ancient hills, valleys and even rivers which would have been as wide as the Nile some 35 million years ago. Great trees once grew there.

Two hundred thousand years ago men were walking across the Sahara hunting large mammals in forests of oak and cedar. And two thousand years ago the Sahara was the breadbasket of the Roman Empire. So what went wrong? The Sahara had fertile but fragile soil. It could only support a limited number of animals and crops, and as the Egyptians and Romans increased their farming, the soil slowly eroded. In a hot, dry climate, it blew away and what were fertile fields turned to rock and sand.

Sadly, it's a story repeated many times in history, and whole civilizations have been wiped out. The Anasazi tribe of indians in New Mexico were wiped out by a prolonged and severe drought in the 1200s.

The worst drought ever recorded in North America struck the Great Plains in the 1930s. For the best part of five years the prairies were seized by hot dry winds and very little rain. Droughts strike there about every twenty to twenty-five years, but when the pioneers ploughed into the prairies they created their own disaster. They tore up the prairie grasses and slaughtered the bison into extinction. To begin with the bonanza harvests looked like a dream come true. The drought started in 1930, but then an intense hot wind in 1932 picked up the soil into dustclouds so thick they blotted out the sun for days and weeks on end. Farmers watched helplessly as their fields blew away. Drifts of soil piled up 21 feet (6 metres) high, burying houses and barns. In May 1934, a cloud of dust stretched from Alberta in Canada to Texas, suffocating birds in the sky and dusting ships at sea 300 miles (480 kilometres) off the eastern coast. In just one storm in 1935, 12 million tons of dust were dumped on Chicago. By 1935 some 850 million tons of top soil had blown away. The clouds of dust were so thick the sun was blotted out. The following year, 4768 people died of heatstroke and breathing problems.

This was the era of John Steinbeck's *The Grapes of Wrath*, and Woodie Guthrie, hoboes riding freight trains, and soup kitchens. Over a million people abandoned farming and fled to the cities where they stayed largely unemployed.

When the rains returned in 1936 measures were taken to prevent drought catastrophes in the future. Windbreaks of trees were planted, less ploughing was done and irrigation introduced. But the lessons of the Dust Bowl are becoming lost. In recent years many of the trees have been uprooted, ploughing leaves the soil dangerously exposed, and erosion is increasing. The

*The Prairie Dust Bowl in the 1930s blew clouds of soil as far as New York. © United States Library of Congress*

prairies are living on a knife edge and it might only take another few dry years to tip the prairies back into another Dust Bowl.

In 1988, drought struck across the American Midwest, starting vast forest fires. That summer, thousands of other forest fires broke out in the US, burning a total of 5 million acres (2 million hectares). The biggest fire disaster in American history tore through Yellowstone National Park in Wyoming. 1.5 million acres (607,000 hectares) of forest were burnt down. It turned into the biggest firefighting effort in history: hundreds of millions of dollars and over ten thousand people were poured into tackling the blaze. But it was all to no effect: the fires burnt for three months.

The 1975–6 drought was one of the greatest natural disasters to hit Britain in modern times, and perhaps the greatest drought this country has experienced in a thousand years. One million people were forced to use standpipes for eleven weeks and reservoirs dried out completely. Grass became desiccated, milk yields fell and lambs took longer to fatten. Root crops were badly affected and vegetable prices rose. Thousands of acres of valuable trees and plantations were destroyed by fire. Farmers' crop losses were estimated at £500 million.

Flora and fauna were badly affected. The shortage of water robbed older trees of the strength to combat disease and the spread of Dutch elm disease broke out in epidemic proportions, killing trees and changing the landscapes. Our rarest breeding birds were endangered, especially the Dartford Warbler which nests on Dorset heaths.

The drought caused enormous financial damage. In the 1980s the hot dry summers dried and shrank the underlying clay over a large part of southern and eastern England, causing houses to crack from their foundations. British insurers hit peak claims of over £500 million in 1991.

One of the regions of the world most vulnerable to drought is the Sahel – Sub-Saharan Africa, 1 million square miles (2.5 million square kilometres), where life expectancy in Ethiopia is forty-six years. The region is dry with a short rainy season and the economy of these countries is so fragile that a failed rainy season pushes the rural population into famine. From 1969 to 1976 and again during the mid-1980s the normal rainy season was delayed or failed. The famines they triggered were massive: in 1973 alone, one hundred thousand people died from drought in the Sahel. The droughts in 1984 and 1985 caused a further half a million people to die of famine. Droughts in early 1991 left over 4 million people facing starvation. All told, there have been about 1 million deaths in the Sahel since 1970.

## Cold

### SNOW

Even in today's warmer climate, snow and ice still sweep the high latitudes and high mountains of the world with a beauty and power no other weather possesses. Permanent snow and ice cover about 12 per cent of the Earth's land surface – a total of around 8 million square miles (21 million square kilometres). 80 per cent of the

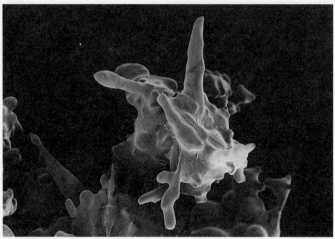

*These recent electron micrograph pictures of snowflakes show some of their variety of shapes – the typical hexagon crystal (above) and the less well-known lumps (below). © Dr William Wergin*

world's fresh water is locked up as ice or snow – 7 million cubic miles.

The six-sided crystal beauty of snow was first recorded by William Bentley, from Jericho, Vermont. He spent his life photographing snowflakes through a microscope and in over forty years from 1885 he took several thousand stunning photographs. And to his amazement he never found two snowflakes the same.

But Bentley wasn't quite giving us the whole picture, because most snowflakes are actually pretty grotty lumps. Recent research shows that only 1 per cent of flakes are symmetrical – the rest are ugly sisters.

The amazing variety of snowflake shapes comes from the temperatures in the atmosphere. At around 30 degrees Fahrenheit (–1 degree Celsius) the ice crystals grow into thin plates. As the temperature drops to 12 degrees Fahrenheit (–11 degrees Celsius) they grow into hollow columns. And dropping further to 5 degrees Fahrenheit (–15 degrees Celsius) is everyone's idea of a conventional snowflake, with star patterns starting to grow.

As the crystals fall towards earth they travel through air of different temperatures and so they each grow in their own unique way, with countless different shapes. No two are ever the same because they never pass through the same blend of air temperatures. That's the wonder of snow.

## COLD TEMPERATURES

The record low temperature for the British Isles is –17 degrees Fahrenheit (–27.2 degrees Celsius) at Braemar in Scotland on 11 February 1895 and again on 10 January 1982. In fact, the whole of Britain was bitterly cold in 1982. Cold weather in Britain is brought on by clear skies. Without cloud cover which acts like a blanket, the heat from the ground escapes. Calm weather conditions allow the air to be cooled near the ground, and because the nights are long in winter they allow more cooling – the further north the location, the longer the nights and the more cooling.

But to put our cold weather into perspective, the world record is –128.6 degrees Fahrenheit (–89.2 degrees Celsius) at the Vostok base in Antarctica, and Canadian and Siberian sites are frequently close to the all-time record.

## VOLCANOES AND COLD WEATHER

The effects of volcanoes have also cast cold spells over the globe. Eruptions in 1815 led to freezing winters and cold summers that again did enormous damage to harvests.

Even by the standards of the Little Ice Age in the nineteenth century, the year 1783 was exceptionally cold. A thin fog cast a veil over the sun for much of the summer over Europe and North America, and the first snows arrived early followed by a severe winter.

But for the first time in meteorology, the appalling weather that year was scientifically explained. Benjamin Franklin, better known for his kite-flying exploits under thunderclouds, attributed the fog to the vast quantities of smoke belching out from the volcano of Hekla in Iceland that summer, and carried by the wind round the world. The dust, he reasoned, blocked out the warmth of the sun and stopped the ground heating up properly. And a couple of hundred years later that explanation essentially still holds true, although the main culprit has been pinpointed as the sulphur shot out by volcanoes. This turns into a corrosive cloud of sulphuric acid which stays airborne longer than dust, absorbing the sun's heat and helping prevent the earth from warming up.

The late eighteenth and nineteenth centuries were a turbulent period for volcanoes. The eruption of Hekla in Iceland in 1783 was followed by one in the Azores in 1811, Tambora in Indonesia in 1815, Graham Island in 1831, Nicaragua in 1835, another Icelandic one in 1875, Japan in 1888 and the Caribbean in 1902.

A study of world weather records in the aftermath of violent volcanic eruptions invariably shows a marked dip in temperatures. In April 1815, the volcano of Tambora in Indonesia erupted, one of the largest eruptions in the past ten thousand years, injecting an estimated 74 cubic miles (100 cubic kilometres) of ash into the atmosphere (compared to 7.4 cubic miles (10 cubic kilometres) from Krakatoa in 1883, and .74 cubic miles (1 cubic kilometre) from St Helena in 1980). After the Tambora eruption, the Thames once again froze over, as it had done through much of the previous century's Little Ice Age. The average temperature dropped by around one degree Celsius, and the next year, 1816, was chronicled as 'the year without a summer' or 'Eighteen Hundred and Froze to Death' as the Americans called it, when frosts struck in June in New England and Europe suffered the worst wine harvest since records began in 1482. In Switzerland, Germany and France the price of grain almost trebled and food riots broke out in many parts of Europe.

A volcanic eruption in the Azores in 1811 led to a bitter winter in 1812, and was a major factor in the defeat of Napoleon's army in Russia. After a successful battle

*Volcanic ash eruptions can block out so much sunlight they cool the whole world.* © *NASA*

at Borodino, the French army reached Moscow on 14 September 1812. The following night the Russians burned most of the city, destroying the supplies and shelters Napoleon needed for his own troops. He ordered a retreat on 19 October, and then succumbed to the savage climate.

The cold became intense after 7 November, on the 9th fell to 5 degrees Fahrenheit (–15 degrees Celsius) on the 17th was –15 degrees Fahrenheit (–26 degrees Celsius) and on 3 December fell to –35 degrees Fahrenheit (–37 degrees Celsius). Napoleon's original army of 378,000 had already been cut by supply problems, disease, desertions and battle before being decimated by the cold.

But the most apocalyptic of all the nineteenth-century volcano eruptions was Krakatoa, a small island between Java and Sumatra which erupted on 27 August 1883. It exploded with such force that its noise was the loudest thing in recorded history. Its dust and smoke shot up into the stratosphere where it was blown around for years afterwards, creating a white veil over the sun and turning sunsets into deep crimsons as it scattered the light. [See Bishop's Ring]

More recently, when El Chicon in Mexico erupted on 4 April 1982, its smoke plume circled the globe within a month and temperatures dropped worldwide. And the eruption of Mount Pinatubo in the Philippines in June 1991 shot 15 million tons of sulphur up into the atmosphere as a vast acid cloud and cooled global temperatures by about half a degree.

But all these eruptions pale into insignificance compared to the eruption of Toba in Sumatra. Admittedly it happened 73,500 years ago, but geologists believe it was the greatest volcanic eruption for the past million years. Geological records reveal a sudden cooling at about the time of Toba's eruption. Its dust was so great it is thought to have triggered the last ice age. The snowfall in the northern hemisphere had been increased so much that it greatly enlarged the permanent snow cover over Canada, reflecting sunlight, cooling the Earth even more, and the planet flipped into an ice age.

## AVALANCHES

Avalanches are the terrifying face of snow: as much as a million tons of snow hurtling down slopes at speeds approaching 200 miles per hour (320 kilometres per hour) crushing everything in their paths.

Avalanches are formed by a special set of weather conditions. The sun thawing the top layer and freezing it again produces a hard icy layer. If fresh snow falls on top it can easily slide down, but from the surface there's no way of knowing of the danger, which is what makes skiing off-piste so dangerous. Skiers venturing off on their own on fresh slopes (off-piste) risk triggering the giant – an avalanche can be set off just by the weight of a single skier or even a loud noise.

Once the avalanche starts a dense core of snow gathers speed, picking up more snow as it goes. As its speed increases, the snow may rise and become airborne. It is now riding on a cushion of air without friction to slow it down, and the avalanche suddenly goes into overdrive, reaching speeds up to 200 miles per hour (320 kilometres per hour).

The fastest measured avalanche struck at Glärnisch, Switzerland on 6 March 1898. It reached 217 miles per hour (349 kilometres per hour), and travelled 4.3 miles (6.9 kilometres) in just over a minute. It charged across a one-mile wide valley, shot up the opposite slope and then fell back into the valley again.

The momentum of snow is so great that it sends out

an invisible shockwave of air, blasting almost everything ahead of its path. The energy inside the avalanche is so intense that the ice underneath it melts, and once the avalanche grinds to a halt the water freezes back to ice. So any poor soul caught and surviving the avalanche can often be entombed in ice soon afterwards and die.

Avalanches are surprisingly common – there are around one hundred thousand each year just in the American Rockies, but most are in uninhabited areas where they pose no threat. Yet avalanches have caused massive catastrophes in the past. When Hannibal tried to invade Rome by crossing the Italian Alps, he lost sixteen thousand of his troops in avalanches. When Napoleon crossed several Alpine mountain passes en route to the Battle of Marengo in northern Italy in 1800, he instructed his advance guard not to 'cry or call out for fear of causing a fall of avalanches'.

The world's worst avalanche disasters struck during the First World War when Italian and Austrian troops fighting in the southern Tyrol realized they could kill more of the enemy by using their guns to trigger avalanches. The sound of the guns set the snow moving and in one day thousands of men were killed by avalanches. At the time censorship withheld news as to what sort of 'heavy weapon' lay behind the incredibly devastating mortality of the slopes, but estimates of the toll during the three winters of the war now number sixty thousand, and some authorities say that figure is too low. Bodies from those avalanches were still being found in 1952.

And now with skiing becoming more popular, the number of people killed by accidental avalanches has grown. Ski resorts now take the risk of avalanche very seriously with special avalanche protection squads working round the clock every day assessing the risk and triggering controlled avalanches to avoid accidental ones.

If you are the victim of an avalanche and feel the ground suddenly slip away from you in a cloud of surging snow, try to stay airborne by paddling your hands and arms underneath your body. It's not much advice, but it's the best there is. Because if you sink inside the avalanche and get buried you risk suffocating, often within half an hour. The trouble is that most survivors or witnesses who see their friends buried in an avalanche run off to fetch help. By the time they return with help it's usually too late.

Avalanches are a terrifying sight, and have given snow a bad name, but that's not entirely fair, because snow can actually *save* lives. Snow is a heat insulator because it traps air in between the snowflakes, a bit like cavity-wall insulation. That's why a lot of plants can survive under a blanket of snow but are killed by a severe frost on a clear, cold winter's night.

It's snow that saved two women climbers on the north face of Ben Nevis in February 1995 for two days and a night. Kim Roden and Zoe Green became stranded in a blizzard, and, knowing their mountain survival training, they dug a snow-hole to shelter from gale-force winds. With just malt loaf and glucose tablets they survived the ordeal suffering hypothermia, frostbite and exhaustion.

And of course the Inuit indians (eskimos) know well of the insulating power of snow. Igloos are still made from snow with great skill. Firstly, the snow has to be just the right density – too soft and it will crumble, and too hard and it will break up. But once the igloo is built it keeps its owners draught-free and a good 10 degrees warmer than the outside. Not that many Inuit spend their lives in igloos these days, but they do use them as lodges on hunting expeditions.

### ENGLISH AVALANCHE

A blizzard during Christmas 1836 blanketed England in snow, but was particularly severe over the Sussex Downs. It also culminated in the worst single snow disaster in British history.

The snows started falling on Christmas Eve and on Christmas Day a blizzard blew up: the sky was pitch black, snows fell heavily and the wind howled and whipped up large drifts 10–15 feet (3–4.5 metres) deep in Lewes. By Boxing Day the blizzard had cut Lewes off, and in nearby Brighton two people on the streets died of cold. But at the foot of a cliff in Lewes a large overhang of snow threatened the street below, and when cracks started appearing in the snow residents below were warned to evacuate, but they took no notice.

At 10.15a.m. on 27 December the ridge of snow collapsed, and an avalanche fell about 350 feet (107 metres) and smashed onto the houses below. Fifteen people were trapped, eight of them died either of suffocation or crushed under the wreckage of their houses. The next day another avalanche fell and hampered the rescue efforts further, but the damage was already done. The place is still commemorated today in a pub called *The Snowdrop Inn.*

### SNOW AND WAR

Snow in the mountain passes stopped Alexander from continuing east into India in 330BC and a century earlier Hannibal with his elephants incurred losses in the Alps because of snow. In the thirteenth century snow blocked the Moors from Spain in their effort to enter France.

But of the wars in history, snow and cold had enormous impacts on the Second World War, and some historians say it even won the war for the Allies in Europe.

Perhaps the greatest effect came from the Finns' near-defeat of the Russians in the three-month 'winter war' of 1939–40.

The Russians invaded Finland to secure their borders against potential invasion by Germany and they expected to sweep through Finland to Lapland in ten to twelve days. Shooting began on 16 November 1939, with 36,000 Finns outnumbered by 1,500,000 Russians – a staggering ratio of forty-two to one. But they had snow on their side. Wearing white camouflage sewn from bed sheets, the Finns launched guerrilla raids on skis to attack the Russians. The Finns attacked them from the rear and sides and dived into snowbanks to hide. They struck in the middle of the night and in blizzards and fogs. The Russians were totally ill-trained and ill-equipped for this guerrilla warfare. The Russians fought only along roads and open fields with tanks. Snow slowed their advance to no more than 5 miles per hour (8 kilometres per hour) at best and whenever they tried to cross frozen lakes they found themselves booby-trapped.

Something like half a million Russian troops were

killed, largely from the cold. But in the end the Russians won by sheer force of numbers. The Finns were made to cede the eastern part of their country, but their incredible resistance allowed them to keep the rest of their nation – a unique position for any of the countries bordering Russia at the end of the war.

Observing the Finno-Russian war, the Germans realized that the Russians were badly equipped, trained and organized. From this they assumed the Russians to be weak, a grave miscalculation. On the contrary, the bitter Finnish experience taught the Kremlin that coping with snow must be fitted into army training and tactics, and by the time Hitler invaded Russia in 1941, Stalin's troops were as prepared as the Finns themselves had been earlier.

The German invasion of Russia advanced rapidly in 1941. Even when the winter began early, this was to the Germans' advantage, because instead of the usual heavy rains making the roads impassable, the ground was frozen and allowed trucks and tanks to be moved. But the Germans were completely unprepared when the weather grew much colder.

Snowfall began as early as October 1941, and heavy snow began about 7 December, with the snow cover in Moscow and Leningrad estimated between 28–59 inches (710–1500 millimetres) restricting the mobility of both armies. The deep snow also reduced the effectiveness of mortar shells and preventing heavy tank guns from being used. German mines often failed when the snow cushioned the fuse and detonator.

German machinery failed in the bitter weather. The extreme cold froze the mechanisms of rifles and machine guns, breech blocks of artillery became absolutely rigid, recoil liquid in artillery pieces froze stiff, tempered steel parts cracked, springs broke like glass. The Germans had to light fires under their artillery whereas the Soviets used low-temperature lubricants developed following the Finno-Russian War.

The Russian T34, KV1 and KV2 tanks had better mobility over snow because they were lighter, had wide tracks and good ground clearance – a big advantage over the German tanks. The Russians also used ski troops trained in Siberia following the disastrous Finno-Russian War. The Russians had ponies used to winter weather, whereas the German horses came from the milder climates of Western Europe and died in the cold.

The Russians could anticipate German attacks because sound travels faster in very cold weather and the noise of the German troops advancing over heavily crusted snow deprived them of any surprise.

The German troops were only equipped with light clothing, and heavier winter clothing didn't arrive in time. The temperature dropped to –49 degrees Fahrenheit (–45 degrees Celsius) on 30 November, yet the Germans still had not received winter coats. This led to a drive amongst German civilians for winter clothing and skis, but few arrived before February 1942. By the end of 1941 the Germans had lost one hundred thousand men from frostbite, and by the end of winter over a quarter of a million. Thousands more died from pneumonia, 'flu and trenchfoot.

Although the Red Army lost millions – dead, wounded and captured – by December 1941, they had mustered enough replacements from their vast manpower. But the German losses were virtually irreplaceable, and by April 1942 had reached 625,000. The siege of Stalingrad and Moscow was lifted, the Germans were forced to retreat, and the tide of the whole war in Europe turned to the Allies, thanks in a large part to the intense cold and snow of the Russian winter.

## Weather in Art

It's all very well looking back on the records to find out what the weather was like years ago, but what do you do if the records don't exist or they're too patchy? Apart from historical traces of the climate left behind in tree rings and ice cores, there's a much more civilized way of slipping back through time, and you don't need a chainsaw or thermal underwear to get there.

Landscape paintings give us all sorts of clues to the past climate. Historical climate expert Hubert Lamb from the University of East Anglia has studied hundreds of canvases for climate trends. He looked at Pieter Brueghel the Elder, of the sixteenth century, who recorded the merrymaking of Flemish peasantry in their daily lives. His artworks started off with fairly warm sunny summer weather, but in the 1560s he suddenly switched to cold snow-swept landscapes. This change began with *Hunters in the Snow*, depicting a group of men returning from a hunt set against a frozen lake. It was at this time that the winter of 1564–5 struck – the longest and most severe for well over a century. Brueghel became so infatuated with the wintry scenes that he repainted many of his earlier pictures with snow.

Cloudiness also tells a lot about the climate, and climatologist Hans Neuberger looked at a staggering twelve thousand canvases, dating from the period 1400 to 1967, to find any trends in cloud cover, as reported in the journal *Weather* in 1970. Hardly surprisingly, he found Mediterranean subjects had far clearer skies and better visibilities than British paintings, none of which featured a clear sky throughout the entire historical period! But the range of cloudiness seemed to give some useful insights into our past weather.

But the real revelation was finding that cloudiness increased from the fifteenth to seventeenth centuries, particularly as the Little Ice Age took grip about 1550, and then faded away again during the nineteenth and twentieth centuries. Even taking into account artistic licence, the overall trend seems to have been unmistakable, that the climate was a lot cloudier two or three hundred years ago.

There's probably no better example of the artistic weather record than Joseph Turner. Because he was obsessed with the light of the sky, clouds and sea, Turner has given us a stunning insight into the climate of the early nineteenth century. His glorious red skies were a particular sign of strong atmospheric powers at work, because this was a time when volcanic eruptions in the Azores in 1811 and Tambora in 1815 had shot clouds of dust across the globe. That dust cooled the earth and scattered the light, filtering out the blues in the low sun and giving sumptuous red sunrises and sunsets.

# *Tampering with the Weather*

There have been many attempts at changing the weather, from the days of indian raindances onwards. But whether they work or not is a moot point, because it's often notoriously difficult proving the effectiveness of weather modification.

### RAIN

The science of rainmaking was started by Nobel Laureate Irving Langmuir. He had originally won a Nobel Prize for chemistry, but during the Second World War, together with his collaborator Vincent Schaefer, he grew increasingly interested in meteorology and started looking at how snow and rain formed. Langmuir and Schaefer were both keen mountaineers and often climbed to the weather observatory at the summit of Mount Washington in New Hampshire during the winter. What amazed both of them was that the clouds at the top of the mountain often stayed as water instead of snow, even though the temperatures were well below freezing. This was nothing new to conventional meteorologists, but to the two weather novices it sparked off experiments into how water remained unfrozen – 'supercooled' in physics jargon.

Schaefer discovered he could make the same supercooled mist by breathing into a refrigerator ice-box. And then he tried to turn the mist to snow by sprinkling it with dust onto which ice crystals can form – 'nuclei' in scientific parlance. So Schaefer tried dozens of materials from soot to graphite, but all without success until he had an amazing stroke of luck. On a hot summer's day in July 1946, Schaefer's ice-box was too warm, so he dropped a piece of frozen carbon dioxide (dry ice) into the box. Suddenly, as if by alchemy, thousands of perfect tiny snowflakes formed. It was the magic breakthrough, and yet ironically it had nothing to do with nuclei – the vital factor was the excessively cold temperature of the dry ice. This made ice crystals form at the critical temperature of –40 degrees Fahrenheit (–40 degrees Celsius) whether there was dust in the air or not. It seemed like the magic wand for making precipitation from clouds had finally been discovered and Langmuir made brave predictions of weather on demand, helped by his Nobel status.

A few months later, Schaefer carried out the first aerial experiment by sprinkling 3 pounds (1.4 kilograms) of finely ground dry ice from an aircraft onto a supercooled stratus cloud. The results were totally staggering. Within five minutes snowflakes started falling from the cloud. It was so dramatic that a large hole opened up in the cloud where the dry ice had been dropped. In fact, in later tests they cut out the trade mark of General Electric in a bank of cloud using dry ice!

It appeared to be a dramatic vindication for Langmuir's optimism about weather modification, and of course the press loved it. The wave of excitement triggered an enormous upsurge of interest from other scientists, including a crystal expert, Bernard Vonnegut. But he felt that dry ice wasn't ideal because it only triggered a shower of snow that would fall anyway, and it often evaporated before reaching the ground. So he searched for a true nucleating agent, and found that silver iodide crystals fitted the bill because its atoms were arranged very much like those in ice crystals. And he succeeded in making snowflakes from pure silver iodide and supercooled water droplets at only –25 degrees Fahrenheit (–4 degrees Celsius). So Vonnegut's discovery sparked a new wave of seeding clouds.

The US military establishment and Weather Bureau climbed aboard the bandwagon in 'Project Cirrus', the first large-scale scientific project in weather making. Commercial businesses sowed rainclouds for farmers and by the early 1950s almost a tenth of the area of the USA was being cloud-seeded in an industry worth $5 million a year.

Unfortunately the bubble eventually burst when the results of seeding failed to meet its promises. Precipitation was often slight and unpredictable. Yet even today, claims of successful rain bursts from seeding can appear fairly impressive, although they still fall within the range of natural weather variations. That doesn't mean to say that rainmaking doesn't work – it's just that it can't be conclusively proved by statistics.

We now know that successful rainmaking needs a cloud with a copious supply of supercooled droplets, and for that to occur temperatures need to be within a critical range. Unfortunately the ideal clouds for this are those over mountain ranges – hardly the most promising rainmaking areas from a farming point of view.

The only other promising avenue is 'bumping up' cumulus clouds, those big puffy cauliflower-head rainclouds that sometimes turn into thunderstorms. Seeding should in theory form extra ice crystals and lift the top of the cloud higher and so trigger much greater precipitation. Unfortunately the match between theory and practice still remains elusive.

Nevertheless, a cloud seeding operation has been running in the Santa Barbara area for the past fifteen years. The local water agencies give the clouds an extra boost by spraying silver iodide into the clouds from aircraft and from the ground. It's claimed that the annual rainfall has been increased by up to 15 per cent on the lowlands and 25 per cent over the nearby high hills.

### FOG

To date, the most successful and consistent weather modification is fog dispersal. It started in the Second World War when bombers returning to Britain from night raids on Europe had trouble landing in fog. So operation FIDO was set up – the Fog Investigation and Dispersal Operation. Burning drums of oil warmed the air above the runway, burning off the fog, as well as lighting a path for the returning airmen. In two and a half years FIDO allowed over two thousand fogbound planes to take off or land from British airbases. It cost 15 million gallons of gasoline, but at $100 to $500 a minute the operation was considered too expensive and also dangerous for commercial flying, and it was stopped at the end of the war.

Today, fog dispersal at airports is done using a variety of methods. The simplest is to blow warm air into the fog. Alternatively, the fog can be seeded with liquid gas which takes up heat from the air. Or the fog is seeded with dry ice. Frozen crystals of carbon dioxide provide minute nuclei for the moisture droplets to freeze onto and grow into droplets which fall to the ground.

### FROST

Frost is another example of weather that can be modified. For the farmers of California's Central Valley a harsh frost can destroy the buds on their fruit trees, ending the season's crop overnight. The peaches are literally nipped in the bud and crops worth up to $89 million a year are ruined in the San Joaquin Valley in California. The farmers use a variety of ways to get rid of the frost. Windmills are used to blow the air and disturb it enough to prevent frost. Elsewhere rows of irrigation trenches circulate water pumped up from wells, although spraying is a more effective way of transferring the water's heat to the air. The air can be warmed using cans of oil called 'smudge pots' which are burnt. This prevents frost but it makes the air thick with oily bits of smut.

### SNOW

What do you do in a ski resort with no snow? With mild winters hitting many world ski slopes in recent years, making your own snow has become a desperate last-ditch attempt at attracting the skiers.

Snowmaking isn't easy or cheap. Water is shot out as a fine spray through a cannon in freezing cold weather, but that on its own isn't sufficient. You also need something for the ice crystals to form onto – they don't crystallize in thin air. In nature they grow on specks of salt or dust floating in the atmosphere. But strangely enough, the best thing for artificial snow is special bacteria grown for the snow. They're harmless, but the snow they create isn't fantastic – it tends to be lumpy and it's expensive to make. But for hard-pressed ski resorts it's better than nothing.

ICE

We take ice very much for granted these days. The invention of the refrigerator brought ice on demand, but in the days before fridges it was a very different picture. In fact, the pre-refrigerator days were so different that ice was one of the most valuable foodstuffs in the world and cold was more a luxury than warmth. And ice was the finest form of cold in summer heat.

Ice has been made by humans for thousands of years, and the first known ice stores were built in Mesopotamia four thousand years ago. Desert civilizations built gigantic north-facing walls and ponds under them to catch the freezing night temperatures, and cut the ice out before the rising sun melted it. The ancient Greeks stored wine chilled with snow in thick-walled buildings.

Charles II introduced ice-houses from France in the 1600s, and ice became so precious that a dish of ice-cream cost £1, or £50 at today's prices. In the eighteenth century the ice-cream industry took off and large ice-cellars were built underneath cities. An interesting reflection on the climate at the time was the wave of ice-house building by wealthy landowners which coincided with the Little Ice Age, when the winters were so cold that the Thames froze over regularly. The landowners used to cut ice from their lakes during the winter and store it in their ice-houses for the summer.

The ice craze became so popular that a trade in ice to the colonies in the tropics started. For example, in 1833 a ship carrying 180 tons of ice was sent to Calcutta. Even though 60 tons melted en route and another 20 tons at its destination, enough got through to make the venture profitable. Alas, the first refrigerator invented in the 1850s routed the ice trade.

## Fog

One day in 1579, when Sir Francis Drake was gallivanting round the world in the *Golden Hind* doing the usual exploring and piracy thing, he came across a mysterious place shrouded in thick fog. The fog lasted so long that Drake was stuck for nearly a month, complaining about 'those thicke mists and most stinging fogges'. Which was a great pity because the 'fogges' hid the entrance to one of the finest natural harbours on the western seaboard of the Americas: San Francisco Bay. Its discovery was delayed by fog for some two hundred years until the eighteenth century when the Spaniards arrived.

Fog, quite simply, is a cloud hugging the ground. And like a cloud, its dense blanket is made of tiny droplets of water so small that it would take 7000 million of them to make a single tablespoonful of water.

San Francisco's famous fogs are caused by cold water from the depths of the freezing Pacific being forced up to the surface by the coastline. When the cold waters hit the warm air on the surface the moisture in the air condenses into a ground-hugging cloud – known to weather people as advection fog. These sorts of fogs are common along shorelines all over the world, but what makes the

Californian fogs so spectacular is the intense cold of the Pacific waters.

It is a truly awesome sight. A bank of fog starts up in the early morning and according to wind and temperature can hang off the shore like a stalking monster, or engulf only part of the bay, or on a really heavy day, roll all the way up to the Berkeley Hills and slop around in the natural basin of the bay like a bowl of meringue. As the day grows hotter the fog is usually burnt off and by evening it has vanished as silently as it came.

The best time of year to see the fog is in the summer when the surface air is hottest and creates the thickest fogs. In fact the fog turns the climate of San Francisco upside down, making July one of the coldest months of the summer on average, because it blocks out sunlight.

### DISASTERS

Fog is responsible for some of the world's worst transport disasters. Probably the worst accident happened on 29 May 1914 in the St Lawrence Seaway, Canada. In the early hours of the morning, in thick fog, the Norwegian Steamer *Storstad*, carrying coal, rammed the Canadian Passenger Steamship, *Empress of Ireland*, travelling from Quebec to Liverpool. The *Empress* was ripped apart in the collision and sank within minutes, taking 1042 lives out of 1367 passengers onboard.

No wonder mariners fear fog. They used to fire guns, bang drums, blow bugles, anything to warn away other ships. And even now under International Maritime Law the smallest dinghy upwards, must carry a bell to warn away other ships in fog.

Fog has also played a major role in some of aviation's

worst accidents, including the world's worst air crash at Tenerife airport in the Canary Islands. At 5p.m. on 27 March 1977, a KLM 747 taking off in thick fog collided with a PanAm 747 taxiing along the same runway. There were 583 people killed without any survivors.

### DUNKIRK

In one of the most extraordinary episodes of the Second World War, fog actually *saved* thousands of lives. In 1940 half a million Allied soldiers were surrounded by a vastly superior German army in Belgium. The Allies retreated to the French port of Dunkirk. Over the next eight days from 26 May, the troops were ferried across the English Channel under intense enemy attack. It could have been a disaster, but for two crucial days a thick fog rolled in, hiding the evacuation from the Germans. That cover was vital in making Dunkirk the largest and most successful wartime evacuation of troops in history.

### BATTLE OF THE BULGE

Fog was also used in the Second World War for cover to attack the enemy .

Following the D-Day landings in 1944, the Allies advanced into Belgium by mid-December. But they soon became overstretched  along a front covering 600 miles (970 kilometres), from the North Sea to Switzerland. In the middle of that line they had no idea that waiting in the heavily wooded forests of the

Ardennes in southern Belgium were two German Panzer armies.

On 16 December a heavy fog fell over the Ardennes and the Panzer tank divisions used it as cover to launch a two-pronged attack on the Allies' line, hoping to cut off and crush the British and Canadian forces at the northern end of the front and destroy the whole Allied offensive. The counter-offensive in the fog took the Allies completely by surprise. Without air cover in the fog they could only rely on their ground troops, who were heavily outnumbered. The Germans soon drove a bulge-shaped wedge into the Allied lines – what became known as the Battle of the Bulge – and surrounded the American troops in Belgium.

But then the fog suddenly lifted on Christmas Eve. Under clear skies, American and British planes devastated the German offensive. On 26 December General Patton relieved the besieged troops, and by 16 January the Germans had been completely routed.

Even though the Battle of the Bulge inflicted some heavy damage on the Allies, it actually helped to shorten the war. The Germans had spent so many resources on the offensive they had nothing left in reserve to defend the Rhine, and left the way open for the invasion of Germany from the west – the Allies were astonished at how easy it was to cross the Rhine into Germany.

FOG AND NATURE

Fog may seem menacing, but there are a great many living things which depend on it for their survival.

The coastline of northern California is a good place to start with because the gigantic redwoods have come to depend on foggy weather. The damp fog helps feed the trees with moisture by dripping off the needles onto the ground below, or even by soaking into the needles themselves. Scientists have also discovered in Scotland that pine trees feed off the valuable minerals carried in mists and fogs, and this is probably true also for redwoods.

In the Namibian coastal desert the weird-looking *Welwitchia* plant hangs on for dear life by a slender thread. Its big scruffy leaves flop onto the sand without a hope of seeing rain for months or even years on end. But when the great coastal fogs roll in off the South Atlantic the leaves soak up the wet air like blotting paper.

The same is true for an amazing little beetle also living in the Namibian desert. When the fog rolls in the Namib tenebriond beetle climbs onto the crest of a sand dune where fog condensation is greatest. There it sticks its bottom into the foggy wind and collects the minute droplets of foggy water on its back, letting the water trickle down to its mouth.

Another beetle uses engineering to catch the fog. The Namib dune beetle digs narrow trenches in the sand perpendicular to the fog's wind. The fog collects in the ridges and collects more water than the surrounding sand. The beetle then runs along the trench drinking the water.

The Australian lizard, *Mulloch hapridus*, doesn't even have to think about drinking fog. It just absorbs the moisture into its skin and funnels it down to its mouth.

Jackals lick condensed fog or dew from the surfaces of rocks. And humans have used something similar. During the Second World War the *Dunedin Star* ship was wrecked on the Skeleton Coast of Namibia. An aircraft was sent to rescue the survivors, but that unfortunately crashed. The one good thing was that the crashed aircraft's wings allowed water to condense, and the survivors licked the condensed fog droplets off the wing surfaces each morning until they were eventually rescued.

Elsewhere, fog provides an even more secure lifeline. In the village of Chungungo, high in the Andes Mountains of Chile, there is so little rain that the only way to get water is to trap fog. In a recently installed project, a large array of nets strung out on the mountainside catches the fog and drips it down into tanks, catching up to 13,000 gallons (60,000 litres) a day

## Dew

On the island of Tenerife, off the west coast of Africa, rainfall is in such short supply that farmers turn instead to dew for irrigation. They plant vines in sunken hollows which trap dew. On cold nights the dew forms in these hard mud bowls and the water runs down towards the centre, irrigating vines.

## Frost Hollows

Within 12 miles (19 kilometres) of the suburbs of London is a town whose night climate appears almost exactly similar to that of Braemar in the Aberdeenshire plateau, which is one of the coldest inhabited regions in the British Isles. The average minimum temperature for Rickmansworth from 1906–1935 was only 0.5 degrees Celsius warmer than Braemar. As a result, Rickmansworth has a growing season about five weeks shorter than nearby towns. It also scored one of the biggest swings in daily temperature in British weather records – a diurnal range of 50 degrees Fahrenheit (28 degrees Celsius) in July 1941.

Before the railways were built, Rickmansworth's climate was pretty much like anywhere else in the home counties. But when the Victorians built a high railway embankment across the valley, cold air flowing down from the surrounding hills was trapped in the valley – the ideal frost hollow.

Heavy frost can itself be a big problem simply because it grows so heavy. In March 1969 a heavy frost in Yorkshire brought down power and telephone lines, and even the television transmitter at Emley Moor on the Pennines collapsed under the weight of rime frost – a thick coat of feathery white ice which forms when an icy wind blows in freezing fog.

## Smog

The diarist John Evelyn wrote in 1661 that 'The city of London resembles rather the face of Mount Etna, the Court of Vulcan, or the suburbs of hell, than an assembly of people . . . the air is here eclipsed with such a cloud of sulphur that the sun itself is hardly able to penetrate.'

Even in the thirteenth century air pollution was so serious that a commission was set up to investigate the causes. The problem was burning wood fires and later on coal for homes and industries like the lime kilns used for construction.

London has long been bedevilled with smog caused by coal smoke. Dickens wrote in *Bleak House* in 1853 of Esther Summerson talking to Mr Guppy: 'I asked him whether there was a great fire anywhere? For the streets were so full of a dense brown smoke that scarcely anything was to be seen. "Oh dear no, miss," he said, "This is a London particular."'

*Coalsmoke in olden days created smog, acid rain and disease.* © *Royal Meteorological Society*

Perhaps the strangest phenomenon of the pollution was the story of the peppermoth. Before the industrial revolution, this ordinary looking moth was a greyish silver colour, and its colour blended in well with trees

and stones. But as black soot covered the urban landscape, strains of the peppermoth developed a black
colour which blended in well with the new pollution.
It's one of the finest examples of Darwinian evolution
driven by atmospheric pollution.

The smoke from coal fires also gave off sulphur dioxide, and when it mixed with oxygen and moisture in the
air turned to sulphuric acid which we know now as acid
rain, eating into stonework, metalwork, and  causing
breathing problems. London is basically shaped like a
shallow bowl, and in calm weather cold air can sit in the
bowl and be trapped by warm air sitting on top of it like
a lid, trapping the coal smoke near the ground. The
smog then had no escape route and rapidly built up at a
frightening rate into the London pea-souper, – a thick,
greeny-yellow smog. Only when the lid of warm air was
blown away could the smog disperse.

And then on Friday, 5 December 1952, Londoners
woke up to find the worst smog in history, when daytime simply never arrived. The city was enveloped in a
thick yellow smog and it stayed dark for five days.
Visibility dropped to less than one foot in some places,
traffic almost came to a standstill and people experienced an almost maddening claustrophobia. Hanging in
the air were thousands of tons of black, sooty particles
of tar and sulphur dioxide gas, mostly from coal fires.
The sulphur dioxide created an acid cloud with the pH
of a car battery. By the time the smog cleared, some
four thousand people had died or were dying of chronic
breathing problems. Undertakers ran out of coffins and
florists out of flowers. Most of the deaths were probably
caused by the smog's acid irritating the lungs and chok-
ing people to death.

That great smog shook up the politicians; four years

later legislation was passed to make London smokeless and a decade later the difference was breathtaking. Londoners could actually see their city.

There is still one particular day of the year when we are susceptible to pea-souper fogs. Firework displays on 5 November give off so much smoke that under the right weather conditions they can cause smog. A temperature inversion prevents the bonfire and firework smoke from escaping, a large concentration of soot particles in the air builds up, and as the pollution cools in the air it sinks to the ground in an acid smog. This happened on 5 November 1993 when the temperature inversion in the previous few days had already trapped coal smoke in Belgium and France, killing eleven people and leaving at least 260 more admitted to hospital with breathing difficulties. French and Belgian authorities blamed badly ventilated homes with coal stoves for a build up in lethal carbon monoxide gas.

But those temperature inversions that gave rise to pea-soupers now bring another urban air blight – smog from car exhausts. The waste gases from vehicles are turned by the sun into a toxic smog, and when the warm air on the ground is capped by cold air sitting above (or vice versa) the smog has nowhere to go and builds up into a filthy yellowy-brown cloud.

Mexico City has the worst smog in the world. In 1990, Mexico City exceeded World Health Organisation guidelines for air quality for 310 days of the year. At the last count, 13 thousand tons of pollutants per day are spewed into the air above the city. Traffic is the major cause: 3 million vehicle exhausts belch out volatile organic compounds and nitrogen oxides and high temperatures and sunlight cook these into ozone. Like London, Mexico City is also a bowl-shaped metropolis, and cold air easily gets trapped by a lid of warm air. With light winds and strong sunshine the pollution can stew for weeks on end. And to make matters even worse the City's high altitude at 7000 feet (2100 metres) makes the air so thin that people have to breathe in more heavily polluted air than at low altitude. High ozone levels produce acute health problems – children especially suffer from coughs, phlegm, wheezing and asthma and it's estimated that some fifty per cent of the entire population suffer some form of sickness at any one time from the pollution.

Los Angeles suffers its own smog problem for the same reasons as Mexico City – a bowl-shaped metropolis, too much traffic, and lots of sunshine to turn the fumes into smog. Recent research in Los Angeles suggests that smaller particles, especially soot from burnt oil and diesel buses and trucks, are more dangerous than ozone, as they enter deeper into the lungs. A lot of these tiny particles stay afloat in the smog and make a coloured haze which cuts down visibility. But vehicles are only part of the problem. There is also industrial pollution and some other bizarre sources. Recent research from Los Angeles shows that 6 per cent of the haze there is actually caused by particles from cigarette smoke and barbecued meat.

## Natural Smog

Even though industrial pollution has been around since the Iron Age, photochemical smog has been around for millions of years, and it's been given off by plants!

Take a look over pine covered mountainsides from Scotland to Australia, and there it is – nature's very own photochemical blue atmospheric haze. In fact, the smog is so strong that mountains have been named after it: the Smoky Mountains of Virginia or the Blue Mountains of Australia.

The haze is made by plants, and pine trees in particular, constantly 'sweating' volatile organic chemicals like terpenes – those heady pine tree scents beloved of lavatory cleaner manufacturers. When this perfumed discharge hits sunshine it turns into a murky aerosol which scatters blue light, a distant cousin of the smogs of Los Angeles and elsewhere.

The tree-made smog rises and falls during the day, peaking at around noon and also in the autumn just as the Los Angeles smog does. Natural smog is also affected by the weather. Rain washes it back down to earth, and the electricity in the air, say before a thunderstorm, makes the haze worse by somehow ripping off wax from pine needles and adding to the atmospheric aerosol. In fact, natural photochemical haze easily outweighs our own human-made smog. Each year five times more plant smog is given off than man-made particle pollution.

## Aurora

The night offers its most fantastic light show in the coldest parts of the world. Around the Arctic and Antarctic Circles, the sky lights up with vivid blues, greens and

*Auroras are created by the sun's solar wind lighting up the sky like a giant fluorescent light. Folklore says that storms happen after a strong aurora, and there's some evidence that it might be true. From* L'Atmosphère *by Camille Flammarion*

reds in huge vertical streamers dancing in the atmosphere.

This beautiful aurora display is a sign of colossal magnetic storms raging on the sun, creating a surge of electrically charged particles which spew out in a solar wind through space at the speed of light – the fastest wind in our solar system.

The magnetic solar storms which create the auroras are greatest when the number of sunspots is largest, when the stream of charged particles from the sun is most prolific. This solar activity follows an eleven-year cycle, and so the frequency and intensity of the auroras follows the same pattern.

When the storm hits Earth, the upper atmosphere protects most of us from the bombardment. But the charged particles in the solar wind are drawn down into the Earth's poles following the lines of the Earth's magnetic field. As they are dragged down, the electrical particles excite the gas molecules in the atmosphere like a gigantic fluorescent tube lighting up into different colours with the various different gases – red for nitrogen, green for oxygen, and so on.

What isn't so widely appreciated is that the auroras affect us on the ground. They can also cause damage to communications and power supplies, as happened on 8 March 1989 in Quebec province. A huge solar electrical storm erupted and the electrically charged particles blew up electrical transformers on the ground, knocking out the power supply to the whole of Quebec province, and plunging it into darkness for nine hours.

This sort of damage demonstrates the violence of solar flares, but if they affect electrical installations can they alter the weather? There is an old Scottish saying that 'The first great aurora of the autumn is followed by

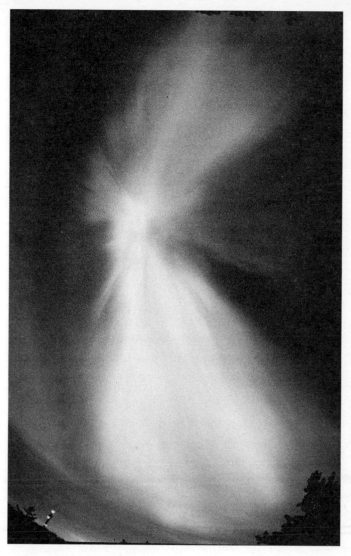

*The massive electrical energy from the sun's solar wind
that produces auroras also interferes with electrical
power supplies and communications on the ground.*
© *Pekka Parvianen*

a storm in two days.' Only now are we realizing that solar flares *do* affect our weather. Scientists have recently found some evidence that a severe aurora deepens depressions in the Gulf of Alaska, strengthening the storm systems that later strike North America. It's possible that the ions in the upper atmosphere affect our weather, but we don't know exactly how . But there is evidence that the Earth's magnetic field affects our weather in other ways, as the next section describes.

## Magnetism

Joe King of the Appleton Laboratory noticed that the contour lines in the Earth's magnetic field bear a striking resemblance to isobars on a map of atmospheric pressure drawn around the true north pole. He suggests that the two are actually linked, and this is why the circumpolar flow of westerly wind, which dominates temperate weather, is sensitive to solar activity. Whenever there are sunspots, there is magnetic disturbance in our atmosphere, a strengthening of the Earth's field, and a tendency for severe wind storms to break out over the sea. When the sun is quiet and our field is correspondingly weak the winds do seem to drop, producing calmer warmer weather everywhere.

Goesta Wollin at Columbia Observatory in Palisades, New York, found twenty years ago that in past epochs whenever the Earth's magnetic field was weaker the planet was warmer. He examined magnetic records from more than forty observatories around the world and it was very clear that in places where the intensity of the magnetic field had fallen it was followed by warmer average yearly temperatures, whereas an increase in magnetic field led to a drop in temperature. He then looked at how the Earth's field changes over months and years, and these too matched the changing weather.

What's important is not necessarily the strength of the field, but how fast it changes. Wollin proposed that the salt water of the oceans is behaving like a gigantic dynamo with the Earth's magnetic field. As salt water is good at conducting electricity, the great ocean currents flowing around the world generate a massive electric current like a dynamo. And when the Earth's magnetic field changes it affects the speed of the ocean currents. This then alters the vast distribution of heat around the globe, and that changes the climate.

Wollin's fellow scientists are sceptical. But if it's true, then there might be a chance of predicting climatic warming or cooling two or three years in advance based on observations of the fluctuating state of the magnetic field.

## Earthquakes and Weather

According to common sense there should be no link between earthquakes and the weather. Earthquakes are seismic shifts in the Earth's crust, the weather is shifts in the Earth's atmosphere. But in 1994 an extraordinary paper was published in *Nature* by a Japanese geologist,

Masakazu Outake, claiming that the weather might trigger earthquakes.

Historical records going back centuries show that all of Japan's thirteen major earthquakes over 1300 years struck during the autumn and winter, and the chances of that happening by coincidence are a thousand to one. It's during these seasons that the atmospheric pressure is greater, and Outake calculated that the extra 10 millibars of seasonal atmospheric pressure in winter would press the equivalent of 210 pounds' (95 kilograms) weight on each square yard of ground, enough to trigger an earthquake on the fault lines.

## Earthquake Lights

Huge efforts are being made to find warning signs to predict earthquakes, but no one has yet made a successful forecast of an earthquake. Nevertheless, strange electromagnetic disturbances have been detected several hours or days before some earthquakes strike. One recent example was a quite strong burst of electromagnetic activity picked up a day before the massive Kobe quake in Japan in January 1995, which killed 2500 people.

The daily Yomiuri newspaper reported various strange lights just before and after the quake. Many people from Kobe and nearby towns saw aurora-like lights or flashes in the sky, and a fireman saw a bluish-orange light above a road during the quake. These disturbances fit in with many other historic sightings of strange lights in the sky linked to earthquakes. The lights can come as streamers, balls, sparkles or 'slow' lightning. Following a quake in November 1930 in the Idu Peninsula, Japan, scientists collected some 1500 reports of mysterious lights in the sky, and reported them in the science journal *Nature* in 1931 and 1932. They were usually bluish, often looking like the rays of the sun or ball-shaped, and at night they could be brighter than moonlight. Another survey during a swarm of earthquakes at Matsushiro in 1965–7 reported in *Kakioka Magnetic Observatory*, 1968, collected more sightings of balls of light and incredible luminous spectacles over the tops of mountains. One theory to explain the lights is that they are created when the enormous pressures in a moving geological fault squeeze the rocks and produce what's called a piezo-electric voltage, turning mechanical energy into electrical charge. The theory goes that an intense electrical field, perhaps 100,000 volts per square metre, ionizes the air and produces the glowing lights.

# THE LIVING
# WORLD

# Forecasting with Plants and Animals

The weather affects the behaviour of plants and animals in all sorts of ways, but trying to make accurate forecasts from them runs into huge problems because they are often extremely unreliable. Which puts paid to much weather folklore, for instance there's no truth that cows lying down are a sign of rain on the way, because cows also lie down if the weather is going to be fine. But there are some pretty striking bits of animal behaviour which show how well-tuned the natural world is to the weather. Later on we'll look at the way climate affects living things, and how they're affected by changing climate patterns.

## BIRDS

Birds are supposed to be clever little barometers, and some have their own weather proverbs, like robins:

> *Robin singing high, fine and dry*
> *Robin singing low, too wet to mow.*

For as long as anyone can remember, robins forecast rain within twenty-four hours when they sing on low branches with their tails down, but singing on high branches with their tails up they signal fine weather. And maybe there's something in this because robins are very stroppy about their territory, and need song-posts to trumpet their patch. Only if the weather turns bad will they take shelter and warble a few muffled notes.

Some birds have such good reputations as weather forecasters it's earned them special nicknames. The male mistlethrush is one of the few birds that sings when a thunderstorm is approaching, hence its nickname the storm cock. The green woodpecker is sometimes known as the rain bird whose laughing call is supposed to herald rain.

The storm petrel is a seabird that got its name from the way it behaves before a storm. Sailors and fishermen believed that when this ocean wanderer was seen close to the shore, stormy weather would soon follow.

The way that many birds fly in the sky tells a lot about the atmospheric conditions. Rooks fly low in the sky and tumble if it's going to rain, and if they fly high it is a sign of fine weather. High-flying swifts and swallows are usually pretty good signs of good weather the next day because they are feeding on insects which stay close to cover when rain is due.

### THERMOMETERS: CRICKETS, FROGS AND SNAKES

Crickets are one of nature's noisy thermometers., When the temperature at night is below 55 degrees Fahrenheit (13 degrees Celsius) the average cricket is completely silent, and then just about 55 degrees Fahrenheit it chirps at 60 clicks per minute and the rate steadily increases with rising temperature.

The Abyssinian mountain frog, *Rana wittei*, comes from the marshes of the Ethiopian highlands and Mount Kenya's northern slopes. It too is a living thermometer, croaking as long as the temperature remains above 32 degrees Fahrenheit (zero degrees Celsius) but it falls suddenly silent the instant the temperature drops below freezing.

Some people believe that you can tell the temperature by listening to a rattlesnake. When the snake becomes excited its tail vibrates and the frequency is supposed to vary with the temperature, falling to nothing at 32 degrees Fahrenheit (zero degrees Celsius) and rising to about 100 rattles per second at temperatures of 99 degrees Fahrenheit (37 degrees Celsius) increasing by 2.7 rattles for every degree rise.

BEES

Of all the insect world, bees have an impressive reputation for sensing the weather:

*When the bees crowd out of their hive,*
*The weather makes it good to be alive.*
*When bees crowd into the hives again,*
*It's a sure sign of storms and rain.*

Bee weather-forecasting probably works because bees are very fussy about the weather. They adore flying in warm weather over 69 degrees Fahrenheit (20 degrees Celsius), low humidity and moderate wind speeds of less than 4 miles per hour (6.4 kilometres per hour) on clear sunny days. On dull days they need an extra 3.6 degrees Fahrenheit (2 degrees Celsius) before foraging. So low temperatures, little sunshine or high winds are pretty awful bee days, and they make far less honey.

Beekeepers often say that they don't like going near hives before a thunderstorm because the bees are so bad tempered. How the bees can predict a storm isn't clear, although the sudden darkening of the skies does trigger a rush back to the hive. But bees may also be sensitive to the build up of static electricity in the air, and although there has been little research on this, beekeepers have often noticed that bees avoid flying near power lines, perhaps because of the electric fields given off around the cables.

## WASPS

The fearsome reputation of wasps is a bit of a myth. Wasps are not nearly as strong flyers as bees and need much calmer weather conditions to buzz around in. In fact, a fit human can easily outrun a flying wasp. Wasps also need warm and humid summers to make a good swarm, and a mild winter to survive in large numbers.

## BUTTERFLIES

Out of all our native insects, none can be so pernickety about the weather as butterflies. They are sun-lovers *par excellence*, hell-bent on sunbathing to sustain their forages amongst the flowers in search of nectar. The sun is an extraordinary factor in their lives because being cold-blooded creatures, their muscles can't work hard enough to fly unless they are warm enough.

So badly do they need solar energy that most species flying up to a bridge will shy away from its dark shadow, preferring to take the long way round by flying up and over in sunshine.

There are even some butterflies that seem to be able to forecast weather, rather than reacting to the immediate conditions – these are the Orange Tips which live happily in light woodland as long as there are glades and open spaces. They close up their wings just before a cloud obliterates the sun. On a changeable day, in the late afternoon, they can take up roosting positions earlier than usual if a large bank of clouds appears in the sky. So they seem to anticipate cloudy weather.

### BEETLES

Rain in many parts of the tropics is the only sign of a change in season, and signals the start of mating. And there's probably no finer example of the power of rain than the sex life of the Panamanian fungus beetle. The male remains an inactive virgin in the dry tropical heat of early April. Only when the first heavy rains of the season come, in mid-April or early May, do the males suddenly become sexually active and start their wooing and cooing of suitable mates. Rainwater is somehow the vital ingredient for turning on the males, and neither drinking water nor artificial rain substitutes for real rainfall. How the rain works is unknown.

## FROGS

Frogs and toads are seen in large numbers during wet spells but don't necessarily give advance warning of rainfall, though excessive croaking of frogs generally points to rain.

## WORMS

Everyone knows that worms come up to the surface when it rains. Just look at birds yanking out inches of writhing *Lumbricus terrestris* from the ground like spaghetti. But worms actually try to take precautions against the weather and predators, as Darwin discovered: 'Worms seize leaves and other objects, not to serve for food, but for plugging up the mouths of their burrows.' Darwin felt that shelter from the cold was an important reason for the worms plugging up their burrow which maybe helped prevent flooding during showers. Some worms even practise stonemasonry. They heap tiny stones into tumuli over their burrows and if the stones are removed the worms come back out at night and drag them back with their mouths, their tails fixed in their burrows. Darwin even saw one drag a stone weighing 2 ounces (57 grams) back to its home.

## SPIDERS

Spiders have a long folklore of weather forecasting because of their sensitivity to weather. Rain is their chief preoccupation, and small wonder: after spending a fortune in time and energy spinning a glorious web they don't want it torn to shreds by heavy raindrops. So, many spiders respond rapidly to heavy rainfall by cutting out large sections of their webs, quickly collapsing them. Many others assume 'rainfall postures', hanging straight down beneath their webs with their front legs stretched out below to act as guttering and drain the rain off the webs.

Spiders hang their webs to supports using suspended threads. According to folklore when spiders spin these supporting threads short the weather is unsettled, but if they make them long the weather is often supposed to be set fair for several days. On the other hand, when spiders are seen crawling on walls more often than usual, rain should ensue; if they work during rain, the cloud will soon clear.

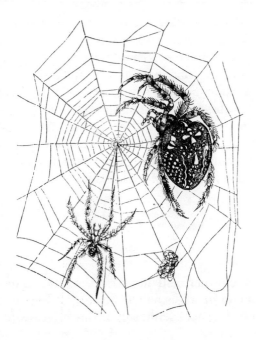

*When you see gossamer flying*
*Be sure the air is drying*

Spiders often love to parachute around on silky threads
of gossamer, drifting through the air up to a record altitude of 16,400 feet (5000 metres) in the Himalayas.
Because spider gossamer is affected by humidity and also
wind speed, it is an indicator of the weather. Ballooning
is ideal on warm days with light winds, typical of summer. On these occasions, ballooning by hundreds or
thousands of spiders will probably help to cut down over-
crowding in local areas, and there is always the chance
that they land somewhere suitable to colonize.

### LEECHES

The medicinal leech is an uncanny predictor of weather
because it behaves as a natural barometer. Dr
Merriweather from Whitby in Yorkshire used this to
good effect in the Great Exhibition at Crystal Palace in
1851. He put leeches into bottles partly filled with water.
If they stayed at the bottom it forecast fine weather but
just before a weather change they moved up the jar, and
if it was about to rain they climbed to the very top of the
jar where they knocked into a bell, which rang a weather
warning.

### FLOWERS

Flowers can perform short-term weather forecasting,
by opening or closing their flowers, although they are
not always reliable. Flowers do not like getting their

pollen wet so many of them close their flowers before rain comes. Two particularly sensitive flowers are the bindweed *Convolvulus arvensis* or the Scarlet Pimpernel, also known as the Poor Man's Weather Glass because of its weather-forecasting talents.

Even the flower's pollen sacs sense moisture. In the plantain, the anthers squeeze shut on dewy nights or during wet weather, protecting the pollen inside. The movement can be surprisingly fast: anthers of the unfortunately named Bastard Toad-flax *Thesium alpinum* shut up within thirty seconds of being moistened.

Flowers also have a keen sense of warmth. The passing of a cloud is enough to close sensitive flowers like gentians, crocuses and tulips. They sense the slight change in temperature – sometimes a mere 1 degree Fahrenheit (half a degree Celsius) is enough to close a crocus. And the fastest flower mover is reputed to be a gentian, *Gentiana quadrifaria*, which is said to close in ten seconds if the temperature drops fast enough. These movements are made by rapid flower growth. In cool weather the lower surface of their fused sepals/petals grows faster and closes the flower over. But in warmer weather the upper surface of the flower grows faster and the flower opens up.

One clue why flowers go to such extraordinary lengths to move with the temperature is that they tend to be plants growing in cold places. In the brisk sunshine of early spring when the first flowers bloom, the open flowers trap heat like miniature solar collectors. The few insects on the wing fancy a bit of warmth, so the solar heated flowers are a welcome invitation to shelter, and the insects pollinate them in return.

One flower has gone into solar heating in an even bigger way. *Dryas octopetala* has flowers that swivel round like satellite dishes following the sun through the day. The sunshine it collects keeps the flowers a couple of degrees warmer – and that attracts insects. It's also been proved to help incubate the seeds of the successfully pollinated flower afterwards.

## How Plants Cool the World

Plants also affect the weather. They evaporate water from their leaves by opening or closing tiny sphincterlike pores called stomata. This loss of water is called transpiration and it keeps the plant cool and draws up liquids and salts through the plant. But the quantities of water involved are quite staggering. An acre (0.4 hectares) of grass between May and July transpires over 500 tons of water. This colossal evaporation actually affects the local weather, because the water vapour lost by the plants makes the air more humid – a tropical rainforest is humid partly because the plants are transpiring. In turn, the humidity helps clouds form and drop rain which the trees feed on, and so the water cycle goes round and round.

But when forests are destroyed on a large scale the local climate changes. The air becomes drier, clouds are less common and rainfall is severely cut. At Mahabeleshwar, south of Bombay, the surrounding hills have been severely logged and annual rainfall has been severely hit, cut from 400 inches (1000 centimetres) a year to just over 236 inches (600 centimetres). The pleasantly warm summers have now become oppressively hot.

The loss of rainfall from cut forests can have some other unexpected effects. The Panama Canal needs a constant supply of fresh water to replace the water lost each time a ship enters or leaves the canal. The surrounding densely forested mountains feed fresh water into the canal, but ecologists found that as the surrounding forests were cut down by peasant farmers the canal was running low. Urgent conservation measures have now been taken to protect the surrounding forests to save the canal.

Upsetting the water balance of forests may even cause calamities much further afield. Cutting down a forest in Brazil not only reduces rainfall locally but also affects the unnatural spread of deserts in nearby Peru, although it's not clear how this works.

## The History of Climate and Nature

Nature has always changed when the climate changed. Now we're facing a rapid rise in global temperatures and wildlife is again changing. In this next section we'll look at how wildlife, plants and diseases changed in the past, what is changing now and what we can expect in the near future.

### THE LAST ICE AGE

Ten thousand years ago woolly mammoths and their cousins the mastodons roamed Europe, Asia and North America during the last Ice Age, feeding on tundra and conifer trees. Prehistoric people in France hunted reindeer, bison and great mammoth on grassy plains and tundra – which we know from the drawings they left behind in their cave homes.

### PRE-BOREAL

After the Ice Age, summer temperatures in Britain grew warmer and winters were milder, more like the climate of the South of France today. As the ice sheets retreated, the food of the mammoths and mastodons of spruce and tundra was replaced by deciduous trees. As the old pine forests died out, the big animals died with them. Hazel is sensitive to cold summer weather and was much more widespread in Norway and Sweden than it is now. Holly, ivy, foxglove and primrose were much more sensitive to the winter cold and were spread further into northern and eastern Britain than they are now.

The small-leaved lime tree grew across Britain in the balmy climate. Today's climate is cooler and our early July temperatures in the north are too low for the tree's pollen to work properly. So the lime tree's range barely extends into Yorkshire. But as global warming brings back those balmy summers of ancient times we can expect the species to advance back into its old home in northern Britain.

*The last great Ice Age, over 20,000 years ago, saw the world's climate zones drastically shift. Whilst the woolly mammoth (top) roamed today's temperate regions, the Sahara was a lush grassland with elephants and giraffes, as seen in prehistoric cave paintings (bottom).*

### IRON AGE

Around 1000BC the climate turned wet, cold and stormy at the start of the Iron Age in Britain. Boglands grew large in the uplands and Scotland and many of the settlements there were abandoned.

### ROMANS

The cold lasted until about 450BC, when temperatures rose, which is when the Roman Empire started expanding. When the Romans colonized England in 55BC, they introduced vine growing as far north as Northumberland. Vines are especially sensitive because they need 50 degrees Fahrenheit (10 degrees Celsius) before breaking their buds open in springtime – a drop of just one degree during this time can set them back by ten days.

The Romans probably also introduced malaria to Britain. The disease was rife in Roman Italy, although it wasn't the virulent, tropical sort familiar today. The microscopic malarial parasite needed warm and humid weather to develop inside its host mosquito; generally speaking, that means an average 59 degrees Fahrenheit (15 degrees Celsius) in July.

The malaria was carried by three different mosquitoes, mostly in the marshes of East Anglia, the Thames and Severn estuaries and eastern Scotland. But its first major inroads into the British population were not recorded until the fourteenth century, as pictured in Chaucer's *Nun's Priest's Tale*:

*And if it do, I dare laye a grote,*

*That ye shul have a fevere terciane,*
*Or an ague that may be yore bane.*

The word *ague* in medieval literature was malaria. It was a seasonal disease peaking in spring and autumn, and the worst epidemics occurred in the years with hot summers when the mosquitoes would have flourished. Amongst its victims the most famous was Oliver Cromwell who was reported to have died of malaria.

It's difficult to say how many people suffered British malaria. By the time figures were collected in the mid-nineteenth century it was starting to decline, thanks partly to a series of wet and cold summers which helped to kill off the malarial parasite. The Victorians also inadvertently checked malaria by draining marshes and improving sewage disposal which helped eliminate the mosquito's breeding grounds. Yet infections lingered on even into the twentieth century, with 566 cases recorded between 1917 and 1952.

### NORMANS

From around AD900 to 1300 the climate grew exceptionally warm. Remote places like Greenland were so warm and pleasant the Viking colonists grew barley, oats and rye. In North America Indians settled marginal lands in the north-west, whilst many tribes in the southern desert states suffered drought and in some cases died out, such as the Anasazi in New Mexico [see The Drought Hazard].

It's no coincidence that the Normans felt at home when they invaded England. These islands were basking in a long period of balmy climate. This was a boom time for agriculture, when the Normans took advantage of the high temperatures and replanted many of the vineyards the Roman colonists had originally grown. Vines were flourishing as far north as Yorkshire, and the hills of Northumberland were farmed up to 1000 feet (320 metres). Many upland places like Dartmoor were resettled. Scotland grew prosperous on its agriculture. With long growing seasons raising good harvests, the English economy boomed and lent the financial muscle to the great era of cathedral building that followed.

And as most of the natives soon realized, Norman cuisine was a great improvement on the old Anglo-Saxon stodge, but unfortunately there was one problem. The Normans introduced rabbits and reared them in warrens, but once these animals escaped they went feral and became a national pest. What makes this story so significant is that rabbits are Mediterranean creatures, which thrive on mild winters and warm summers and adapted well to the balmy British climate in those days.

## MEDIEVAL COLD

The climate started deteriorating in the 1300s. Vineyards were abandoned in England and in Germany the vines had to be moved 600 feet (200 metres) down slopes to survive. The Viking settlements of Greenland and Iceland grew so weak their populations fell rapidly.

Disease grew to epidemic proportions. The unusually wet conditions encouraged fungal diseases, including one of the worst ever recorded outbreaks of food contamination. It was ergotism, or St Anthony's fire, caused by ergot blight which blackened kernels of rye during damp harvests. Even a tiny proportion of these poisoned grains baked in a loaf of bread would cause convulsions, hallucinations, gangrene and ultimately death. In fact, the hallucinogenic substance in ergot is the basis of LSD. With the harvests growing so poor, the starving peasants were forced to eat ergot-contaminated bread and so the epidemics of ergotism grew virulent.

The ergot also induced visions of beasts and wild animals. These were times when the legend of werewolves reached huge proportions and when werewolf trials were commonplace. Apart from the ergot-induced visions of wild beasts, real wolves actually turned into man-killers. When the climate took a nosedive in the fourteenth century, with wet summers and bitterly cold winters, wolves grew so hungry they started entering villages and towns and killing people. During one of the worst winters in 1439, fourteen people were killed by wolves in Paris.

The terror of the man-eating wolf then grew into the legend of the werewolf – humans covered in hair, with clawed hands and small, flat, pointed ears.

The rural population was already shrinking in the first half of the century before the Black Death arrived. From surveys of tax records we know that starvation, cold and ergot killed more people than the plague, which swept England later, from 1348 to 1350. No doubt the poor health of the population helped them succumb to the disease.

MEDIEVAL WARM

In the early 1500s cannabis became a popular fibre crop in eastern England, and in 1533 Henry VIII passed a law ordering farmers farming more than 60 acres (24

*Vineyards flourished in the balmy medieval climate of England, as shown in this 13th century illustration. The fine weather produced bumper harvests of all crops, helping finance cathedral building.*

hectares) to sow a portion of hemp or flax for rigging for the Royal Navy. Cannabis needs a warm climate and it started dying out as the climate cooled.

## LITTLE ICE AGE

One of the most dramatic climate events was the Little Ice Age, about three to four hundred years ago when the winters turned so cold the Thames froze over and harvests failed during the sunless summers. All of which had a knock-on effect on our wildlife. By the mid-seventeenth century many butterflies were lost and in the eighteenth century Arctic seals were often seen off the northern coast of Britain. Elsewhere, walruses migrated from northern to southern Greenland and polar bears walked into Iceland from Greenland across pack ice.

The deteriorating climate also led to an interesting change in furniture-making. In the late seventeenth and early eighteenth centuries, walnut from France was very popular in English furniture-making, with its hardness, dark colour and intricate grain patterns. But walnut trees are vulnerable to intense frost at about –4 degrees Fahrenheit (–20 degrees Celsius) and below, and a bitterly cold winter in 1709 decimated the walnut trees in France. Timber supplies ran so low that in 1720 the French government banned walnut exports, and, faced with the sudden loss of their favourite wood, the English furniture-makers turned instead to mahogany from British Honduras, which rapidly took over and the value of imports soared from £276 in 1722 to almost £80,000 by the end of the eighteenth century.

Another indicator of the climate of the Little Ice Age was the European wine harvests in France, Germany and Switzerland. Climatologist William Burroughs writing in the journal, *Weather* in 1985 records how the date of the start of the vine harvest was a ceremony recorded in chronicles and how it became stalled by cold weather. The wine harvests fluctuated wildly, with strings of bad years like the 1590s and 1690s and fine periods like the 1630s and 1680s.

The late sixteenth and early seventeenth centuries were another time when rains wrecked harvests and created serious famines. It's not known how many people died of ergot outbreaks [see Medieval Cold] but it had an impact on the events leading up to the French revolution. Bad weather and disastrous harvests infected with ergot resulted in mass hallucinations in Brittany in 1789, leading to widespread panic and irrational fears of food being stolen.

## POTATO BLIGHT

The weather in northern Europe in the summers of the mid-nineteenth century turned exceptionally wet, and helped spread a disease which led to starvation and mass famine.

In 1845 the summer was particularly wet, and provided the ideal conditions for the spread of the potato blight fungus. The blight only spreads in great humidity, and for spores to infect plants the leaves have to be wet, the humidity must be over 90 per cent, and it must be over 50 degrees Fahrenheit (10 degrees Celsius).

The blight first appeared in Belgium in June 1845 and by September it had reached Ireland: the potato crop was devastated. The potato was the staple diet of the population and widespread famine broke out. The following summers in Ireland stayed exceptionally wet and warm and the potato blight continued destroying the potato harvests. Over the following fifteen years an estimated seven hundred thousand people died from starvation and disease and another million emigrated to America and Australia. In all, over 30 per cent of the population of Ireland died or left.

### TWENTIETH CENTURY COLD

Yet even during more recent cold spells, particularly the hard winters of 1946–7 and 1962–3, Arctic and sub-Arctic species once again moved south and reoccupied territory last held during the Little Ice Age. The snowy owl, for example, used to be confined to northern Scandinavia and other Arctic regions but during cold winters it was seen more regularly further south and even attempted to colonize Shetland in 1963.

## Global Warming and Plants

Now that the present climate is warming up, it's already affecting a huge range of plant and animal life, and in this next section we'll look at the effects the changing climate is already having and is likely to have in the near future.

These past few years have been some of the most exciting and baffling in living memory. Spring seems to arrive at least a month early, sometimes bringing mini heat-waves, and telling spring plants to rush headlong into flowering and trees and shrubs to open their leaves early. A survey of trees in America shows their leaves have been opening about 11 days earlier over the last 30 years. Autumn merges seemlessly into a later and fairly nondescript winter with southern England having hardly had any snow for many years except for the winter of 1990–1.

Already we can see that fast-spreading warm climate plants with very light, wind-blown seeds are moving northwards. For example, the stunning lizard orchid (so-called because its lower lip hangs from the flower like a lizard's tail), spread rapidly between 1900 and 1940 from Kent northwards and westwards over southeast England. Arctic flowers on the Norwegian island of Spitzbergen are spreading northwards and Antarctic grasses are spreading southwards.

But our warmer climate might not necessarily be a good thing. In 1990 another mild spring brought out ornamental cherries, horse chestnuts, clematis and many flowers six to eight weeks earlier than expected. Then hard frosts struck in early April and wreaked havoc on some of this early growth. Rhododendrons were stopped in their tracks, and wisterias and fuchsias shrivelled.

Trees might well suffer the worst of the warmer climate. Mild winters and early springs are already the cause of apple crop failure because flowers develop prematurely. Apart from the danger of frost, early flowering is often out of step with the bee pollinators. By the time the flowers have matured and withered the bees might just be taking off. Studies show that a 2 degree Fahrenheit (1 degree Celsius) rise in maximum average spring temperature might be enough to cut apple harvests by about one tonne per hectare.

A milder climate could cause our wild plants big problems. Springtime in the English countryside might never be the same again. According to ecologists at Sheffield University, populations of bluebells, snowdrops, wild daffodils and other spring flowers could be cut and in some areas pushed out altogether. Because these plants grow in the chill of winter and early spring they score a competitive edge over other plants. So cow parsley, goosegrass, dandelions and garlic mustard which don't flower until late spring could start crowding out our traditional spring plants. Worse still, many unpleasant aliens from hotter climates are waiting in the wings to smother even these plants as they find our milder winters to their liking. They include such vigorous weeds as prickly lettuce and Canadian fleabane. Already the Japanese knotweed and giant hogweed have become notifiable weeds, which means that gardeners must control them.

Plants in southern England may try to find refuge further north, whilst others, unable to reach a colder home, could die out. Rare upland species are at most risk, like the beautiful spring gentian of Teesdale. Part of the problem with these types of plants is that they need cold weather during the winter so that they can break bud or germinate their seeds the following spring.

On the face of it, it should be easy to predict what will happen to plants. Temperate plants will oust arctic and alpine flora and tropical plants will push out temperate ones. But in reality the picture will be much, much more complicated than that.

The effects of global warming are still only a figment of computer model imaginations, but there is enough known about the world's flora and how it reacts to temperature for us to make an educated guess. One model designed by scientists at the Goddard Institute of Space Studies (GISS) in New York shows how the world's vegetation might look in fifty years' time.

Some areas will respond much more than others. The greatest change will not be in Yorkshire but in the far north, in the Arctic Circle, where the vast, treeless tundra will shrink at an alarming rate. Sandwiched between the ice cap and the great conifer forests, tundra exists where the soil is frozen for much of the year and the growing season is too short for trees. Instead, it is covered by sedges, mosses and stunted shrubs. But when the climate warms the frozen soil will melt, the conifer forests will spread north, and the tundra will be pushed right up to the limits of the northern land mass. The loss of the tundra will in turn affect the animals such as moose that are adapted to survive its harsh conditions, or which migrate there in summer to breed.

Overall, the change of climate predicted by the GISS model will be remarkably fast. The tundra will shrink noticeably within a decade. At the same time, crops in the American wheatbelt may fail as drought becomes a regular feature of the prairie climate. Elsewhere, changes might be for the better. The GISS computer predicts more rain over Saudi Arabia and parts of Australia, where the deserts might turn green.

Meanwhile, in Britain the look of our landscape will be radically altered as winter temperatures rise faster than summer ones. For the first time, broadleaved evergreen trees such as the oaks of the Mediterranean will be able to survive our milder winters and oust our traditional broadleaved deciduous trees, such as beeches and oaks. We can also expect changes in forestry as well. Spruce and many other conifers will suffer in the mild winters because they need to endure a certain number of days of cold temperatures before their buds can break. They could be replaced by sweet chestnut (currently confined to Kent) red and turkey oak, red alder, box tree and field maple. Already, timber trees such as Sitka spruce are receiving their barest minimum of winter cold. Foresters are now beginning to realize that trees planted now ready for fifty years' time will have to meet a very different climate, maybe like that of south-western France. So perhaps we should be planting French saplings instead of homegrown ones. Global warming is indeed a complicated affair.

## Agriculture

This is already affecting our agriculture, with vines and maize being grown in southern England. By 2030 some experts believe that maize and sunflowers could be grown over most of England, but dairy farming will be forced into northern England and Scotland. Currently grain maize ripens only in the extreme south-east of England, and elsewhere it can only be used for silage. It's been estimated that a 2.7 degree Fahrenheit (1.5 degree Celsius) rise in average temperature will let maize ripen up to south Yorkshire and Lancashire. This sort of warming is expected in the middle or end of the next century. With temperature rises like this, southern England could grow soyabean and navy beans which are used as baked beans and are currently imported from the United States.

The past twenty years have encouraged another grape

renaissance, with vine-growing spreading from the south of England up to Cheshire. And the future promises more. Temperatures are rising and the risk of late spring frosts receding. If the warming carries on we may well see a Château Glasgow sometime in the next century.

## Global Warming and Animals

As the world climate warms up, wildlife and plants are all responding in their own ways. Mediterranean and sub-Saharan creatures are invading Britain, whilst pests such as aphids and cabbage white butterflies are increasing to plague proportions during our hot, humid summers.

### BIRDS

Bird migrations are very sensitive to the weather. As Europe grows warmer almost every type of migrating bird has responded by changing their flight times, paths or even veering off into new lands – a potent sign of our changing climate.

In fact, bird migrations have been shifting through-out the twentieth century as temperatures have steadily climbed higher. The lapwings of Finland only became established in Finland during this century as the climate grew warmer, and during the sixties they found the weather improving so much they pushed much further north in springtime.

The Orkney and Shetland Islands are another good indicator of bird behaviour in the warm climate. Dippers colonized Orkney in the early twentieth century, probably because of the milder conditions then. On the other hand, the snowbunting and long-tailed duck from the cold Arctic tundra used to breed in Shetland in the nineteenth century when it was colder, but withdrew this century as it grew warmer.

In autumn everyone expects the reverse, with birds heading south towards warmer climes. But the timing of the bird exodus is also changing. Sparrows and many other temperate birds are delaying their migrations as autumn arrives later.

Some birds have even completely changed their compass directions. The blackcaps, a common European species of warbler, quite sensibly fly south to the Mediterranean for the winter. But in the 1960s a few tough birds from Germany and Austria switched north-west instead of south, landing in Britain rather than Spain or Morocco. There they happily survived the winter, and apparently liked it so much that today almost a tenth of their native population – some ten thousand German and Austrian birds – have chosen Britain as their new popular winter resort. Yet, strangely, the native British blackcaps still insist on flying off on their old winter migration routes to the Mediterranean.

The shift in European bird habits is now so dramatic that some birds have given up migrating altogether. In the last century, European thrushes used to breed in central Europe and then overwinter along the Mediterranean. Today, half the thrush species have given up migrating because they enjoy the winter so much, and now remain in central Europe all year round.

## MOTHS AND BUTTERFLIES

Most attention on the warmer climate has focused on butterflies, and they are very sensitive to the weather. For most species it seems that temperature and weather affect emergence, and conditions must also be warm and sunny for the adult to fly, feed or mate. So if the weather is bad the newly emerged adults remain dormant.

The white admiral butterfly spread from south-east England into the Midlands as summers became warmer in the 1940s, whilst peacock butterflies started spreading northwards and are now found well into southern Scotland due entirely to the improving weather.

### URBAN ISLAND SNAILS

Urban areas are warmer than the countryside. Just look at your local weather forecast, and the built-up areas are often about a degree or two warmer than the surrounding area. The waste heat seeping out from buildings and industry is one factor, but there is a meteorological reason as well. When the sun heats a city the buildings soak up the heat and then give it off again. That's why cities are always warmer at night than the countryside, as heat is slowly released from roads and buildings.

But there is probably no more dramatic example of urban heating than *Arianta arbustorum*, a snail living in and around Basel in Switzerland. Over the past ninety years the snail has become extinct at several sites around Basel because the city has grown too warm. The snail's eggs are killed off in the heat, and the only places where the snails have survived are higher up and cooler.

### FISH

Populations of fish are changing their movements around the oceans, which is ringing a few alarm bells. Fish are sensitive to hot or cold water and so their distribution is related to sea temperature. Global warming has been warming the world's oceans for some time and new patterns of fish distribution have been recorded for decades.

Take pilchards, that much maligned relative of the sardine. They are a southerly species which has become more plentiful around Britain's waters as sea temperatures have been rising in the English Channel and North Sea.

But there is a much more dramatic case of how global sea warming has changed commercial fishing. It's the cod. This vital commercial fish doesn't like waters colder than 36 degrees Fahrenheit (2 degrees Celsius),

*Evidence of global warming? A rare Mediterranean*
*sunfish caught off the south coast of England in the hot*
*summer of 1990.* © The News, *Portsmouth*

and if you draw a line of sea temperature of 36 degrees across the North Atlantic you then have its northernmost limit.

In the last century there appears to be no record of cod off the waters of western Greenland so the sea could well have been under 36 degrees Fahrenheit (2 degrees Celsius). But sometime at the turn of this century, cod from Iceland colonized the southernmost tip of Greenland, and since 1917 steadily advanced northwards up the continental shelf of Greenland's western coast with warmer sea temperatures. Between 1917 and 1932 it had progressed over ten degrees latitude.

### FOREIGN WILDLIFE

The warmer weather this century has attracted other wildlife. And if there's any doubt how significant the rising temperatures are, then moths are a dramatic indicator. About a dozen species of birds and more than forty species of moth have tried colonizing Britain from the Continent.

Foreign spiders have been drawn to our newly hot and humid climate. Take *Steatoda nobilis*, a cousin of the black widow spider. It somehow hitched a ride from the heat of the Canary Islands and easily transferred to the gardens of Portsmouth and its surroundings. One woman went into fever and pain for several hours after being bitten. Meanwhile, 1-inch (2.5 centimetre) long woodlouse spiders from the Mediterranean have been marching and biting through London and the Thames Valley, including one woman in south-west London whose bitten leg ballooned to twice its normal size .

A larger alien wasp has gradually been invading the nation. The media wasp *Dolicho vespula media* made sensational headlines about ten years ago when it established itself in southern England from the eastern Mediterranean. It was billed as a monster-sized ogre, but despite the hype the media wasp is truly a large placid wasp, not much bigger than English queen wasps, and it doesn't want to sting unless you sit on it or strike its nests. But the scare headlines resurfaced when *Dolicho vespula saxonica* – a close relative to the media wasp – also appeared in 1987 in Surrey and again spread through southern England. No one is sure how the media and saxonica wasps established themselves here, but it's no coincidence that they arrived during a spectacular run of hot summers and mild winters.

Turtles have now been found off the English coast, which was previously too cold for them. Also, the American snapping turtle has found a home in Hampstead Heath's ponds, after being deliberately released there.

## Pests

Not that any of this should come as much of a surprise. Plagues of aphids and cabbage white butterflies have developed, whilst indoors bedbugs and catfleas have reached bumper proportions. All of them have thrived on the hot weather.

The mild winters are bringing unpleasant surprises of their own. It may be no coincidence that 1989 was one of the worst years on record for greenfly infestation of garden and crop plants. They survived the mild winter of 1988–9 well and a warm, early spring allowed them to disperse quickly. The aphid invasion was so intense that by early summer there were fears that stocks of insecticide might run low. Since aphids also spread plant viruses, crop diseases have been rife too.

The only helping hand in the aphid explosion is a booming population of aphid predators. The summer of 1990 was a good one for ladybirds, and even in winter gardeners have noticed large numbers of them popping out of hibernation on mild days to pick off overwintering greenfly.

The Summer Fruit Tortrix Moth is a good indicator of warmer climate. Its caterpillars can bring ruin to orchards by feeding on apples, eating away the surface and making the fruit unsaleable. The moth is already here and probably came from the Netherlands and Germany where it is particularly common. For forty or more years the moth was only confined to the eastern tip of Kent, where the climate is just warm enough to keep it happy. But then in the 1980s the moth broadened its horizons and spread alarmingly through the major fruit-growing regions of south-east England, from Sussex to Suffolk. This was also a time when the weather became warmer, and particularly during the hot summers of the late 1980s and early 1990s the spread has accelerated.

Of all the garden pests, it's no wonder that slugs are one of the most sensitive to weather. Unless their wet, slimy coats are kept moist they risk death from dehydration. So when it turns dry, hot, or even cold the slugs burrow deep down into the soil and hide there until conditions improve again.

This moist lifestyle is reflected in slug pellet sales. In a typically wet year we spend about £7–8 million on pellets, but during the dry summer of 1990 sales plummeted to £1 million. Yet farmers tend to use pellets whatever the weather, which is unnecessary, costly and contaminates the environment. By knowing the weather forecast and the amount of water in the soil, slug activity can be safely predicted and pellets laid at the critical times.

Meanwhile, wild slugs have been suffering far more than their garden cousins, and one species was almost wiped out by the dry summers of 1990 and 1991. The dry summers decimated the youngsters and the population struggled on with middle-aged and elderly adults. Now, thanks to the recent wet summers, the population is bouncing back again with a fine new crop of youngsters.

Rabbits are booming since their introduction to Britain by Norman settlers. Rabbit numbers have fluctuated over the centuries with the climate, and their almost total extermination by the myxamatosis disease campaign of the 1960s. But the population developed resistance to the disease and the rabbits have made a sensational comeback in the past several years thanks to another bout of warm climate. British farmers are now faced with a plague of rabbits reproducing like only rabbits know how in the warmer, milder climate of the past decade or so.

In the near future, if temperatures carry on rising, we can expect a whole host of new pests to start invading England. A prime example is the Colorado Beetle, slightly larger than a ladybird with a similar shape. A hundred and fifty years ago it only lived in the United States, feeding on the sand-bur, a wild plant of the midwest. Then came the gold rush of the 1840s, and when the miners introduced potatoes the beetle developed a liking for the leaves. Since then it has switched its diet exclusively to potatoes. The beetles migrated east and by 1876 had reached the Atlantic coast of America. In, 1922 they were accidentally shipped to Bordeaux in France and reached the northern French coast in 1940. So far they haven't crossed the English Channel because the air of the Channel is too cold. The beetle migrates by flying up into the air and then gliding on the wind. Its metabolism is such that it seems to be capable of flying only when the temperature is around 77 degrees Fahrenheit (25 degrees Celsius). Because temperatures over the sea are almost invariably cooler than this, it stops flying and drowns in the English Channel.

# Diseases

### LYME DISEASE

Lyme disease is already here throughout the whole UK, but much more in the USA because they've more open access to woodland there. It is likely to explode. It's carried by ticks and is potentially lethal. Lyme disease is related to the weather, because it affects the tick that carries it. The symptoms of Lyme Disease very often start off as flu-like signs of high temperature, muscle aches and pains with a localized rash, but if left untreated can develop into a chronic form of arthritis or sometimes dementia. If caught early enough, the disease can be treated well with antibiotics, but if the treatment is left too late the disease becomes incurable.

### LEISCHMANIASIS

Leischmaniasis is a problem around the Mediterranean: Spain, Greece, Italy, Turkey, but more in Tunisia and Libya. It's more obvious in tropical places because they have worse health care.

Leischmaniasis is caused by a microscopic protozoan living in wild dogs. When a midge called *Phlebotomus* feeds on the dogs it contracts the protozoan, and if the midge then flies off and bites a human the disease is transmitted to that person. When it attacks people it develops in various medical forms: skin ulcers which are hard to heal.

*Phlebotomus* doesn't like the cold and doesn't occur

in the UK, but presently it is just opposite the Channel Islands, but probably not indigenous to the Channel Islands yet. We certainly don't want to have it in this country. If we did, we'd have to have more dog control – it is particularly carried in packs of wild dogs in North Africa.

## MALARIA

Malarial mosquitoes are still surviving in our remaining marshes, and as the climate continues warming, native malaria could once again reappear. Even more worrying is what might happen if the rising numbers of people coming into this country with virulent tropical malaria then infect British mosquitoes. In 1990 one tropical mosquito was found near to Gatwick Airport, presumably having jumped off an aircraft, and made newspaper headlines when it bit a local publican. If the temperatures in Southern England rose to 68 degrees Fahrenheit (20 degrees Celsius) the virulent tropical mosquito and its tropical parasite could survive in places like the Fens, Romney Marsh and Essex coastal marshes. Temperatures during the hot August of 1990 were almost high enough for them to breed, and it was only the night temperatures that were slightly too cool. Medical teams already make regular inspections of southern England's marshes searching for the mosquitoes.

## Living Things and
## Carbon Dioxide

Levels of carbon dioxide have risen and been blamed for the rising temperatures of the greenhouse effect. It's reckoned that around 5000 million tons of carbon dioxide are pumped by humans into the atmosphere each year. Carbon dioxide at the levels in the atmosphere isn't harmful to us, but for some creatures it is already having an effect.

### MOTHS

Researchers at the Australian National University looked at how the moth *Helicoverpa armigera*, a major agricultural pest, is affected by carbon dioxide. The moths have special sensors which are sensitive to the amount of carbon dioxide in the air. They need to know this because it helps them to find plants to lay their eggs on. They can pick up tiny concentrations in carbon dioxide given off from plants, and then home in on the signal.

The problem for the moths is that they have become adapted over millions of years to background levels of carbon dioxide up to 290 parts per million. Now the background concentration of carbon dioxide is so high, above 350 parts per million, that their sensors become confused and they fly off in the wrong direction.

PLANTS

Lots of people assume that a world with more carbon dioxide should be good for plants. After all, carbon dioxide is what plants need for making their food by photosynthesis; they're starving hungry for carbon dioxide. Unfortunately, it's not quite that simple.

Measurements taken at Point Barrow, in the remote Alaskan tundra, show that in the past decade, the amount of carbon dioxide has risen every year and that the plants there are making use of this extra carbon dioxide. Yet this will not protect them. The coniferous forests further south will also benefit from the extra carbon dioxide. Because they grow much taller than the dwarf plants of the far north, they will intercept more sunlight and thrive at the expense of the tundra.

Not all plants will use the extra carbon dioxide so well. Different plants use slightly different types of photosynthesis, largely depending on where they live. Our temperate flora can always handle more carbon dioxide easily so they should thrive. But some plants from warmer climates have slightly different photosynthesis and they can't use extra carbon dioxide so well. These plants include some of our most important crops such as maize and sugar cane, and they could be fighting for survival against much more aggressive weeds which can use the extra carbon dioxide, posing a big threat to farmers in the developing world.

## Weather and Health

Like the rest of the natural world, we too are affected by the weather, and it's no surprise that human physical and mental health changes with the weather.

It sounds like a very whacky idea – using the human body as a weather forecaster. Imagine telling atmospheric pressure, humidity, temperature, atmospheric electricity, changeable conditions just from the way you feel. Yet ever since ancient times human ailments have been used to predict weather, and now there is some scientific evidence that it really works.

Sufferers of rheumatism and arthritis are very often aware of a change in the weather. A change in atmospheric pressure before it rains makes swollen joints turn more painful as if they were behaving like barometers. And doctors now believe very sensitive pain receptors in the joints are triggered by the slight change in pressure. A recent study at Tel Aviv University showed that 83 per cent of osteoarthritis patients could foretell a change in the weather from the way their symptoms changed.

The most dramatic cases of human barometers occur on warm, dry days when a cold front moves in and the sky is filled with low clouds. Some people then turn from good to bad health in minutes. A few individuals develop heart irregularities, respiratory distress and in the most extreme cases suffer a seizure.

Another group of weather-sensitive people are those who have had damaged nerves by shingles or a stroke. Cold weather usually makes the pain worse, even when the individuals are inside a warm room.

Apart from changes in atmospheric pressure,

humidity also affects swollen joints, although it's not so clear why. Humidity can also bring on asthma attacks, although the most dramatic cases are on the approach of thunderstorms, when attacks can sometimes reach epidemic proportions. But whether this is because of the change in humidity or the intense atmospheric electricity is not clear. The humidity can trigger the release of countless microscopic fungal spores, and when these are breathed in by sufferers they can trigger an asthma attack. One hospital in Birmingham found in July 1983 a tenfold rise in asthma admissions following a thunderstorm, when large levels of fungal spores had been released.

Yet thunderstorms are known to trigger at least one other very common complaint – migraine attacks, and maybe there is a link between this and the asthma attacks.

Migraine can be triggered by heat, cold, rain, wind, thunder and lightning. Cold weather probably makes muscles tense and that can provoke headaches and migraine.

Thunderstorms can also provoke sheer terror in some sufferers. Thunder phobia takes many different forms: some people lock themselves in cupboards under the stairs, others freeze on the spot.

Weather complaints can reach life-threatening proportions. A recent study of elderly people living all day in well-heated homes showed that just a brief trip outdoors in freezing cold weather could be fatal. The cold weather thickens blood, narrows blood vessels and can lead to blood clots and this then creates the conditions for coronaries and strokes. Added to that are the deaths caused by hypothermia in the cold brought on by poor circulation problems. As if that wasn't bad enough, cold temperatures can also exacerbate pain, such as angina pain, by narrowing blood vessels.

Probably the commonest bodily weather forecasting is from the common cold. Being soaked in the rain and cold doesn't necessarily cause colds, although these conditions could depress the immune system and let viruses in more easily.

A three-year study at the Pennsylvania Health Department noted a significant rise in the number of suicides on days when the barometer dropped substantially. Similarly, studies of atmospheric pressure in Germany and Switzerland have shown how human reactions are slowed by falling pressure from an approaching storm. Tests on over a hundred thousand visitors to an exhibition in Germany in 1953 found that people took longer to respond to a light signal when the weather was bad. A survey of accidents in Munich found that work accidents in a factory almost doubled during bad weather, as well as workers complaining of poor health. Yet another survey in Munich found that of forty-three thousand road accidents, significantly more happened during bad weather. But of all the weather conditions, such as fog and frost, the steepest rise – of 40 per cent – happened on days of falling barometric pressure.

Whether these accidents were caused by low pressure *per se*, or something else linked with it isn't clear. There is some thought that atmospheric electricity also plays an important role in human behaviour. German research shows that road accidents rise by 70 per cent, deaths by 20 per cent and work accidents by 20 per cent during high atmospheric electricity.

Changes in atmospheric pressure might also directly trigger certain health problems. Cases of spontaneous pneumothorax – a rare condition that causes the lungs to collapse without warning – always happen in clusters. Evidence from casualty wards shows that collapsed lungs tend to happen just after a change in atmospheric pressure. Sudden changes in air pressure can rupture the surface of the lung like a balloon, and the lungs collapse.

But weather isn't all bad for health. Sunshine is an important part of our health because it makes vitamin D, essential for keeping calcium in balance to keep bones healthy. Women who spend ten minutes each day in the sun are less likely to suffer from hip fractures in old age because their bones are much stronger.

Less easy to measure is the effect of sunshine on mental wellbeing. The sun feels good because it helps better breathing and hot weather improves blood circulation. Sunbathing can lead to a fall in blood pressure and lower cholesterol. In fact, cholesterol tends to rise during winter and fall in summer, and in a large survey over a number of years, the largest fall in cholesterol was in 1984, which was a spectacularly sunny summer.

Illness brought on by weather is also rooted in pollution. The great London smogs of the 1950s killed thousands by creating fatal breathing attacks. Now urban smog is created by vehicle fumes, and cities such as Los Angeles and London are now issuing pollution warnings to alert asthmatics to the dangers of poor air quality.

And asthma isn't the only condition prey to urban smog. On 15 December 1994, the *Independent* newspaper reported an epidemic of a viral infection which left babies wheezing, brought on by mild weather and poor air quality. Hospitals in London, Manchester, Liverpool, Bristol and Cardiff were all inundated with babies suffering from bronchiolitis caused by a virus which normally peaks during the winter but is exacerbated by pollution.

## Solar Health

When Voltaire visited England he reported the cases of suicide he heard about:

> A famous court physician, to whom I confessed my surprise, told me that I was wrong to be astonished, that I should see many things in November and March, that then dozens of people hanged themselves, that nearly everybody was ill in those two seasons and that black melancholy spread over the whole nation, for it was then that the East Wind blew most constantly.

And those not committing suicide were depressed, and even animals were reputed to be in bad spirits.

Over recent years we've begun to realize that the weather and the Earth's magnetic field have some surprising effects on our mental and physical welfare. Investigations of over twenty-eight thousand daily admissions to several psychiatric hospitals found a trend towards escalation in the number of admissions during stormy days. Three Israeli scientists then discovered that the numbers of first admissions into a psychiatric unit were surprisingly well correlated with solar activity. Over a ten-year period they found that admissions tended to peak during magnetic disturbances in the ionosphere caused by the wind.

Another recent report in the journal *Bioelectromagnetics* (vol. 12, p. 67) found a relationship between visual hallucinations and magnetic solar activity. The solar flares during sunspot activity seemed to match the numbers of hallucinations. Interestingly enough, no cases were recorded in June and very few in December, the summer and winter solstices, respectively. These are times when the solar wind is most in alignment with the Earth's magnetic axis and has the least magnetic disturbance. In contrast, the spring and autumn equinoxes have most magnetic activity and highest number of hallucination cases.

A recent survey in the journal *Biometeorology* of acute psychiatric wards in Antwerp, Belgium, over three years found that bed occupancy peaked in March and November, with lows in August. The pattern was unmistakable for all three years and also matched admissions to the endocrine unit of the hospital. Another study showed that there were more hallucinations following bereavement during magnetic disturbances caused by the solar wind.

How might solar magnetism affect our mental health? Artificial magnetic fields as weak as natural fields affect the pineal gland just below the brain. This gland secretes the hormone melatonin which is implicated in diseases that involve hallucinations. And increases in solar activity are closely related to increased blood coagulability, higher incidence of coronary problems and higher blood pressure, and greater levels of growth hormone and prolactin secretions.

But it's not just mood that's affected by weather. Walter Randall at the University of Iowa discovered an astonishing link between human births and changes in the Earth's magnetism. What particularly interested him was the magnetism at the time of conception, and he found that the conception rate dips around the equinoxes in spring and autumn and peaks at the June and December solstices. A study in Chile showed the pattern is the same in the southern hemisphere. And then he took the work another amazing step further. He and Walter Moos found an eleven-year cycle in conceptions in America, Germany, England and Wales, Switzerland, Japan, Australia, and New Zealand. Over a fifty-four-year period, they all tied closely to the sunspot cycle and the related solar flares and magnetic disturbance on earth. We've got no idea what links this human behaviour to the outside world.

What we do know is that the Earth's magnetic field is sensitive to variations in the solar wind – the stream of electrically charged particles streaming out of the sun. For example, sudden 'gusts' in the solar wind cause 'magnetic storms' on Earth which send compasses in a spin and interrupt radio communication. As the orientation of the Earth in relation to the sun changes gradually with the seasons, so too does the angle at which the solar wind approaches us from space. This in turn causes a rhythmic variation throughout the year in the intensity of the Earth's magnetic field, a rhythm which is most noticeable in very high altitudes within the Arctic and Antarctic circles – as manifested in the vivid auroras of the polar regions. The magnetic index, as it is called, is high around the spring and autumn equinoxes and lowest at the June and December solstices.

# Gender and the Weather

According to William Lyster, a research biologist at the University of London Institute of Obstetrics and Gynaecology, there was a brief boom in boys born in August 1977 which was probably an after-effect of the great drought of 1975–6. He found that in several separate parts of Britain the average sex ratio for births in that month was extraordinary: 140 boys for every 100 girls. The normal ratio is 106 to 100.

Lyster believes that when a drought breaks there is a surge of accumulated trace elements into the drinking water supply. The unusually high concentration, he suggests, affects the formation of sperm. As sperm take about fifty days to mature, in addition to the normal nine-month pregnancy, this leads to a 320-day delay between the effect and its cause. In the case of the 1975–6 drought the starting date is the middle of September, two weeks after the rains started, because the huge drought in the soil at first prevented any large-scale run-off into rivers and reservoirs.

Another extraordinary upset in the genders followed the great London smog of December 1952. Lyster found the available records of a number of London hospitals yielded 109 male births compared to 144 female about 320 days afterwards.

Polluted air might also be the reason for the predominance of girls among the children of male anaesthetists discovered by other researchers. There are also indications that workers in PVC plants and foundries tend to be fathers of girls. How the polluting gases cause all these gender imbalances is not known.

## Ill Winds

There's an old English saying: 'When the wind is in the east, 'tis good for neither man nor beast.'

Whether you believe in folklore or not, this one's got a grain of truth in it. Wind has long been linked with bad things – teachers know that their classes are hell when the wind blows. Children become restless, badly behaved and, some would say, plain obnoxious. Studies of children in the playground of an American school showed that the number of fights doubled when the wind blew greater than force 6. Another piece of research revealed that half of all heart attacks and strokes occurred during wind speeds at force 4 or 5.

Studies of Israel's sharav wind revealed that almost one third of the population suffers some sort of complaint from the wind, ranging from headaches to insomnia. This has been linked to a rise in the concentration of a nerve-transmitter, serotonin, which helps control mood, sleep and blood circulation. The same rise in serotonin was found in the Swiss population during the Föhn. This wind is responsible for traffic accidents rising by a half in Geneva. Human reaction time is affected. According to the Touring Club Suisse, traffic accidents in Geneva in 1972 rose by over 50 per cent when Föhn conditions prevailed. In 1976, the medical department of the West German Weather Station in Freiburg published the results of a four-year study proving that industrial accidents during a Föhn required surgery 16 per cent more often, and other medical treatment 20 per cent more frequently. Deaths from post-operative complications such as heavy bleeding and thrombosis rise so high that some

Swiss and German hospitals try to postpone major surgery until the wind passes.

Los Angeles is occasionally buffeted by the Santa Ana, a hot, dry wind named after the canyon it sometimes blows through. Santa Anas occur when air rushes down from the high inland plateaus and is heated by compression by as much as 5 degrees Fahrenheit (3 degrees Celsius) for every 1000 feet (300 metres) of descent. The natives become noticeably restless during a Santa Ana, as the mystery-story writer Raymond Chandler once wrote: 'Meek little wives feel the edge of the carving knife and study their husbands' necks.' Indeed, one study found that murders rose by up to a half during Santa Anas, no matter if it blew during winter or summer.

The FBI recognizes a 'long hot summer' phenomenon, expecting more murder, aggravated assault and rape between June and September than at any other time. But the Santa Ana seems to supersede this annual cycle, producing short-term local effects whenever it blows, winter or summer. In California's early days, defendants in crimes of passion were able to plead for leniency, citing the wind as an extenuating circumstance.

In 1968, Willis Miller of California Western University collected statistics for homicides in Los Angeles county and compared them with weather records. When the Santa Ana wind blew in 1964 and 1965 there were 64 per cent more deaths than normal.

What in the wind causes these calamities is another matter. It could be the change in air pressure, or humidity, but one idea is the electricity in the air changes its nature. Air normally contains negative ions, but dry winds tend to collect positive ions, mostly oxygen. Air normally contains both sorts of ions but one usually predominates. During a thunderstorm the air is rich in positive ions creating illness, whereas negative ions are created near waterfalls and high mountains and they're even created in domestic showers. But probably the easiest place to get negative ions is by the seaside, where the invigorating air was prized by the Victorians for its healthy properties. Negative ions tend to be in short supply in urban areas, and particularly in dull smoggy conditions. Positive ions are thought to affect adversely the way we feel, producing irritability and anxiety as well as nausea and headaches in about a third of the population who are susceptible to the ions. But negative ions counteract these unpleasant effects.

The charged oxygen affects breathing quite badly, putting the body under stress. And that stress might be the cause of much of the ills.

Studies have shown that an excess of positive ions can trigger the production of serotonin – a nerve-transmitter hormone. High levels of serotonin are linked with migraine and nausea.

In 1991 an outbreak of weather sensitive ailments broke out in America, and could have been because that year was a peak year for sunspots. It's possible that the sunspot activity affects ions in the Earth's atmosphere which disturbs certain people.

## The Economy

Weather has an enormous impact on the economy. With a good forecast, businesses can plan for the weather ahead, and in some industries it's absolutely crucial information. For offshore oil and gas drilling a good forecast is vital for towing rigs out to sea. But other businesses closer to home use forecasting for a wide range of uses.

One ice-cream company reckons that for every degree rise in temperature during the summer, their sales go up 10 per cent. It's with that phenomenal power of weather over commerce that the Met. Office set up a special forecasting bureau for industry. Sales of ice-cream, soft drinks, salad vegetables and summer clothing are just a few cases affected by the weather business. Soft drink sales really take off when temperatures rise above 59 degrees Fahrenheit (15 degrees Celsius) and lager sales soar around 73 degrees Fahrenheit (23 degrees Celsius), for example. But there are also some bizarre insights into the British psyche, especially through sandwich sales. For instance, beef sandwiches go up in cold weather whereas roast chicken takes off when it gets warmer. Hot weather is also good for sausages (perhaps for barbecues) and ready-made meals such as pizza which don't need much work in the kitchen on a sunny day.

Which is why Marks and Spencers, amongst many others, subscribe to the Met. Office service. By paying attention to the weather forecast they can place orders to their sandwich factories for the next day. And they can also help pinpoint seasonal trends, like when there is an instantaneous switch to summer eating after the first weekend of good weather in the year. This is when a large chunk of the nation migrates to their gardens and starts eating barbecues and salads. But strangely, the transformation to winter eating is much more gradual during the autumn.

The temperature range can sometimes be crucial. At

precisely 68 degrees Fahrenheit (20 degrees Celsius), motorway service areas sell 70 per cent fewer hot meals. Clearly, some sort of universal human thermostat diverts the motoring public's eating habits. And the losses can be significant: one motorway catering company lost £70,000 a day in wasted hot meals when the temperature rose above the 68 degrees Fahrenheit (20 degrees Celsius) threshold.

In another case, an antifreeze manufacturer saved £250,000 by pitching its annual marketing and delivery according to weather forecasts instead of the fixed dates traditionally used every year.

But there are even weirder anomalies. The warmer the weather the less bread we buy, except for rolls. Coffee sales at first sight seem to be steady throughout the year, but during rainy periods we drink more coffee and during sunny spells drink more tea. So an awful lot can rest on weather forecasting. Small wonder the Met. Office reckons that hundreds of millions of pounds are wasted in the economy every year because the weather isn't planned for.

## Weather Forecasters

Proper, scientific forecasting began in ancient Greece. The great philosophers Plato and Aristotle were among the first to suggest that weather could be studied in a rational, scientific way. With the Renaissance the world's oceans opened up to trade, so ships had to have advance warning of storms at sea – and they started taking measurements from scientific instruments. Galileo made the first thermometer in the 1600s and some forty years later, his student, Torricelli, built the first practical barometer for measuring atmospheric pressure.

Yet ships were still being lost at sea through bad weather and forecasting took another giant leap forward in the early 1800s when meteorologists came up with the idea of comparing weather conditions observed simultaneously over a very wide area – the 'synoptic' approach. They're the forerunners of the charts we use today. These also provide some of our first weather records. The first meteorological office was set up in 1854 with forty weather stations dotted around the British Isles, taking simultaneous readings to give storm warnings. The mariners were pleased with the results, but weather forecasting became so ridiculed that the first head of the Met. Office, Admiral Robert Fitzroy, eventually committed suicide.

The mathematics of modern forecasting was inspired by Lewis Fry Richardson, a man ahead of his time. In 1922 he described a mathematical technique for forecasting the next day's weather. The snag was that Richardson reckoned on needing an army of sixty-four thousand mathematicians to help solve the formulae in time for the forecasts.

The Second World War was a crucial time for weather forecasting. The German invasion of Russia depended entirely on mild weather but the long-range weather forecast was disastrous. Even though the Germans were well aware of the severity of the Russian winter, they relied entirely on the advice of their weather service led by Franz Baur. He had predicted a mild winter based on statistical probability – the previous two winters had been so severe that he calculated that the chances of a third successive bad winter were too remote to worry about. But the winter of 1941–2 broke all records for the intense cold, plunging to –40 degrees Fahrenheit (–40 degrees Celsius). As we saw in an earlier section, the cold decimated the German attack. Yet even in the face of catastrophic troop losses, Baur still remained adamant that his forecast was accurate.

That statistical approach to weather forecasting almost cost the Allies a disastrous invasion of occupied France on D-Day in June 1944. The invasion plans hinged on the weather but June 1944 was one of the most appalling summers on record with storms whipping the English Channel into a frenzy. But what isn't widely appreciated was the clash between the British and American weather forecasters on whose advice the invasion plans hinged.

Basically, the Americans reckoned they could forecast six days ahead by looking back at past records of similar weather conditions for the Channel, based on statistics. But the Channel storms of June 1944 had few good historical parallels and the Americans played a dangerous guessing game.

The British forecasters, on the other hand, played a lot safer by measuring the weather and calculating from their knowledge of physics what would happen next. But they could only forecast twenty-four hours ahead, and even that was a struggle.

The rift between the American and British forecasters was split wide open by Supreme Headquarters pressing for forecasts up to a week ahead, and especially as the original D-Day planned for 5 June drew near. It rested on meteorologist Group Captain Stagg assigned to Supreme Headquarters to reach a decision.

The American and British forecasts were completely different. The Americans forecast good weather but the British, on the other hand, predicted strong winds and low cloud in the Channel.

In fact, the Channel grew increasingly stormy. At a conference with General Eisenhower and his staff at 4.15a.m. on 4 June, Stagg forecast continued storms and Eisenhower postponed the invasion for twenty-four hours in spite of the enormous logistical problems involved.

But later at 9.30p.m. on 4 June, the British forecasters predicted a gap in the storm fronts as one low was replaced by another racing in from the Atlantic. Eisenhower was persuaded and the invasion was launched on Tuesday 6 June.

And indeed the forecast came true, even though conditions were just on the margins of acceptability. The American beaches Omaha and Utah suffered high gusting winds which scattered the air landings of thirteen thousand paratroops. Wind and waves at Omaha sunk much of the invasion equipment and sent the naval bombardment off target.

As for the Germans, their forecasters completely failed to spot any break in the weather until it actually happened. They too relied heavily on long-range forecasts using historical records, although their twenty-four-hour forecasts were also hampered by lack of information in the Atlantic. As a result, their air reconnaissance and E-boat patrols were cancelled and most senior officers left for wargames in Brittany. So the poor weather had given the Allies perfect cover for the invasion.

The successful British forecast was a major feat at a time when weather predicting was still in its infancy.

Interestingly enough, American forecasters in 1979 re-ran the data from June 1944 through a computer and got much the same results as Stagg's analysis. If the invasion had been postponed again it would probably have been until 19 June when the tides were favourable again. But the weather that day brought the most pro-longed Channel storm in summer for decades. Had the actual D-Day assault been rearranged for then it would have been a catastrophe.

The lessons of the D-Day forecasters haven't been lost. Forecasting has continued to rely on weather mea-surements and the idea of looking at past weather records for clues has been ditched.

## Train Crashes and Weather

The worst railway accident in Britain was caused by the weather. On Sunday, 28 December 1879, a ferocious storm blew across Scotland with winds estimated to be gusting over 80 miles per hour (129 kilometres per hour) and heavy rains bringing flooding to many areas. The gale was howling through Dundee, with chimney pots falling and smashing into streets. On the nearby River Tay, the wind was whipping the water into a swirling white spray and slamming into the new railway bridge spanning the river. This was the Tay Bridge, connecting Dundee to Edinburgh, and was a marvel of its day, car-rying two railway tracks across seventy-four spans made of wrought iron supported on masonry pillars. On its opening it was hailed as a major engineering achievement, and attracted a visit from Queen Victoria.

But only eighteen months later, the storm took a terrible toll on it. As the 7.13p.m. train from Burntisland to Dundee crossed the bridge, the wrought iron middle girders gave way, the bridge collapsed, and the train plunged into the River Tay. Astonished eyewitnesses saw sparks showering out from the engine, presumably as its brakes were slammed on. Only two hours later the storm subsided enough for a steam boat to search for survivors, but none were found. All seventy-five people aboard the train were drowned, and in the calm the following day the first bodies were brought ashore.

The board of inquiry set up in the aftermath concluded that the bridge failed through poor engineering. It had been badly designed, built and maintained, and led to the wrought iron bracing failing. From that disaster, engineering standards were greatly improved, but much more attention was also paid to measuring wind speeds more accurately and taking the strength of wind more closely into account in the design of large structures such as bridges.

But recently the engineer blamed for the Tay Bridge collapse has been redeemed. Sir Thomas Bouch was used as a scapegoat by the Board of Trade inquiry, according to a recent analysis by Professor Swinfen at Dundee University. He concludes that winds gusting up to 100 miles per hour (160 kilometres per hour) were to blame rather than any design or building fault. 'Even if the bridge had been perfectly constructed, it could not have survived that gale,' Professor Swinfen suggests.

One of the strangest railway accidents in Britain took place on 30 October 1863. At about 3.30p.m. the engine shed of the London, Brighton and South Coast railway at New Cross in south London was struck by a blast of wind, possibly a tornado. The doors were open at the time and the wind was unable to escape so it lifted up the roof and blasted open the walls. The resulting debris blocked the shed and the adjoining railway line. Seven locomotives were damaged, one of them derailed, and one man killed. The survivors were dug out of the rubble.

A tornado definitely struck a tragic blow at Reading railway station on 24 March 1840. The station was nearing completion before the start of a new train service between Reading and London, and the steam engine *Firefly* was under time trials nearby. A storm suddenly blew up and with it a tornado struck along the railway line, blasting ballast in all directions, some of it shattering windows in nearby houses. Then it hit the locomotive, weighing 40 tons, and derailed it. One of the men making the timings on the engine's speed was picked up and flung against the bank, coal from the loco was flung in all directions and broke the collarbone of another timekeeper. The tornado approached the station with a scream and a roar and then ripped up the whole station roof weighing some 4 tons, including one unfortunate carpenter who was working on the roof at the time. His body was found 100 yards (90 metres) away buried in debris.

On 27 May 1931 a tornado struck the *Empire Builder* express train travelling at 60 miles per hour (97 kilometres per hour) near Moorhead, Minnesota. The tornado picked up five coaches, weighing about 70 tons each, off the rails. One coach was lifted and carried 80 feet (24 metres) and dropped in a ditch. Fifty-seven passengers were injured.

In 1975, a commuter train from Epsom Downs, Surrey, hit an empty train which was going into sidings

near London Bridge Station and left sixty-one people
injured. The empty train went through a danger signal
because the green 'go' signal appeared to be lit. This
was caused by the alignment of the line, reflecting the
sun's rays from the surface of the locomotive waiting at
the signal. The crash occurred on a busy stretch of line
controlled by one of Britain's most sophisticated signal
boxes. The public inquiry into the crash completely
exonerated the driver and concluded that reflected sunshine on a signal was to blame for the crash.

Snow has also been a problem for British railways.
Large parts of the rail system were brought to a halt in
February 1991 when powdery snow was blamed for
blocking locomotive diesel engines. Despite using high-
tech snowploughs, the trains were unable to run and
much of the rail network was suspended.

But this hardly compares to the hell endured on 9
March 1891, when the West Country Express left
Paddington station in London. At 3p.m. it was speeding
through the outskirts of London when an intense blizzard blew up and trapped the train in huge snowdrifts.
The train eventually arrived in Plymouth four days
later – on Friday, 13 March.

## Crime and Weather

There is increasing evidence that weather has an effect
on crime, and that heat and humidity in particular lead
to rises in rape, theft, murder and burglary. This is
partly to do with the vacation time during the hot

months of summer, particularly August. It may also be no coincidence that many riots happen during summer. The 1967 riots in the United States were sparked off in the hot humid nights of Tampa, Florida, and there was shooting and rioting in Cincinnati. The riots then spread through many other US cities. The rioting in Detroit was the worst in American history with 39 dead, 1500 injured and 3500 arrested.

On the other hand, crime during winter falls off, particularly in January, which is hardly surprising as this tends to be one of the coldest months of the year in the northern hemisphere.

As we saw in Ill Winds, crime is also affected by winds, which trigger a host of violent crimes.

## Crime and the Boys from the Met.

Apart from the effects of weather on the crime rate, the weather is also playing a crucial role at the other end of the criminal process: in prosecution cases. In the forefront of the legal side of weather are the Boys from the Met. – not Scotland Yard but the British Meteorological Office at Bracknell. With a special Forensic Department of ten highly trained forecasters it is proving so popular that up to two hundred legal clients a month are using it, at a minimum charge of £140.

The Met. Office can proudly point to some impressive cases which have turned on their evidence. One of their reports resulted in the acquittal of a man charged with an act of indecency. The alleged incident took place outdoors, but the meteorologists showed the weather was freezing cold that night. In fact it was so cold that it was claimed that human physiology being what it is, the accused man could not have performed the act he was charged with.

Another case was a man accused of soliciting in a public convenience. His defence was that he was sheltering from heavy rain, which the police adamantly denied. But the weather report showed that it was in fact raining heavily at the time. The man was acquitted.

Pathologists have used weather reports to try and determine the time of death of a body, particularly outdoors where the rates of decomposition can often depend on weather conditions. One case involving a corpse in the River Cam narrowed down the time of death to within two likely days using weather reports. As a result several murder suspects were eliminated. Another stunning success for the Boys from Bracknell.

# THE HISTORY
## OF CLIMATE

For the past million years the world's climate has yo-yo'd between warm periods and freezing cold ice ages. The fortunes of empires often have rested on the vagaries of climate. It's important we understand these natural cycles, so we can try and entangle what's happening to our climate now, and what it promises for the future, as we'll see in the next section.

## THE ICE AGES

The cold periods we have known in recorded history are nothing compared to the Ice Ages. Half the world was covered in snow and ice from sixty thousand to ten thousand years ago. Vast sheets of ice a mile thick crushed Canada and the northern part of the United States, northern Europe and northern Asia during the last great Ice Age. Mountains were torn to shreds and all life was annihilated underneath. The weight of ice was so great it pushed continental land-masses down into the Earth's mantle. To give an idea how massive that force was, even now ten thousand years afterwards the crust is still rising in places like Scandinavia and northern Britain where the ice had previously pressed down.

Global temperatures were about 18 degrees

Fahrenheit (10 degrees Celsius) cooler than today's, pushing our familiar climate zones down towards the equator. South of the ice-sheets was a tundra of treeless marshy plains, extending down to southern France. The southern United States was covered in the sort of conifer forests we now see in Canada. And the Mediterranean climate was shifted down into North Africa.

### POST-GLACIAL

The climate grew very warm after the last Ice Age. In fact, it was a degree or two warmer than today, heralding the warmest climate of the past eighty thousand years. And the consequences were dramatic. The icecaps melting at the poles spilled vast pools of fresh water into the oceans, and world sea levels rose rapidly up to 51 feet (37 metres) higher. The rising seas cut off Russia from North America, Britain from the Continent, Ireland from Britain, changing the face of the world.

Ancient civilizations in the Far East, Middle East, and Latin America flourished. Agriculture and cattle rearing date back to 9000BC, and civilizations developed in the valleys and flood plains with irrigation. Communities lived in the Sahara and other areas that are now deserts, and elephants, giraffes, lions and hippos roamed the Nile valley. Birch, oak and beech trees covered much of Britain and prehistoric communities generally flourished about 4000BC, rearing sheep and growing crops.

## WARM PERIOD: THE LITTLE OPTIMUM

Between AD900–1300 the world basked in temperatures about a degree warmer than today's. The Vikings conquered Greenland in the ninth and tenth centuries during this warm period, when the Arctic ice-sheets were retreating and the land really did look green – hence the name Greenland. The Viking colony grew for two centuries until the climate deteriorated during the thirteenth and fourteenth centuries.

Farming on the uplands of England rose 450 feet (140 metres) higher up the hillsides than today's climate allows and Scotland became self-sufficient in food. Throughout Europe the booming harvests lent the financial muscle to the great wave of cathedral building that typified the period.

## MEDIEVAL COLD

Cold wet weather began creeping in again in the thirteenth century, as glaciers advanced, winters grew colder, rainfall increased, and summers were shorter. The growing season became so short that much of the land could no longer be farmed. Starvation set in and the population fell.

Then the temperatures dropped even further and the Norse colonists in Greenland were wiped out because they failed to adapt to the colder weather. They were also cut off by icebergs at sea from their friends in Iceland. We know this from remains found of the colony in Greenland, and also recently from dental research. Tooth enamel traps isotopes of oxygen which indicate the local temperature at the time, and corroborates the archaeological evidence. When the climate briefly warmed in the sixteenth century, European ships returning to Greenland found no living sign of the Norse people, only the deserted ruins of their buildings. The colony had been totally wiped out, and only the Inuit (Eskimos) survived because they were well-adapted to living in the cold.

At the same time that the Greenland colony was being wiped out, the entire population of Iceland was facing its own crisis. The Icelandic sheep could no longer forage and died, destroying a lucrative wool export trade. The temperatures dipped to a low around 1750, and snowfall was common up to June and even in August. Even fishing became extremely difficult because the coast remained locked in ice except for a few weeks of the summer. In fact, it was possible to walk from Greenland to Iceland across the pack ice of the Denmark Strait separating the two islands. We know this because occasional polar bears arrived in Iceland. The population was almost annihilated, falling to about fifty thousand, and the situation became so serious that the ruling Danish authorities considered evacuating the survivors. The nation's fortunes only revived in the nineteenth century when the climate warmed.

On the Continent, glaciers like the Grindelwald glacier were recorded advancing forward from AD1280. In some places the glaciers swallowed up fields, or blocked valleys and formed lakes, and there are records of these lakes suddenly breaking after heavy rains and causing devastating floods.

As for Britain, these were tragic times too. More people died from the cold and wet in the fourteenth century than perished in the Plague (the Black Death of 1348–50) that followed soon afterwards. We know this from parish records and tax records; the population fell to a third from 1300 to 1327 and then the Plague further decimated the numbers. Long, harsh winters, late springtimes, poor wet summers produced a succession of poor harvests. Epidemics of ergot food poisoning brought on by the poor weather devastated the peasant communities. Many villages in upland areas were abandoned such as Wharram Piercy in the Yorkshire Wolds which was settled during the warm spell after the Norman Conquest, but deserted when the climate deteriorated about 1420. But even in the fertile lands of East Anglia, half of the hundred villages recorded there in the Domesday Book of 1086 were abandoned by the time they were hit by plague. Elsewhere, boglands grew in the cold, wet climate and forced many populations out of valley bottoms, which were becoming increasingly flooded, to drier land. Maybe half the population of Britain was wiped out in the appalling climate.

Across Europe, the catastrophic famines brought on by the poor climate followed by the Black Death forced mass migration southwards. From 1315 to 1360 and from 1400 to 1485 many villages were abandoned in one of the greatest periods of human migration in history.

### LITTLE ICE AGE

Following the medieval cold of the 1400s the weather seemed to oscillate wildly. There were some very warm summers and some appallingly wet ones producing floods and failed harvests. The early 1500s were generally warm, but around the middle of the century the so-called Little Ice Age set in – another bitterly cold epoch.

In America, the pioneer settlers faced severe winters and in Europe the glaciers of the Alps and Scandinavia advanced. In the worst winter, ice blocked the harbour of Marseilles for many weeks, the canals in Venice froze over several times, the Tiber River in Italy and Ebro in Spain were frozen and the Swedish armies crossed the Baltic Sea into Germany in 1632 during the Thirty Years' War. Droughts struck in North Africa.

The coldest year of the Little Ice Age was probably 1607–8, known as 'The Great Winter' in Britain. Trees were split open by frost, livestock died of cold and in Scotland ships were trapped by ice floes off the coast of Fife and Edinburgh, and people walked out on the frozen sea to the trapped ships in the Firth of Forth. Starvation was widespread.

The period 1550 to 1750 was the coldest this millennium, although the climate wildly fluctuated and the mid-1660s were so warm drought struck in the summer. An outbreak of plague in 1665 might have been encouraged by the hot weather, and the tinder dry conditions of 1666 helped fan the flames of the Great Fire of London which destroyed thirteen thousand buildings. Nevertheless, the winters were so often bitterly cold that Queen Elizabeth I led her court across the frozen Thames in the winter of 1665. Ice-skating was introduced in 1662.

The Thames froze so deeply that 'frost fairs' were held on the ice. Perhaps the most elaborate of all of them took place in the particularly severe winter of 1683–4. The freezing conditions lasted from early December 1683 to 5 February 1684, and towards the end of January the diarist John Evelyn noted:

The Thames before London is still planted with

*Frost fairs were held on the frozen Thames during the Little Ice Age two hundred years ago.*

booths in formal streets, and with all sorts of trades and shops furnished and full of commodities of all kinds.

Coaches ply to and fro as if in the streets, and there is sliding, bull-baiting, horse and coach races, puppet-plays and other interludes, tippling and other lewd entertainments – so that it all seems to be a bacchanalian triumph, or a carnival upon the water.

Many coastal inlets along the coast were also frozen and ice floated down the English Channel and many wild creatures and farm animals died from the cold that winter.

In all there were ten winters in the seventeenth century when the Thames froze solid, and another ten in the following hundred years or so. The last frost fair was in January 1814, lasting a few weeks.

In Scotland, the Little Ice Age bit even deeper. The cold led to widespread crop failures and famines and in turn spurred mass migration from Scotland. Permanent snow cover grew in the highlands and it was so cold that the ice at one time stretched from Iceland to the Faroe Islands, just 200 miles (320 kilometres) north of the Shetlands; Eskimos visited Scotland and even a polar bear floated there on an ice floe. The dismal climate devastated a succession of harvests, beginning in the 1590s. The climate grew worse in the 1600s until eventually a large part of the population died of starvation. These desperate times started the mass emigration of the Scottish Protestants to Ulster, where James VI evicted the native Irish population from their lands, eventually leading to the Irish troubles of the twentieth century. The ultimate collapse of the Scottish economy eventually led to the Union with England in 1707.

TWENTIETH CENTURY

The four coldest winters in Britain this century were 1962–3 (coldest) then 1947, 1940 and 1917. The winter of 1947 was one of the most punishing cold spells in recent history. The nation's economy was already weakened by the severe post-war rationing of essentials such as food and fuel. The cold lasted seven weeks, and although it wasn't as cold as the 1962–3 winter it caused far more economic damage. It started on 23 January and the country was blanketed in snow until well into March. On 20 February the Dover to Ostend ferry service was suspended because of pack-ice off the Belgian coast.

On 5 February coal transport into London and the south-east ceased. Coal stocks ran so low power rationing was started. Electricity restrictions were introduced in early February with domestic supplies cut off for up to five hours a day. The economy nose-dived, production fell by 25 per cent, exports fell by £200 million, and workers were laid off, which pushed unemployment up to 2 million for a short time. Farming was decimated, with the loss of 4 million of the country's sheep – 20 per cent of the population – followed by a disastrous harvest the next summer because of flooding and rain after the snows melted. The Labour government was forced to make savage cuts in spending, leading to the devaluation of sterling the following year. Many now feel that the winter of 1947 was the turning point which led to a Tory victory at the next general election.

The prolonged winter of 1962–3 was the coldest in England since 1795. In some places snow lay on the ground from Boxing Day until the following April. The impact of the winter was less dramatic than in 1947 because the economy and energy supplies were in better shape. But economic activity still dropped by about 7 per cent and unemployment increased with 160,000 workers laid off. At least forty-nine people were also killed by the direct effects of the severe weather.

# THE FUTURE: FREEZE, FRY OR FLOOD?

What is happening to the weather? From one year to another our weather records are being broken: drought, heatwaves, storms, cold winters, wet summers. The warnings are that we're heading for an apocalyptic global warming, known as the greenhouse effect. Yet not so long ago the alarm was that we were plunging into another ice age sparked by a series of bitter winters in the 1970s. What are we to make of it all?

It's been ten thousand years since the last ice age ended, and as warm periods go this present one has been quite long – but how much longer will it last? Given the history of past ice ages we can expect the next one in thousands or tens of thousands of years' time, but there is one outstanding factor which might prevent it – man-made pollution.

## Ice Ages

It wasn't that long ago that the newspaper headlines were predicting that the next ice age was upon us. Temperatures were actually dropping between 1940 and 1970, and in the bitterly cold, long winter of 1962–3

those fears looked realistic. It looked like the polar ice-caps were growing, and could suddenly flip the global climate into freezing cold.

Because it is such a brilliant white, snow reflects 90 per cent of the sun's light. Without this light there's little heat, which helps keep the world's poles cold. At their peak the ice sheets in the Arctic, Greenland, Siberia, northern Canada and Antarctic cover nearly a quarter of the Earth's surface. These vast icecaps behave like massive freezers, keeping the whole planet from overheating. But it's a very tricky balancing act, because if the snow cover grows too large it can reflect too much warmth and send the whole world into another ice age. Even a small cooling would have disastrous consequences.

## The Greenhouse

Perhaps the only thing saving us from freezing up again is the man-made pollution believed to be keeping the planet warm. Put simply, the Earth is getting warmer because we've polluted it with gases that trap heat. It's called the greenhouse effect because the pollution behaves like the glass in a greenhouse, letting the sun's heat in but stopping it from escaping. What this means in practice is that the Earth gets warmer.

It doesn't sound much to say that the world might heat up an extra 7 degrees Fahrenheit (4 degrees Celsius), but that extra warmth is enough to melt substantial chunks of the polar ice sheets, pushing the levels

*Global warming. The shrinkage of the Rhône Glacier between 1750 and 1860.*

of the world's oceans higher, triggering ecological catastrophe and leading to starvation and civil strife. These
are seen as the inevitable consequences of the greenhouse effect.

If anyone is in any doubt that warmer climates
haven't already arrived in the mountains, take a look at
the melting glaciers in Europe. Records going back over
a century show that glaciers from the Pyrenees to the
Alps are beating a hasty retreat. Warm winters are
already creating more avalanches as well as shorter ski
seasons on average. In February 1995 an iceberg the size
of Oxfordshire broke off the Antarctic ice sheet and the
following month the continent's 600 mile (960 kilometre) long Larsen northern ice shelf was cracking.

Unfortunately, the climate is so complicated it's very
difficult to be sure if the Earth is getting warmer
because of the greenhouse effect or something else.

What we can say for sure is that 1989, 1990, 1991 and
1994 were the warmest four years in the 140-year history of world weather records. The 1980s were already
the warmest decade on record. The average climate of
the world has been getting steadily warmer for the past
eighty years. The past decade has been exceptionally
warm (the seven warmest years since 1860 have
occurred between 1980 and 1991 and the two warmest
were 1990 and 1991). As a result glaciers and ice caps
are melting and that's making the level of the seas rise.

But that's all we're safe to say for certain. Scientists
disagree on how much, when and how the Earth will
warm. Part of the problem is that so many other factors
are involved as well. For instance, the dirty sulphur that
gets belched out from many power stations could by a
strange twist of fate be saving us from the greenhouse
warming. Each microscopic particle of sulphur floating

in the air helps to block out sunshine and keeps us cool!

But if the greenhouse effect wins out what will its effect be? One way that scientists are trying to predict what will happen is by looking back at ancient history to find patterns that could be applied to the future. By collecting fossils and ancient pollen from 3 million years ago, they have found that the earth was 3 to 4 degrees warmer than now, with forests growing as far north as the Arctic coast of Greenland, and the warmer seas reaching up to 115 feet (35 metres) above current levels.

How does that compare to today? Sea level is already rising 0.08 inches (2 millimetres) a year, and at the same time southern England is tilting downwards at about 0.16 inches (4 millimetres) a year. The sea level might eventually rise 8–55 inches (20–140 centimetres), easily topping our sea defences and seriously flooding low-lying coastal areas, deltas, estuaries and river systems. Insurance companies are reassessing the risk of coastal flooding because of climate changes and may charge extra premiums to thousands of businesses with factories and offices less than 16 feet (5 metres) above sea level. Vast areas of East Anglia and sizeable chunks elsewhere in Britain fall below that line, some of them 30 miles (48 kilometres) inland from existing sea defences. Farming has made the situation far worse. Draining the fens, for example, has caused the land to shrink 6–10 feet (2–3 metres).

The greenhouse effect could be very good for some plants. Extra carbon dioxide stimulates plant growth by boosting their photosynthesis by which they make their food, and also helps to cut down their water demands. So plants of the greenhouse world will grow more rapidly with less watering. The warmer nights will also lengthen the growing season.

Unfortunately, not all the benefits of the greenhouse will produce better crop yields. Weeds will also benefit from the extra carbon dioxide, whilst not all crop plants can use the extra carbon dioxide. And then the warmer temperatures might lead to an explosion in crop diseases and bugs, just as the mild winter of 1988–9 brought on a plague of greenfly and their accompanying virus diseases the following spring. So we have to be careful before rushing to conclusions that the greenhouse could be good for crops.

The story for wild plants will be even more bewildering. Natural plants have adapted to their environments over hundreds, thousands or millions of years. The sudden lurch into warmer climates could have catastrophic effects on delicate flora like alpine plants which could be pushed into extinction.

What will life be like in Britain? Some say the summers might be as hot and dry as those in the south of France within twenty years, but others disagree and say there will be no noticeable change, or else we will have extreme fluctuations in local climate.

Our climate is already becoming very erratic. The heatwave of 1976 has parallels in the first half of the eighteenth century during the Little Ice Age. Wild fluctuations were a feature of the Little Ice Age, both at the beginning of that period when temperatures fell and at the end of the period when temperatures recovered again, with periods of great heat interspersed with record cold spells.

Alongside all these uncertainties one of the most alarming prospects is a sudden and catastrophic change which could turn all the predictions upside-down. The big nightmare is what might happen to the ocean currents. Many parts of the world depend on the quirks of ocean currents for their climate: Britain and the rest of north-west Europe get generally milder winters because of the enormous amount of heat released by the Gulf Stream. It behaves like a central heating system – its boiler is at the equator where the tropical seas absorb energy from the sun, equivalent to 20 million nuclear power plants. Then as it sweeps up into the North Atlantic it gives up the heat like a massive radiator, and keeps the British Isles 10 degrees Fahrenheit (6 degrees Celsius) warmer than the latitude should allow. The fear is that a gigantic thaw of ice from the Arctic will release so much fresh water into the North Atlantic it will knock the Gulf Stream off course, and that, ironically, would make north-west Europe much colder in the winter.

Less well known is the 'Atlantic conveyor': every winter at about the latitude of Iceland, relatively salty water rises as winds sweep the surface. Exposed to the cool air, the water releases heat and then sinks to the bottom again. The heat given off is equal to 30 per cent of the yearly input of the sun's energy to the North Atlantic. Studies of the last ice age suggest that this current may be particularly vulnerable to small changes in salinity and temperature. Like the Gulf Stream, if the current failed we could end up substantially cooler instead of warmer. What a paradox!

If Britain carries on getting warmer it will affect the economy. The millions of Brits flying off to the Mediterranean sun might be reversed and spend more time and money in the UK. And when you consider that the UK tourist industry is already a larger employer than the NHS the economy could take a big boost.

In fact, tourism is the biggest moneyspinner in

Scotland where up to 15 million tourists a year visit, so any improvement to the climate could be an enormous benefit. But warmer winters could conceivably melt the Scottish ski resorts into obliteration. There's a real fear that within thirty years global warming could also melt some of the world's other marginal ski resorts, from Canada to Australia.

## Floods

Floods are the single biggest natural disaster threat to humans. [See Floods.] Of all natural disasters, floods claim 40 per cent of lives lost. They cost about $16 billion a year in damage, and the likelihood is they'll get worse as some 750 million people in the world live close to coasts and rivers.

Another alarming prospect is that sea levels are rising with global warming. That's no idle speculation; the Government's own Policy Committee on Climate estimated that by 2030 levels will rise 7 inches (18 centimetres) and 17 inches (44 centimetres) by 2070.

The biggest fear is a repetition of the 1953 flood, when three hundred people were killed in England, and more than 1800 on continental Europe. On 1 February 1953 a high spring tide whipped up by a storm across the North Sea burst the Dutch sea defences, drowning 1835 people, leaving 300,000 homeless and flooding a tenth of the country's surface area.

The risk of a 1953 flood surge has shortened considerably, from a 1 in 150 year chance in 1953 to a 1 in 35 year chance now. Estimates are that a similar sized flood would kill at least ten times more people in England. Already reeling from gargantuan storm damages across the world, insurers are hiking up their premiums to low-lying areas. Britain is indeed heading for stormy waters.

It's not just London at risk. Floods will threaten 500 million people worldwide, but particularly in places like Alexandria, Shanghai, Bangkok, Hong Kong, Tokyo, Rio de Janeiro, New Orleans, Leningrad, Hamburg, Venice and London. These are the cities most vulnerable to flood, partly because they are all built by the sea or on river estuaries. The effects of global warming are often being worsened by subsidence caused by draining underground water supplies. Bangkok and Shanghai could be facing sea level rises 6 feet (1.8 metres) higher in a hundred years' time. In Hong Kong the land reclaimed from the sea would be most at risk, while the whole of Alexandria could theoretically disappear. And as for Bangladesh, the World Bank estimates that defending it from floods could cost at least $10 billion over twenty years, and even then there are considerable doubts whether engineering could do much good.

Trying to defend against floods by engineering often causes more problems than it solves, and the experience of New Orleans serves a useful lesson. For fifty years engineers have been trying to make the Mississippi safe from flooding by building a massive system of embankments, reservoirs, floodgates and channels. Unfortunately the net result has been an ecological disaster and may ironically make flooding worse. As a result of the engineering, some 40 square miles (104 square kilometres) of salt marsh in the delta sinks into the sea each year. Unfortunately, marshes are probably the best defence against floods, yet in forty years' time the coastline might be so severely eroded that it reaches the outskirts of New Orleans. There is even talk of having to move the port of New Orleans.

Meanwhile, on the opposite side of the world, there is a frightening reminder of how fast sea levels are rising. Three hundred Pacific coral atolls making up six countries, as well as the Maldives in the Indian Ocean, are already feeling the waters lapping over their shores, destroying fresh water supplies and crops. When they eventually disappear, who will be next to go under?

In 1994 evidence from satellite measurements showed that the world's sea levels are rising twice as fast as had been thought. Waters were thought to be rising by about .06 inches (1.5 millimetres) a year, but half a million satellite readings suggest that seas have been rising by 0.1 inches (3 millimetres) over the previous two years.

## Storms

Storms may increase and become more intense. Hubert Lamb at the University of East Anglia has found that Britain has suffered some of its worst storms during times of rapid climatic change. Going into and coming out of the Little Ice Age produced some apocalyptic tempests.

The 'Grote Mandrenke' (drowning) North Sea storm of January 1362 drowned an estimated 100,000 people and was probably the greatest North Sea flood disaster in recorded history.

The worst storm that hit Britain in more recent history struck in 1703 when 8000 people died. One scientific explanation is that the very cold weather clashed with warm air coming up from the tropics. That difference between cold and warm is exactly what breeds storms, and the greater the temperature difference, the bigger the storm.

And so in recent times we suffered two massive storms in the space of only three years. In 1987 and 1990 storms left behind over £1 billion worth of damage. [See Violent Storms in Britain.] On the other side of the Atlantic, hurricanes with the highest rated force number 5 have battered the Caribbean, when by statistical chance they should only come once every hundred years. It all looks like we are in a very stormy spell, but is there more to come?

The official answer is equivocal. The Met. Office says that it was a bit of a coincidence that the 1987 and 1990 storms came so close together, and maybe they're right. They also say that it's highly unlikely that those storms were the face of global warming.

But on the other side of the Atlantic there has been a marked rise in hurricanes. These are very particular sorts of storms because they need to feed off water over 76 degrees Fahrenheit (23 degrees Celsius), spawned in the waters off the west coast of Africa. Hurricane Gilbert which struck Jamaica and the Yucatan Peninsula in 1988 (the strongest-ever recorded Caribbean hurricane), Hurricane Hugo which hit south Carolina in 1989, Cyclone Ofa, the strongest ever Pacific cyclone in 1991 in the South Pacific. Cyclone Val less than a year later was even stronger than Ofa. And Hurricane Andrew in the United States in August 1992 was one of the worst storms this century, with gusts of up to 170 miles per hour (270 kilometres per hour) and is estimated to have cost $20 billion of damage. Just a few weeks later Cyclone Iniki wrecked Hawaii.

As for Britain, climate modellers at the Met. Office's Hadley Centre are suggesting that as the Atlantic warms up our storms might start closer to our shores. That is bad news on two counts: it gives less warning of a storm approaching, and, worse still, the storms will be much fresher and stronger.

Unfortunately, climate models are notoriously inaccurate, particularly when you're dealing with long-term climate changes that are only poorly understood. But another way of trying to predict storminess in the future is to look back at our recorded history.

## Ancient Droughts

So is the end of our civilization nigh? The prospect of the greenhouse effect warming the globe slightly over the next few decades is sometimes dismissed as unimportant compared with natural fluctuations of temperature from season to season and even from day to day. But changes in temperature of one or two degrees, no bigger than the ones we are likely to experience over the next twenty years, have had profound influences on human cultures over the past two thousand years.

Professor Hubert Lamb at East Anglia University has found changes in climate coincided with major upheavals in past civilizations. For example, the spreading influence of Buddha (d. 483BC) and Confucius (d. 479BC) with their acceptance of suffering, both coincided with a long period of extreme cold in China up to 200BC .

Periods of adverse climate can trigger disasters such as the medieval famines, mass migrations like the Scots' colonization of Ireland, the collapse of civilizations such as the Roman Empire, and spark off wars. Perhaps the most succinct lesson we can learn about failing to adapt to a changing climate is from the Vikings. They were encouraged to colonize Greenland by a period of mild weather and the accompanying retreat of North Sea ice in the ninth and tenth centuries. During the thirteenth and fourteenth centuries, though, temperatures dropped by about two degrees and the Norse colonists were completely wiped out because they failed to adapt to the colder weather.

The lessons of the past are stark: adapt or die. Or alternatively we must find ways of controlling the greenhouse, if indeed it is already upon us.

Pretending that climate change is nothing to worry about is like postponing paying your bills – the longer you leave it the worse it gets. And if you never pay up the consequences are, of course, dire.

And that is pretty well what happened to dozens of cultures throughout history that failed to adapt to changes in their climate. The price they eventually paid was the collapse of their civilizations.

It happened to the Canaanites in biblical times, about four thousand years ago, when the weather grew dry and their crops shrivelled up. Instead of using the well-established technology of irrigation, they turned to religion and built more temples to appease their gods. It didn't take too long before their whole way of life collapsed and they had to abandon their farms and towns and become nomads.

Much the same happened to the early Mayan civilization of Yucatan in Central America two thousand years ago. The climate slowly turned drier and the Mayan rulers responded by granting themselves more power to organize food supplies better. But of course that didn't address the fundamental problem of what to do with less water. It also turned the ruling class into a corrupt elite, and when the climate turned even worse the farming system collapsed, famine became rife and the whole civilization disintegrated.

The same story can be repeated many times, but one culture at least learnt their lesson in time. About a thousand years ago, the Chimu people of northern Peru had a thriving agriculture and prosperous economy, but then they suffered a sudden period of drought. So they used intensive irrigation and survived. In fact, they did so well they ransacked their neighbouring tribes' lands which hadn't adapted.

Of course, the interesting question is whether we too will adapt in time or go the way of the Maya, the Canaanites and so many others.

# WEIRD WEATHER FACTS AND FIGURES

The atmosphere contains one and a half billion cubic miles of air and some 3400 trillion (million, billion) gallons of water floating around up in the Earth's atmosphere.

The average cloud only lasts about ten minutes.

Cloud droplets are very small, about a ten thousandth of an inch across, a thousand times smaller than a raindrop.

The biggest clouds in the world are cumulonimbus, climbing up to 6 miles (9.7 kilometres) high and holding up to half a million tons of water.

The power of a typical thunderstorm about 0.6 miles (1 kilometre) across is equivalent in energy to about ten Hiroshima-type bombs.

Lightning discharges about a million volts, peaking at between 10,000 and 40,000 amps, travelling at 186,000 miles per second (300,000 kilometres per second) and heating the air to up to 86,000 degrees Fahrenheit (30,000 degrees Celsius).

Sunbathing on sunny days with clouds in the sky can be dangerous. Clouds can reflect so much ultraviolet light from the sunlight they dramatically increase the ultraviolet reaching the ground.

The rainiest place in the world is Mount Wai'ale'ale in Hawaii where it rains on average 360 days a year – or there are 5 days in the year when it *doesn't* rain!

The wettest place in the world is Tutunendo in Colombia, where it rains an average 463.4 inches (1177 centimetres) in a year.

The driest place on Earth is Wadi Halfa in Sudan, with less than one-tenth of an inch (2.5 millimetres) average annual rainfall.

The tiny droplets of water that make fog are so small that it would take seven thousand million of them to make a single tablespoonful of water.

Heatwaves can increase the murder rate. In New York in 1988 the temperature stayed above 90 degrees Fahrenheit (32 degrees Celsius) for 32 days and the murder rate soared by 75 per cent.

The miners of Wagga Wagga, a mining town in Australia, have to put up with daytime temperatures averaging 90 degrees Fahrenheit (32 degrees Celsius) all the year round. So they've ducked the heat altogether and built an entire town underground where it stays cool all year round.

The highest temperature recorded on Earth was 136.4 degrees Fahrenheit (58 degrees Celsius) in the shade, on 13 September 1922, at Al'Azizyah in Libya, in the Sahara Desert.

The largest desert in the world is Antarctica. It only

gets about 5 inches (127 millimetres) precipitation a year – just slightly more than the Sahara.

The coldest temperature on Earth was –126.9 degrees Fahrenheit (–88.3 degrees Celsius) recorded at Vostok, in the middle of Antarctica.

Permanent snow and ice cover about 12 per cent of the Earth's land surface – a total of around 8 million square miles (21 million square kilometres). Eighty per cent of the world's fresh water is locked up as ice or snow – 7 million cubic miles.

The largest single snowfall was 102 feet (31 metres) of snow – enough to completely engulf a ten-storey block of apartments – in the winter of 1971–2.

The largest snowflakes in the world fell on 28 January 1887, measuring 15 inches (38 centimetres) across by 8 inches (20 centimetres) thick across Fort Keogh in Montana.

A single snowstorm can drop 40 million tons of snow, carrying the energy equivalent to 120 atom bombs.

The worst American snow tragedy happened on Sunday, 11 March 1888, when four hundred people were killed, and thousands were either marooned or buried for days in towns and trains, in drifts up to 50 feet (15 metres) high.

The worst blizzards are in Antarctica where wind speeds regularly reach 120 miles per hour (193 kilometres per hour).

The fastest measured avalanche struck at Glärnisch, Switzerland, on 6 March 1898. It reached 217 miles per hour (349 kilometres per hour).

The largest ever hailstone in the world fell on 14 April 1986, in Bangladesh, weighing 2.25 pounds (1 kilogram). The hailstorm killed ninety-two people at Gopalganj.

The largest piece of ice to fall on Earth was an ice block 20 feet (6 metres) across that fell in Scotland on 13 August 1849.

The worst flood in recent recorded history was the overflowing of the Yellow River in China in 1887, when an estimated 6 million people were killed. But in 1332 the Hwang Ho river in China reputedly drowned over 7 million people, and a further 10 million died from the resulting famine

The fastest winds on Earth are inside a tornado funnel, spinning at up to 300 miles per hour (480 kilometres per hour).

The most violent tornado in recorded history struck on 18 March 1925, killing 689 people, injuring 1980 others, destroying 4 towns, severely damaging 6 others and leaving 11,000 homeless across Missouri, Indiana and Illinois.

The windiest place in the world is Port Martin, Antarctica. In this desolate spot the average wind speed over a year is 40 miles per hour (64 kilometres per hour), that's gale force 8, for over a hundred days a year.

The fastest ever recorded gust of wind on the surface of the world was recorded at Mount Washington, New Hampshire, USA, on 12 April 1934.

# Select Bibliography

Alexander, D. *Natural Disasters* (UCL, London, 1993).

Battan, L.J. *Weather in Your Life* (W.H.Freeman, San Francisco, 1983).

Breuer, G. *Weather Modification: Prospects and Problems* (Cambridge University Press, Cambridge, 1979).

Burrows, W.J. *Watching The World's Weather* (Cambridge University Press, Cambridge, 1991).

Carpenter, C. *The Changing World of Weather* (Guinness Publishing, London, 1991).

Corliss, W.R. *Rare Halos, Mirages, Anomalous Rainbows and Related Electromagnetic Phenomena* (Sourcebook Project, Glen Arm, Maryland, 1984).

Corliss, W.R. *Lightning, Auroras, Nocturnal Lights, and Related Luminous Phenomena* (Sourcebook Project, Glen Arm, Maryland, 1982).

Dennis, J. & Wolff, G. *It's Raining Frogs and Fishes* (HarperPerennial, New York, 1993).

Devereaux, P. *Earth Lights Revelation* (Blandford, London, 1989).

Eloise, E. & Paamanen, L. *The Winter War: The Russo-Finnish Conflict, 1939–40* (Scribner's, New York, 1973).

Elsom, D. *Earth* (Simon & Schuster, London, 1992).

File, D. *Weather Facts* (Oxford University Press, Oxford, 1991).

Frydenlund, M.M. *Lightning Protection for People and Property* (Van Nostrand Reinhold, New York, 1993).

Gaskell, T.F. & Morris, M. *World Climate: The Weather, The Environment and Man* (Thames and Hudson, London, 1979).

Gates, P. *Spring Fever* (Fontana, London, 1993).

Goldsack, P.J. *Weatherwise: Practical Weather Lore for Sailors* (David & Charles, Newton Abbot, Devon, 1986).

Gribbin, J. *Future Weather* (Penguin, London, 1982).

Holford, I. *The Guinness Book of Weather Facts and Feats* (Guinness Superlatives, London, 1977).

Inwards, R. *Weather Lore* (Senate, London, 1994).

Lamb, H.H. *Climate: Present, Past and Future* (Methuen, London, 1977).

Lamb, H.H. *Climate, History and the Modern World* (Methuen, London, 1982).

Lockhart, G. *The Weather Companion* (Wiley, New York, 1988).

McEwan, G.J. *Freak Weather* (Hale, London, 1991).

McWilliams, B. *Weather Eye* (Lilliput Press, Dublin, 1994).

Meinel, A. & Meinel, M. *Sunsets, Twilights, and Evening Skies* (Cambridge University Press, Cambridge, 1991).

Minnaert, M.G.J. *Light and Color in the Outdoors* (Springer-Verlag, New York, 1993).

Moss, S. & Simons, P. *Weather Watch* (BBC Books, London, 1992).

Officer, C. & Page, J. *Tales of the Earth* (Oxford University Press, New York, 1993).

Soyka, F. & Edmonds, A. *The Ion Effect* (Dutton, New York, 1977).

Tromp, S.W. 'The relationship of weather and climate to health and disease,' in Howe, G.M. & Loraine, J.A. (eds) *Environmental Medicine* (Heineman, London, 1973).

Tufty, B. *1001 Questions Answered About Hurricanes, Tornadoes and Other Natural Air Disasters* (Dover, New York, 1987).

Wilson, F. *The Great British Obsession* (Jarold, Norwich, 1990).

# Acknowledgements

The author would like to thank: Professor Derek Elsom, Dr Terence Meaden, Christopher Rowe, all from the Tornado Research Organisation (TORRO). Martin Gorst, Yavar Abbas, Sonia Harding and Liz Seymour from Pioneer Productions all for their excellent help with information. Especial thanks for kind use of their photographs to: Warren Faidley, Dr Alistair Fraser, *Ealing and Acton Gazette*, *Harrow Observer*, Esko Kuusito, Munich Re Insurance, NASA, National Archives (America), National Severe Storms Laboratory, 'The News' (Portsmouth), Pekka Parvianen, United States Library of Congress, Dr William Wergin.